B54 056 60

Rebe... is the former dig... magazine. She is a columnist for the Telegraph Women's section, and has written for *Metro Online*, *Marie Claire*, the *Guardian*, the *Saturday Telegraph*, the *Independent*, *Stylist*, *Glamour*, the *i* paper, *Indy100*, *Look* and the *New Statesman* amongst others.

She is a regular contributor to *Sky News* and ITV's *Good Morning Britain* as well as appearing on *This Morning*, Radio 4's *Woman's Hour*, LBC, *Channel 5 News*, *World At One* and the BBC World Service to discuss her work.

She graduated from Royal Holloway's Creative Writing MA in 2015. Her debut novel, *Perfect Liars*, was published in 2019 and her second, *Truth Hurts*, in 2020.

Rebecca lives in London with her husband.

TWO WRONGS

Rebecca Reid

CORGI BOOKS

TRANSWORLD PUBLISHERS
Penguin Random House, One Embassy Gardens,
8 Viaduct Gardens, London SW11 7BW
www.penguin.co.uk

Transworld is part of the Penguin Random House group of companies
whose addresses can be found at global.penguinrandomhouse.com

First published in Great Britain in 2021 by Corgi
an imprint of Transworld Publishers

A CIP catalogue record for this book
is available from the British Library.

ISBN
9780552177382

For my agent, Eve White

PROLOGUE

Chloe knows that she should be dancing. She should be laughing and jumping around, not caring about the photographer recording the entire thing or the idea that someone might be judging her. She wants to. Really, she does. But she can't bring herself to do it. The boning in her dress is digging into her waist, stinging her skin, and her feet hurt. She feels silly. The song changes, and she stills. She looks across the room to see if Rav has noticed, if he is sharing the same memory she is. But he isn't looking at her, he's dancing. Laughing. The sickly pop song hasn't catapulted him back to that time, that place. She staggers back to the table, to sit down.

Chloe gulps at a glass of cold water, trying to steady her breathing. Thankfully, the song ends. But the tightness in her chest isn't going anywhere. Rav is still drawing focus on the dance floor, doubled with laughter as he, his brother and his newly minted sister-in-law, Meghan, do some ridiculous dance, one that everyone knew in the noughties. The canopy above them is studded with fairy lights and everywhere she looks she can see flowers. Fat, sexy white roses.

Rav pulls his mother up on to the dance floor; she's perfect and pristine in a pale yellow suit. To Chloe's surprise, she allows it. All eyes are on them. Chloe can see why. They're so beautiful, all of them, they manage to make the silly movements look good. Chloe slips off her shoes. They're high, with red soles. An unsuitable Christmas present from her mother-in-law, worn today in an attempt to gain favour. What time is it? She and Rav had agreed that they would leave at midnight.

Chloe doesn't want to be a killjoy. She loves Rav's brother, and his new wife. Admittedly, she wishes that Rav's parents weren't quite so blatant in their favouritism, but that isn't the happy couple's fault.

She takes a sip of wine, smiling at her husband and his family as they throw themselves around. Rav looks lit up from the inside. They've been together for what? Fifteen years? But sometimes she can't quite believe he's hers.

Chloe feels a tap on her shoulder and turns, fixing her face into a smile. It's a woman, about the same age as her. She's wearing very high heels. Chloe's face is level with her torso.

'Hi,' the woman says, gesturing at herself. 'Corinne. I did Engineering with Max and Rav. I don't know if you remember?'

'Of course,' lies Chloe. 'How are you?'

The woman takes her reply as an invitation, sinking down on to the chair across from her. She leans towards Chloe, her breasts tipping forward, straining against the V of her shiny red dress, and puts her hand on Chloe's thigh. 'I hope you don't mind,' she says, a conspiratorial expression on her face, 'but I just have to ask. We've been talking about it on our table – saying we'd always been curious.' She stops herself, seeming to realize that she's not making any sense. 'Sorry,' she says. 'What I mean is, we've been talking, and we were wondering.' Corinne pauses, like she's taking a run-up, and then asks: 'What happened to Zadie?'

1
NOW

'What are the chances that they've forgotten all about tonight and they aren't coming?' moaned Rav from the sofa, limbs splayed over the pale blue velvet.

The major benefit of living in such a tiny flat was that they could have a conversation while in two different rooms.

'Somewhere between zero and fuck all,' Chloe called back from the bedroom, a mascara wand poised just below her eyelashes. Brown mascara was all she could face putting on. It was too hot for anything more than that. 'Might I remind you,' she said, smiling into the mirror, 'that these people are our best friends? You do actually like them.'

'They're both total pains in the arse.' Rav sighed.

'Not mutually exclusive. Besides, if you had your way, we'd never see anyone.'

'True,' he replied. 'If I had my way, I'd spend every weekend in bed with you.'

Chloe laughed as she pulled on a T-shirt. It was only

Guy and Lissy coming over, to introduce their new baby. Ancient friends, so no need to make much of an effort. And, if she allowed herself an uncharitable thought, it wasn't as if Lissy was exactly a style icon.

'What if we just don't answer when they get here?' Rav suggested, poking his head around the bedroom door. His hair was mussed from spending all afternoon lying on the sofa reading the papers. 'We could turn all the lights off. Close the windows.'

Chloe drew her hair into a bun, enjoying the relief of pulling the warmth of it away from her sticky neck. The ends were dry, but her roots were looking dark – the eternal tug of war that came with being a bottle blonde. 'Too hot for that. We'd melt.'

'Hide outside?'

'Their house overlooks our garden. Remind me never to commit a crime with you – you'd be useless.' Chloe pushed him into the kitchen. 'Have a beer. You'll be glad when they're here.' Rav did this a lot. Invited people over, cramming their diary with social engagements and then complaining about them just before they started.

Rav pouted. 'Will I?'

'Yes. You always are. You love Guy. You'll be talking to him about rugby all night. It'll be me who gets stuck talking mucus plugs and second-degree vaginal tearing with Lissy.'

Rav smiled. 'We'll never be like that, right?'

'Not if we don't have kids.'

Rav cracked open a bottle of beer. 'Blasphemy.'

'Oh, come on, we could be one of those really chic couples who have loads of money and a really small dog, or a bird or something.'

He laughed. 'My mother would murder me.'

'I think you'd find she'd murder me.' Chloe reached up to kiss Rav on the lips. 'She'd never hurt her little prince.'

The doorbell rang. 'Fuck,' said Rav. 'Too late.'

Chloe hovered in the galley kitchen, then took a bottle of white wine out of the fridge and got glasses down from the shelf. Pouring the yellow liquid, she watched Rav pull the door open and throw his arms around Guy, who was handsome but had the shell-shocked look of a man who wasn't entirely prepared for fatherhood.

'Mate! Who is this?' Chloe watched as Rav dropped to his knees to get face to face with the carrier. The extent to which Rav liked babies always seemed at odds with everything else about him.

'She's sleeping,' said Lissy, clearly trying to sound like she didn't mind whether Rav woke baby Claudia up or not. Lissy's hair was still wet at the ends and the skin under her eyes was violet. So she was doing all the night feeds, then.

'Hello, you,' said Chloe, beckoning Lissy through into the living room and pressing a glass of wine into her hand. If she had asked whether Lissy was drinking, she would have had to endure a half-hour monologue about how Lissy had read all the breastfeeding research – not just the NHS guidelines, which were designed to cater to the 'lowest common denominator', but proper medical studies in the *BMJ* – which miraculously proved that Lissy was allowed to drink as much Sauvignon as she wanted. It was easier not to ask.

'Shall we sit outside?' asked Rav, pushing the sliding doors open so that the kitchen and garden became one long room. Chloe winced, knowing that once they got outside Rav would light a cigarette – downwind of the baby, but in the same postcode, which would make Lissy furious. Lissy would stew all evening then finally snap and say something before she and Guy went home. She beckoned Rav into the kitchen and told him not to smoke around the baby, at least not until Lissy had finished her first glass of wine. Leaving Guy and Lissy fussing over their sleeping daughter, she started to chop an avocado for the salad.

'Hey' – Rav caught her arm as she closed the fridge – 'you didn't mean that before, about the bird thing?'

'What bird thing?'

'Having a bird and loads of cash and no kids.'

'Oh.' Chloe fixed her face into a smile. What a time to ask. 'Of course not.'

Relief flushed on Rav's perfect face. 'Phew.'

Chloe forced a laugh. 'Can you imagine? What would you do?'

Rav laughed. 'God knows. Come outside.'

'I'll be out in a minute – just let me put the fish in.'

As expected, Guy and Rav spent half an hour on cricket then another on rugby, or rather the upcoming rugby season, while Lissy recounted every moment of her birth, including a ten-minute monologue on how the midwife had said she was the 'best prepared' mother she'd ever delivered. Chloe smiled and nodded in all the right places, and tried to ignore the pang of sadness in the back of her chest at the knowledge that Lissy was lost to her, probably until she herself had children. It had happened slowly, over the course of the pregnancy. The questions 'And what have you been up to?' or 'And how are you?' seemed to have been subsumed by the growing life inside her. By the time baby Claudia was born, Lissy's ability to ask a single question about Chloe's life had completely disappeared. Lissy had been the longest hold-out of Chloe's friends, but it had been inevitable.

Zadie wouldn't have been like that – though, Chloe realized, she might actually have children by now. Zadie was the type to either do it early, or late. Either she would have accidentally had twins with mad names in her early twenties, or perhaps she would have waited until she was forty and done with wildness, popping out a placid little thing without any of the fuss of IVF. Either way, she wouldn't have been the type to transform in mother-hood, Chloe was sure of that. She tried to quash the thought. She had resolved not to indulge in these little fantasies about her friend, about the life she might or might not have had. But something about the question Corinne had asked at the wedding had derailed her self-control. In the month since, Chloe had found herself wondering again and again. It was as if the question were a shovel, dislodging the tightly packed earth that Chloe usually kept on top of that corner of her mind.

A couple of hours later the sun had set and the plates of food had been practically licked clean. Claudia had, miraculously, stayed asleep for the entire evening so far and, in spite of herself, or rather in spite of Lissy, Chloe was having a nice time. She topped up each glass of wine, revelling in the cooler air, grateful that she might be able to sleep under the covers later.

'Supper was amazing, Chlo,' said Guy. 'We've been living off ready meals for the last week.'

'No, we haven't,' said Lissy sharply. 'They're not ready meals. They're frozen meals I prepped before Claudia was born.'

He nodded. Clearly, he knew that arguing with Lissy while she was so hormonal you could almost see the oestrogen coming off her skin was a pointless undertaking.

'You should come to us next time,' said Lissy.

'Of course,' Chloe said. 'I could cook at yours, if you wanted. We would have come to you tonight . . .'

'No, no,' Guy said. 'We wanted to come here. It's a treat to be out of the house.'

Lissy opened her mouth, probably to say that she had left the house every single day, actually. But Guy kept talking. 'How's next Saturday?'

Rav shook his head. 'We're busy. Week after?' Everyone got their phones out and started the complex negotiation of attempting to make plans.

It didn't use to be like this. When Chloe and Rav had first moved to London, two years into their relationship and desperate to be in the city, they'd rented a flat in the same Georgian house as Guy and Lissy. The four of them had been in and out of each other's flats, sunbathing on the roof, getting pissed in the shared back garden, cobbling together roast lunches in their cramped kitchens. But then, eighteen months ago, something had shifted. It was as if Guy and Lissy had suddenly decided that it was time to be grown-ups. They had bought a house on the next street and Rav had decided that it was time to move somewhere smaller to save up for a house. Which was how they'd ended up living in this place. It was lovely – the kitchen led out into the garden, the ceilings were high and the windows were huge, but it was unquestionably small. Every cupboard was topped with boxes, every piece of furniture had suitcases and storage boxes shoved underneath it. She and Rav were almost literally bursting out of the place. 'Soon,' Rav kept saying, 'we'll buy somewhere bigger.' Chloe sometimes looked at their joint bank account and wondered how Rav could be so sure when the numbers there stayed so solidly mediocre.

Occasionally, when Rav was out, Chloe would look on property websites as if they were hard-core porn. She would tease herself with the huge, comfortable places they could afford to buy if they weren't locked into a prestigious postcode where only people with generous parents could live. Unlike most of their friends, they hadn't ever had a loan from the bank of mum and dad:

Chloe because her stepfather was so hideously tight, and Rav because – well, Chloe wasn't entirely sure why. She assumed he had always been too proud to ask.

As she carried the blue-and-white plates to the dishwasher she turned to Rav and said, sotto voce, 'Nice save.'

'What?'

'Getting out of next Saturday. I can't do two weeks of birth chat in a row.'

Rav laughed. 'It wasn't a save. We're out next Saturday.'

'It's not in the diary.'

'Really? I'm sure I told you.'

Chloe shook her head. 'No. What are we doing?'

Rav put the salad bowl down on the side, pulled a bottle of wine from the fridge and, as he headed outside, said, 'Having dinner with Max.'

'Excuse me?' she replied to Rav's turned back. But he was already in the garden, falling cheerfully into a chair. Chloe stared at him through the doorway, her lips parted and suddenly dry, her head painfully tight.

'Chlo, Chlo, look what Claudia is doing!' said Lissy in a stage whisper. Chloe picked up the jug of water she had refilled and, dazed, went back into the garden to appreciate the spit bubble baby Claudia had created.

'You're pissed off,' said Rav as Chloe wiped the garden table. Lissy and Guy had finally left. They had talked a lot about being exhausted but seemed to think it would be more fun to stay and get stuck into the wine than to take the baby home and get some sleep.

'I'm fine,' Chloe snapped. She wasn't sure why she said it. It was such a cliché, claiming she was fine when she was so clearly angry.

'I know you're not his biggest fan . . .'

Chloe wheeled around to glare at him. 'So why did you say we'd see him? Why didn't you ask me?'

'I didn't think it would be a big deal.'

'Well, it is.'

'He was a mate, and he feels bad that we lost touch when he went to Australia. Now he's back in London and he wants to see us. He's got a new girl on the go, they're getting married, and he wants the four of us to have dinner. Don't you think it's possible that he might have changed in over a decade?'

Chloe turned, knowing that what she was about to say would hurt Rav but no longer inclined to care. 'Mates? You think standing on the side-lines laughing at his jokes and telling him how brilliant he is makes you "mates"?'

Rav blinked slowly and pushed his eyebrows together, clearly stung. She was being cruel. It shouldn't hurt him, to think that someone he hadn't seen since his early twenties hadn't rated him. Hadn't thought he was especially 'cool'. But Rav was easily bruised.

'I'm sorry,' she said. 'I didn't mean it.'

'It's fine.'

'No, it's not. It doesn't matter whether he liked us or not – it was years ago. I should let it go.'

'I can cancel. Tell him we're double-booked. It's just that—' He stopped.

'What?'

'He was hinting at there being some work. Said he'd bought a big building near Melbourne and he was looking for someone to sort it out.' He swallowed. 'It'd be a lot of cash, Chlo.'

Chloe could hear the yearning in Rav's voice and knew that it wasn't just about the project. Of course he wanted the money and the prestige, but it was more than that. It was about wanting to be back in Max's world, illuminated by his reflected glory. He'd always loved it when they'd first known him, and while she might try to convince herself that they'd both grown out of it, the desire for Max's attention, she knew in Rav's case it wasn't true.

'It's okay,' she said, wishing she had the willpower to deny him. 'We'll go.'

She pulled out a pen and wrote 'Dinner with Max' in the shared diary which lived on the kitchen table. As she looked down at the wet blue ink, a twisting, griping feeling formed under her ribcage.

ZADIE

Zadie's finger rested on the button for the electric window of the car. She pressed it down, then pulled it up, flicking the window a centimetre up, a centimetre down. She used to do the same thing in the car with her parents when she was a child on the way back to school on a Sunday night. She would wait to see how long her mother would ignore it before shouting at her. But the driver in the front seat, neatly dressed in a navy-blue suit, didn't notice. Or if he did, he said nothing. She stopped pressing the button, just in case he could hear over the hum of the road and it was annoying him.

She watched the other cars passing, looking through their windows at the children, dogs, suitcases in them. Occasionally, a car filled with boxes and bags and rolled-up duvets would pass and she would wonder if they, too, were on their way to start university. Presumably with their parents.

Her mother had been apologetic about not dropping her off. 'I would have done, darling,' she had said, 'but we're away that weekend. And it's not like you've never been away before. You know, other people who get dropped off by their parents,

15

this is the first time they've ever left home.' She'd clearly been trying to assuage her own guilt more than anything else.

It was true. Zadie had been leaving home for months at a time since she was eleven. This wasn't the big sticking-plaster rip that other people found it to be. In fact, it was coming as quite a relief. A summer at home with her parents breathing down her neck, obsessing about whether she was eating, worrying about who she was seeing – it had been almost unbearable. 'Out of sight, out of mind' was a maxim that suited the Lister family down to the ground.

The driver indicated and turned off. The world felt quieter as soon as he pulled on to the new road, flanked by sloping green hills. Pretty. She had been to visit before, of course. The previous year, while Max had been 'studying', which seemed to mean playing rugby and convincing some sweet, spineless friend to do his academic work for him, she had visited all the time, convincing her house mistress that she was going home and telling her parents that she was at school. But it was different now. She was going to be with him properly. Like adults. No more waiting up at night, hoping he would call her from some party, inevitably surrounded by beautiful girls, while she was locked up fifty miles away at school. And it wasn't going to be all about Max, either. She was going to find her own friends. Her own place.

She had sworn to her parents, who had clearly been furious that she'd got into such a good university, where her boyfriend just happened to go, that she would make her own life. And while she lied fluently to them, in this instance she really meant it. Max's friends were painfully dull, obsessed with which school people had gone to, who people's families were, and talked endlessly about sport.

'Will it be your first year?' asked the driver, cutting through Zadie's daydream of a group of like-minded friends who wanted to visit galleries with her or paint huge, messy canvases together.

'Yes,' she said. 'First term of the first year.'

'You must be a smart cookie, getting in here.'

Zadie laughed. He wasn't wrong. Her teachers had almost choked when she'd announced that she wanted to come here. But six months in the library, doggedly learning everything she'd ignored in previous years, and here she was. 'I'm reading History of Art. It's a bit of an easy option.'

'Doesn't sound easy to me.' He caught her eye in the wing mirror and smiled.

He pulled into the car park of the halls, which was filled with teenagers and suitcases and weeping parents. Zadie watched as a pretty blonde girl followed a slender woman and a bald man up the path. She had an armful of books and a dazed expression, as if she had arrived somewhere wonderful. Zadie considered her, considered all of them. She could do as she had promised her mother she would. Unpack into whatever box-sized bedroom she had been assigned. Make friends with the girls on her hallway. Do everything she had been doing at boarding school for the last seven years, all over again. And a little part of her wanted to. When was the last time she had done something the 'normal' way? But she had promised Max. She had come here for Max. They'd spent the entire summer excited about finally living together like grown-ups. How would he feel if she suddenly turned around and said she wanted to have the bog-standard university halls experience, rather than living with him?

She leaned forward between the two front seats and gave the driver her most persuasive smile.

'Would you mind taking me a tiny bit further? It's called Archer Crescent.'

The driver looked unconvinced. 'I promised your parents I'd drop you here.'

Zadie laughed and put her hand on his arm. 'I know, but that was because they were worried I'd try to convince you to take me to the airport so I could run away to Aruba and live naked on a beach for the rest of my life. This is just a little change of address.'

He raised an eyebrow but indicated left, turning towards the pretty crescent where Max's parents had insisted on getting him a house, and away from the halls, where her parents had equally insisted that she would live.

Her mother was so obsessed with the whole thing she'd even braved having lunch with Max's mother, who she couldn't stand. 'We're like a really boring Romeo and Juliet,' Zadie had laughed to Max.

The houses, which sat on a little hill, were tall and golden with pastel-coloured front doors. They looked out across the rest of the town; it was green and gold and teeming with possibilities. Halls was all well and good, but how could she be expected to resist moving in here? Finally, after years and years of hiding, making up alibis and snatching days together on holidays or over school exeats, Zadie would be able to be with Max. Really be with him.

The driver insisted on helping her drag all her suitcases and boxes out of the car. After she had piled everything up on the front steps of Archer Crescent, she went to give him a £20 note. But instead, for reasons she couldn't quite understand, she found herself throwing her arms around his neck and planting a kiss on his cheek. He flushed, but didn't seem unhappy about it.

'Good luck with it all,' he said, smiling at the floor. 'Work hard, but don't forget to have some fun as well.'

'Thank you. It's going to be great.'

2
THEN

Greg panted as he dropped the suitcase on the uneven wooden floor. There was a sheen to his bald head despite the fact that it was cold outside – crisp and blue in a way that only October ever was.

A helpful-looking student adviser had offered to carry the bags to Chloe's new room, but Greg, always keen to play the adoring stepfather for the outside world, had insisted that he didn't need any assistance.

'My hero!' Chloe's mother, Louise, smiled, putting her arms around Greg's neck. Her touch made his blue shirt stick to his back. 'What would we do without you?' she laughed. Chloe considered telling her mother that without Greg she wouldn't have needed to pack such heavy suitcases because she would want to come home more than once a term, but that would prompt an argument, and there was no point.

'Thanks, Greg,' she said, eyes firmly on the empty pin-board on the wall behind where he stood. He didn't reply.

'I wonder who your room-mate is going to be,' her mother said, her voice aspartame. She went to the door, looking at the little metal frames which held the names of those who lived inside. On the left, Chloe Sanders. On the right, Zadie Lister. 'Zadie,' she said, as if it was the most astonishing name she'd ever heard in her life. 'Very exotic.' She made 'exotic' sound like it rhymed with 'toxic'. Her mother didn't approve of unusual names. 'It's all so exciting, isn't it?' she added, looking around the room.

Chloe nodded. 'It's nice. I didn't realize I'd be sharing.' The room was wide and rectangular with a high ceiling. Each side had a double bed, a sink, a chest of drawers and a wardrobe, all made of the kind of pine that was virtually impossible to damage. She wondered what it would originally have been, before it was part of a halls of residence, when it was still a country house. Spartan and pragmatic as it was, nothing could take away from the height of the ceilings, the cornicing around the top of the walls and the huge sash windows.

Greg snorted. 'If it's not to your liking, we can take you home, madam. Or see if there are any rooms at the Ritz?'

It wasn't worth replying. 'You guys can go,' she said to her mum. 'It's a long drive.'

Her mother swallowed. Was she genuinely about to cry, or was this for Greg's benefit, all part of the heroic single-mother act? Chloe scolded herself internally, not for the first time, for being angrier with her mother for marrying Greg than she was with her father for walking out on them fifteen years ago.

'I can't believe we're here,' Louise said, her voice cracking. 'I can't believe that we got here, all on our own.' She turned to Greg. 'I was the same age she is now when I had her, and we made it, the two of us.' She pulled Chloe into a hug. None of what her mother was saying was untrue. But Louise was doing the thing she always did, performing for an invisible camera. Ever since Chloe could remember, her mother had been acting out a film, casting herself as the tragic but beautiful heroine left to try and raise her daughter alone. This, Chloe supposed, was the closing scene. She'd drive off into the sunset with Greg (the fact that Greg was the antithesis of a romantic hero didn't seem to matter much) and the credits would roll. Louise had done her job. Everyone would have to agree that she was a Good Mother.

'Love you,' Chloe said weakly into her mother's apple-scented hair.

Louise picked her handbag up off the unmade bed, holding it on the crook of her skinny brown arm. 'If you want anything, you just call. All right?'

Chloe nodded, surprised at the constriction in her throat. She'd been counting down to this since Greg had moved into their little house six years ago, literally and metaphorically sat his fat arse between Chloe and her mother on the leather sofa and commandeered the remote control, replacing their marathons of *America's Next Top Model* with wrestling.

'You guys should get going,' she said, squeezing her eyelids shut.

'You're right,' said Greg. 'Your new mate will be here before long.' He gestured at the empty bed. 'You don't want us embarrassing you when your roomie shows up!'

He didn't know how right he was. Zadie was supposed to be her first friend here – someone to debate literature with, to stay up all night talking about love, life and the future with. And that wasn't going to happen if Greg asked her whether she followed WWE before Chloe had had a chance to find out what books she liked. She watched as they disappeared through the door, down the stairs. She followed their figures through the window, her mother's slender hand clamped in Greg's shovel-like one.

It was difficult to know where to start. With the bed, she supposed. She pulled the tape off the box labelled 'sheets', the contents lovingly ironed by her mother, and made the bed. Then she put her books on the shelves. She took out her speaker and thought about putting some music on, but the idea of picking what she'd be listening to when Zadie arrived was too much to deal with.

There was a knock at the door and the nerves swelled in Chloe's chest. This was it. Her first meeting with her room-mate. A small blonde girl with thin eyebrows put her head around the door, smiling. 'Hi,' she said. 'I'm Lissy.'

Oh. Not Zadie. Chloe fixed her face into a smile. 'Chloe,' she said.

'A group of us from the corridor are going down to the pub. Do you want to join?' She looked around the room.

'Oh, wow, you're sharing. Bad luck . . .' She paused, seeming to realize that she was being rude. 'But I mean, it might be fun. Everyone in America shares a room at uni. My cousin lives in Florida.'

Chloe drank in the girl's jeans, zip-up jumper and trainers – the same outfit everyone back home wore; she even had the same shade of lipstick. She looked across at the unmade bed. 'That's really nice of you,' she said, 'but I think I'm going to wait for Zadie to arrive.'

'Zadie?'

'My room-mate.'

'Oh.' The girl smiled. 'Cool. Well we'll be at the George if you both want to join later.' She disappeared, leaving a faint smell of Impulse body spray behind her.

Four hours later, Zadie still hadn't arrived. The empty bed and shelves stood in stark contrast to her own side of the room, covered with books, fairy lights and posters.

She should go down to join Lissy and her friends. But something inside her recoiled at the idea. Besides, what if she went and sat with them at some sticky table in a pub and they talked about what A levels they'd done and what subject they were studying and if they had boyfriends, the same stupid conversation she'd had a million times back home, and, in her absence, Zadie arrived?

University, it turned out, was a lot like college. Lectures. Seminars. Essays. Girls swishing their hair and not speaking up in case their intellect made them less desirable to the boys, who talked at length about books they probably hadn't read. Chloe's conviction that she would be transformed into a latter-day bluestocking with reams of friends who sat around drinking and discussing art was starting to wane.

A few weeks into term, on her way back from a lecture, Chloe paused on the corridor outside her room, noticing that the door, which she was sure she had locked, was ajar, and that from inside was coming a sort of rustling noise. She pushed the door open, standing back, and looked in, framed by the wooden rectangle. In the middle of the room was a tall, thin girl with masses of blonde hair. She wore a dress which might have been a silk dressing gown, and she was pulling items of clothing from an old-fashioned suitcase and shoving them into the chest of drawers on her side of the room.

'Hello?' Chloe said after a moment.

The girl looked up and smiled. 'Hi,' she said. Her voice was breathy. She didn't stop; her movements were fast and fluid. Chloe stood fixed to the spot, as if to step into her own room would be an intrusion. 'Are you Zadie?' she asked, after what felt like an hour. The back of her neck was hot.

'Yes,' the girl replied. 'Can you pass me that?' she asked, pointing to a folded silk eiderdown sitting on her desk.

Moving slowly, feeling like she'd entered some alternative universe, Chloe picked it up. It was the sort of thing her mother would have bought a cheap copy of from BHS then proudly displayed in the guest room at home. Zadie took it from her and arranged it over her bed, which, after six weeks of being rudely naked on her side of the room, was finally made up.

'Thanks.'

'What are you . . .' Chloe tailed off. It was an obvious question. It made perfect sense to ask it. But she felt stupid anyway.

Zadie stopped moving, running her hands through her hair and wrapping it up into a knot on the top of her head. 'Sorry,' she said, 'you must think I'm an actual loon. Don't worry, I'm not taking your room. You must have been so pleased when you realized you were getting a double to yourself.'

Chloe had no idea what to say to that, so she put her bag down on her desk and retreated to her bed, pulling her knees up to her chest. *No*, she wanted to say. *I wasn't pleased at all. I wanted you to come.* But that would sound insane. 'You're not staying?' she asked instead.

Zadie tipped her handbag upside down on the chest of drawers, spreading the detritus over it. She took a step back, admiring her handiwork, then looked up, as if realizing she needed to answer the question. 'No,' she said. 'Well, I mean, I'm staying here at college. I'm just not staying here-here.'

'It's not—' Chloe paused, but the words came out in spite of herself: 'It's not me?'

Zadie looked aggrieved. She came to sit on the bed next to Chloe, putting her hand on her arm. Chloe's stomach twisted at the intimacy of the touch.

'God, no,' said Zadie. 'Sorry, I'm being useless, I should explain. My parents are coming this afternoon and I need them to think that I'm living here.'

'Why?'

Zadie sighed. 'It's such a saga, but – don't think I'm awful, all right? So, they're a bit over-protective, kind of controlling, and they'd be furious if they found out that I wasn't staying here. It was part of the deal of them letting me come.'

'So where do you actually live?'

'With Max. My boyfriend. We've been together for years so, obviously we wanted to live together. But my parents are such psychos, if they find out that I'm not living here, then they'll probably stop paying my fees or something obscene like that.' She delivered the information at a million miles an hour, so fast that Chloe could only just follow what she was saying. 'Anyway, my little brother, he's such an angel – I mean, not an angel at all, he's been thrown out of about seven boarding schools – anyway, he warned me they were making a "surprise visit", which clearly is code for coming to check that I'm doing as I'm told. So when they get here I need them to think that I'm living here. With you.'

Chloe frowned and slowly got to her feet. Shyly, she pulled the blankets into a tangle on Zadie's bed. 'Then you need to make your bed look like you've slept in it. Won't they be suspicious if it's too neat?'

Zadie's face lit up with a huge smile. Her teeth were white, with a tiny gap between the two front ones, an imperfection that would have spoiled someone else but only stood to make this girl more beautiful. 'You're so right. They'll think I'm trying to hide something if I'm too tidy. I used to get about fifty demerits a term for having a messy room at school.' She turned to look at the neat collage of photos above Chloe's bed and the fairy lights wound around her bedframe. 'You're tidy,' she said. It didn't sound like a compliment.

'My mum is a neat freak,' Chloe admitted. 'It wasn't much of a choice in my house.'

'Mine, too!' exclaimed Zadie. 'She fires every cleaner we have because they don't do it like she would.'

Chloe's mother would never have allowed anyone else to do their cleaning, even if they could afford it. 'So does mine,' she heard herself say. Why had she said that? *Stupid*, she scolded herself. If Zadie ever met her mum, she'd know they weren't the sort of people who had a cleaner. That was an even more stupid thought. Why would Zadie ever meet her mum? She only needed Chloe's help to fool her parents and then she'd disappear again.

Lissy, the girl down the hall, had explained one evening in the pub about the kind of people who lived off campus. There had been a group of them at the bar, ordering bottles of champagne and laughing. Lissy said that there were a few of them, boys who were only at college here so they could row or play rugby, and their girlfriends. People with money and country houses who went away most weekends and considered the town a little low rent. Lissy had given her a conspiratorial smile, as if to say that she and Chloe were a different, lower sort of person.

'I've got a lecture in a bit,' Chloe said, taking her books down from her shelf. 'I should get going.'

'Is there any chance you might be able to come back later?' Zadie asked. 'When my parents are around?' Her eyes were big and her face pale. How could someone so confident and beautiful be that scared of her parents?

'Of course,' said Chloe. 'I'll be back by three.'

'You are the absolute best.' Zadie threw her arms around Chloe. 'I mean it. You're the best room-mate I've ever had.'

Chloe returned on the dot of three o'clock, but Zadie's parents, clearly full of suspicion, had turned up early. They looked exactly as Chloe had imagined. A rail-thin mother with a razor-sharp bob and a fur gilet. A smiling father with a round stomach encased in a navy jumper and with Gucci loafers on his feet.

'Hey!' said Zadie, a little too loudly, as Chloe opened the door. 'I was just going to make some coffee, but I can't remember where I've put the cups.'

Afterwards, Chloe would replay this afternoon in her mind, bathing in the glory of getting it right, for once. 'Yours are in the dishwasher in the kitchen,' she said, without missing a beat. 'We can use my ones – I think you put them in that cabinet?'

'Zadie,' said the older woman, pointedly. Chloe tensed,

thinking she was about to call their bluff. 'You haven't introduced us.'

'Sorry, sorry. This is Astrid,' Zadie said, pointing at her mum. 'And this is Bob.' Chloe flushed at the idea of calling Zadie's parents by their first names and resolved not to call them anything at all.

'Hi, I'm Chloe,' she said shyly. She caught a flicker pass over Zadie's face and realized that Zadie hadn't known her name until that moment.

'Nice to meet you, Chloe. How's living with Zee?' asked Zadie's father.

'It's great,' Chloe said. 'She's a fantastic room-mate.' She noticed a slight frown on Zadie's mother's face. 'Though I wouldn't mind if she was a little bit tidier . . .' she added, smiling. The Listers laughed. Why was it that people liked to bond with strangers by saying mean things about the person they had in common?

'You let me know if her laundry basket starts taking over the entire room,' said Mrs Lister, gesturing at the basket in the corner of the room which was in fact stuffed with Chloe's clean clothes with a couple of Zadie's most garish garments on the top.

'I will.'

After a quarter of an hour the Listers made their excuses, citing a weekend party a few miles away with friends. Chloe could just picture them driving away in their four by four, smiling to each other, all the panic they had been feeling about Zadie having broken her word washed away by the visit. Mr Lister pressed a wad of £20 notes into his daughter's hand as he left, instructing her to 'buy your lovely friend a drink at the pub tonight'.

The girls watched as they disappeared down the hall, and once they were safely gone Zadie jumped up and down. 'You were fucking brilliant!' she exclaimed. 'That stuff about me being messy – urgh, you were just so great.' She squeezed Chloe tightly. 'I owe you.'

She began stuffing things back into her bag.

Chloe felt her face fall. 'Not at all,' she replied. 'I had fun.'

Opening the door, Zadie turned back. 'Wait,' she said. She pulled out a surprisingly old-fashioned phone and held it out. 'Call yourself, so I have your number? And come over to the house some time. You should meet Max. He's the best, you'll love him. Everyone does.'

A warmth spread through Chloe's body as she put the number into Zadie's phone.

3
NOW

Rav had been in a bad mood all day, and while Chloe
was usually quite happy to jolly him along, since his
announcement that they were going to see Max she had
rather lost her taste for it. And, anyway, it was his own
fault that he was hung over. He and Guy had hit the bottle hard, Guy presumably because it had been so long
since he had been allowed out, and Rav in solidarity. He
had spent the day lying on the sofa watching cricket
with the sound turned off and the curtains closed, complaining that his head hurt and asking Chloe to bring
him glasses of cold water. Eventually, she had gone into
the bedroom and shut the door, told Rav to have a
sleep on the sofa until he felt better and told herself that
she was going to spend the afternoon Marie Kondo-ing
her wardrobe. But then she'd found a black silk dress
buried under some old jumpers. It had Zadie's name
taped in the label. All Zadie's clothes had been labelled,
because she had gone to boarding school. She took the
dress out, and before she could stop herself she was

peeling off her clothes and putting it on. She hadn't worn it since Zadie had disappeared. It was dated now. And too small for her. But running her hands over it felt like going home.

Did Zadie still dress in the mad, beautiful way she had when they were teenagers? Or would she have turned out like her mother, neat in cashmere and silk, buying her clothes from a handful of boutiques and having them all tailored so that they fitted perfectly?

After she had given in to the dress, it seemed pointless to try to resist all the other cravings. Her fingers were itching. So she peeled off the dress, hung it back in the wardrobe then let the floodgates open. As usual, she started by typing various different Zadie-related search terms into Google – her name, her full name, her full name with her date of birth – then had a little look on the major social platforms. Five minutes, tops. Nothing ever came up. But because Rav had been so resolutely grumpy and she had nothing else to do it was too hard to resist going in for a proper deep dive, the sort she had stopped allowing herself years ago. She looked up all Zadie's siblings, whose privacy settings were up to the max. Searched for her parents, her cousins. She even read the newsletter of the village she grew up in, as if Zadie was going to be mentioned for winning a cake-baking contest or growing a really big carrot. Still nothing came up. Then it occurred to Chloe that some people had their social media accounts under nick-names, so she had tried out various ideas. An hour later she was exhausted, and faintly ashamed of herself for getting sucked into such a hole.

She went into the living room. 'I'm going to have a glass of wine,' she said, perching on the edge of the sofa. 'Do you want one?'

'Absolutely not,' said Rav. 'I don't know how you can.'

'I didn't drink as much as you did last night.'

Rav got up and immediately stubbed his toe on the coffee table. He swore, then kicked the table, which obviously hurt even more. 'This fucking flat.'

'Is that what this is really about?'

'What?'

'The sulking. The mood. Is it because of the stuff Guy was saying last night, about them having the extension done and turning the basement into a gym?'

'I don't know what you're talking about.'

'You're jealous. Of the house. You get upset because they've got that huge place and we're renting this one.'

Rav frowned. 'I don't care that they've got a big house. I'm happy for them.'

It took all Chloe's self-control not to roll her eyes. Rav was not happy for them. At all. He and Guy had been casually competing with each other ever since they'd first met in their last year at uni, gently spurring each other on. One of them would edge ahead by getting promoted or shaving five minutes off their run time, and the other would be inspired to do better, to earn more, to move faster. But then Guy's ancient grandfather had died and left Guy a small fortune, which, combined with Lissy's not insubstantial salary, had secured them a breathtaking town house, the likes of which Chloe and Rav could only drool over on Instagram.

Chloe didn't care especially. But Rav did. And the unspoken echo that surrounded Rav's misery was the fact that if Chloe earned proper money like Lissy, rather than the pittance (Rav's word, not hers) she took home from teaching, they would be able to afford something much more impressive.

Chloe decided that today was not the day to get into an argument about it. 'It's normal to be jealous of other people. They both had shit tons of help from their parents. We don't have that. My parents haven't got any money, and yours don't want to give us any, which is completely fine.'

'They offered.'

'What?'

But Rav had gone into the kitchen and didn't seem to hear. He reappeared a few minutes later with a mug of tea for him and a glass of wine for her.

'Thanks. Your parents offered what?'

Rav was looking into his mug, avoiding her gaze. 'My parents offered to help us get a house.'

This was the first she'd heard about it. She reached for the remote, trying to keep her tone casual and light. 'But that's good news, so why do you look so miserable?'

'If we get pregnant.'

Chloe's finger hovered over the 'on' button. 'I'm sorry?'

'They said they'd buy us a place if we get pregnant.'

'If I get pregnant.'

'What?'

'We don't get pregnant, *I* get pregnant. You get an orgasm. I get fat feet and a ripped-up vagina.'

Rav winced. 'You said you wanted children.'

'I do.'

'We're in our mid-thirties.'

'I'm aware.'

'They'd help us get a place. Somewhere around here. Somewhere like Guy and Lissy's.'

'In exchange for giving them a grandchild.'

'I know, it's not exactly the most "no strings attached" offer.'

Chloe put the remote down. 'It's the Pinocchio of offers.'

'But if we were planning to have a baby anyway, why don't we just take them up on it, get the house, get on with having kids, get our life moving?'

'I like our life.'

'I like our life, too, but come on. All our friends have kids. We love kids. We've always said that we want children. Your job is stable. My job is stable. How could it possibly be a bad idea?'

He was right. Obviously, he was right. If two healthy people in their mid-thirties who had some disposable income and the prospect of a stable home really wanted children, then it was a no-brainer. But recently Chloe had felt herself getting restless. Feeling trapped by their flat, her job, their friends. All of it was so . . . neat. So identikit. It was a slightly cooler, more urban version of what her mother had chosen for her life. They were increasingly able to share conversations about gardening and bedlinen. At some point in the past she had stopped being young-young and slid into the strange twilight world where people referred to her as 'the lady' when they were instructing their kids to move out of the way for her, where she never got ID'd when she was buying wine. Having a baby felt like the last nail in the coffin, an admission that she really was an adult. And she would not just be an adult, but a mother.

It was fine for Rav. He would be a cool dad. Disneyland, and endless games. Breaking the rules that Chloe made. She could see it all perfectly clearly. She would be in charge of making things run properly. The glue that held the entire thing together. And Rav would be the one the child wanted cuddles and stories with. The glitter that made life fun.

Chloe knew she wasn't the most exciting person in the world. She wasn't even the most exciting person in most rooms. But there had been a time when it felt as if that might change. As if there were some sparkle inside her that just needed to be released. Glitter potential. Somehow, having a baby felt like the final admission that the magic wasn't going to happen. She sighed.

'Okay. Let's start trying.'

The look of hope on Rav's face twisted her heart. 'Really? You're really ready to start trying?'

'Not exactly ready, no.'

'Well, no one's ever really—'

'Ready. Yes, I know.'

'You're sure?'

'I'm sure.'

Rav wrapped his arms around her and inhaled, breathing in the smell of her hair like he used to when they were young and completely obsessed with each other. 'Thank you,' he whispered. He rubbed her back suggestively. 'Maybe we could start trying right now?' His hangover seemed to have magically healed itself. Chloe laughed and leaned in to kiss him, wondering how long it would take her to come to regret what she'd just promised.

4

NOW

Every Saturday afternoon since they had moved to London Rav would disappear on to the Heath with his friends from school and play cricket in the summer or rugby in the winter. He would only be gone for three or four hours, leaving her to get her marking done during term time or just revel in the bliss of being alone during the holidays. Long, silent baths, dedicated excavations of her sock drawer, Saturday afternoons held the boring joys she'd once watched her mother indulge in and sworn she'd never take to herself.

She felt obliged to watch Rav play one cricket and one rugby match a year – 'socials' organized by some ham-necked friend of his (or rather, the ham-necked friend's wife). On these occasions she turned up, stood on the side-lines looking pretty and made polite conversation with the other wives. To Rav's credit, he never asked for more, and didn't ever complain that, unlike his friends' wives, she bought their contribution to the match tea from Sainsbury's. Nor did he ever try to embroil himself with the people she worked with or crash their trips to the pub. He came to every production her school put on, clapped until his hands hurt and told Chloe it was brilliant even when it wasn't.

The system worked. It was a square of fabric in the middle of the patchwork quilt of their marriage. And yet today, for the first time in as long as Chloe could remember, Rav had cancelled. He'd made an excuse that morning about his back hurting, giving too many details about the twinge in his lower spine. And rather than leaving her to her lovely, peaceful day, he had stridden around, getting ready too early to go out and making her nervous. Chloe wanted to ask why dinner with Max was so important that he was willing to cancel something he never, ever cancelled, even when she wished he would. But Rav was (quite rightly) embarrassed about his slavish admiration for Max and would lash out if she pushed the point.

She unscrewed the lid of the gold pot and pulled out her eyeliner brush. Was it worth the risk? The rest of her face was finished, skin painted with a foundation which was the right shade in winter but a little too pale now, and dusted with bronzer. Eyes a combination of four almost identical shades of gold-brown. Lips painted away by her foundation then drawn back on. She put the brush to her lid and drew it across the lash line, a perfect graphic black stripe. Admiring her work, she smiled. She wasn't dressed yet, still sitting on the bed in her knickers and bra. But her hair was behaving and if she could just make the second eye match the first one she'd be pleased with herself.

Max would love this, came a bitter mewl from the back of her head. *He'd love the idea that you're sitting here, painting yourself for him. Thinking about an outfit for him. Trying for him.*

'It's not for Max,' she said out loud, as if saying it into the room made it any more true. 'It's for Rav. It's for me.'

She put the brush back to her lash line and was beginning to pull it across when a voice sounded from behind her.

'Well, hello sexy,' said Rav.

Instinctively, Chloe turned her head, to see her husband standing in the doorway. 'Fuck!' she yelped, realizing she'd put a black line across the side of her eye. 'Fucking fuck.'

'Bad time? Was that my fault?'

'Yes,' ground out Chloe from between her teeth. 'Very, very your fault. You shouldn't sneak up on me.'

'Sorry,' he said, resting his head on the door frame. He was so tall the top of his head almost brushed it. 'You look great, though.'

Chloe made a noise a bit like a laugh. 'I look like I'm in *Brighton Rock*.'

'*A Clockwork Orange*.'

Chloe scrubbed at the side of her face, looking into the mirror. She got the eyeliner off, but it took all her foundation with it, leaving an oddly pink patch of skin behind. 'What?'

'You look like you're in *A Clockwork Orange*. That's the one with the fake eyelashes. *Brighton Rock* is about gangs in the thirties.'

'I know,' she snapped, feeling stupid. 'That was what I meant.'

Rav raised his eyebrows but seemed to think better of making a fuss. He disappeared into the living room, humming as he went.

She had known that. She knew far more about books and films than Rav did. She didn't answer. Instead she turned to the wardrobe, looking for her navy dress. It was round-necked and short-sleeved with a fitted waist. She called it her 'boring dinner-party dress'; it was the one she took out when she wanted people to think she looked nice but not think any further than that.

'Is that what you're wearing?' asked Rav, coming into the bedroom, his hair freshly pushed back with water, beads of it on his skin. Even when he was irritating her, even when he was forcing her to go to dinner with the person she could stand least in the world, she couldn't help noticing how obscenely beautiful he was. His mother's skin tone, her huge eyes. His father's cheek-bones. Long, lean muscles.

'Yes,' she said. Then she weakened. 'Did you have something else in mind?'

'No, no,' he replied, dragging a towel over his head.

Chloe cocked her head to one side. 'Really?'

He put his hands up as if she were pointing a gun at him, trying to laugh his way off the wafer-thin ice. 'I just thought that pink one from the other day was nice, that's all. It was a bit more . . . party.'

The 'pink one' was a short, silk dress with spaghetti straps and a flirty skirt. She'd bought it out shopping with Lissy. She had only tried it on because she'd been so agonizingly bored of hearing about nipple shields, but when she'd looked in the mirror at herself she'd wondered if the dress had some sort of magic. A heavily pregnant Lissy had said something about wanting to jump in front of a bus because she was so fat and had then compelled Chloe to buy it. It was a dress for a better evening than this one.

'If you want to give Max something pretty to look at,' said Chloe, doing up the buttons on the front of her dress, 'you're welcome to borrow the pink one.'

Rav shook his head and fastened the buckle to his belt. 'Do you really still hate him so much?'

Chloe spritzed perfume on her wrists. 'Are you calling the Uber or am I?'

Perhaps he knew he was in dangerous territory, or maybe he didn't want to hear the answer. Either way, he picked up his phone and left the bedroom. 'I'll do it,' he called back.

Chloe had just finished redoing her eye make-up – not as neatly as the first time – when Rav shouted, 'The car's going to be here in two minutes.' He was already standing on the doorstep. 'Ready?'

She picked up her bag. 'Ready,' she said, closing the

bedroom door behind her and pulling the skinny strap back up her shoulder. Rav grinned. 'You changed.'

'I did.' She smiled. 'Entirely for your benefit. Have you got the wine?'

Rav held up two bottles of fancy-looking Malbec. He'd clearly slunk off somewhere impossibly grand in Mayfair on his lunch break yesterday. Between the wine and the bunch of flowers she'd bought that morning they'd already spent a decent £75 on this evening. She wanted to tell Rav that he should stop bothering, that Max would never be impressed by something as mediocre as a bottle of wine, and that Rav would lose points in his eyes for doing something as pedestrian and middle class as bringing two bottles to dinner. But she couldn't bring herself to. There was a fizz to Rav's mood, the same excited bounce he always got when they were doing something new, when he felt he was about to break new ground. So she smoothed her hair instead and picked up the flowers. 'I suppose we'd better go, then,' she said.

'You never know,' said Rav as he closed the front door behind them. 'You might even enjoy yourself.'

No fucking way, thought Chloe, as she walked to the taxi.

5

THEN

'Who's the boy?' asked Lissy, putting a fistful of Bacardi Breezers down on the pub table, two for each of them. She had to raise her voice to be heard above the deafening Rihanna song.

'What?' replied Chloe. She took a long drink of the sugary pink liquid, hoping that if she drank enough of it she would forget that she was having the exact same night out she used to have at home.

'You've been staring at your phone all evening,' said Lissy. 'There's definitely a boy. Right, Sam?' She raised her eyebrows at her friend Samantha, a sweet, plump girl with a moon face who also lived on their corridor.

Chloe shook her head, watching as Lissy counted her change back into her wallet, which had a picture of a puppy wearing a tiara on it, then zipped it back into her sensible bag. In their second week, Lissy had tried to talk all the girls on their corridor into going to a talk about staying safe on campus. Chloe had said no, and been subjected afterwards to Lissy going on about putting your keys between your fingers as an anti-rape method and carrying hairspray to use as mace on anyone who attacked you.

'So, who is he?'

Chloe shoved her phone into her pocket. 'No one,' she said. 'It's not a boy.' Which was true. The person she was waiting to hear from, the person she'd woken up every morning praying to have a text from, was Zadie. There was no way to explain that to Samantha and Lissy.

'There's nothing to be embarrassed about,' Samantha assured her. 'They're all the same. Ian still hasn't messaged me.'

Samantha had watched too many reruns of *Friends* on Channel 4 in the common room and had told her long-term boyfriend, Ian, still back at home in the Midlands, that she wanted to go 'on a break'. Ian was presumably now making hay while the sun shone. Chloe tried to stop her eyes from rolling back into her head. On the table next to them was a bigger group, screaming with laughter and buying round after round of shots. Lissy was leaning across her to talk to Samantha about Ian's text silence. Chloe tried to scrape up some enthusiasm for the conversation. It wasn't difficult. She only had to throw in a 'You're too good for him' or 'You should get over him by getting under someone else' and she'd be golden. She should do it. Samantha and Lissy had been kind to her. Yes, their *Sex and the City* marathons and obsession with home-made face masks were a long way from her vision of university, the hoped-for debates and literary salons, but it had to be better than nothing.

Something buzzed against her thigh. Jumping, she scrabbled for her phone, pulling it out. 'Busy tonight? Z x,' read the screen.

'She's blushing!' said Samantha.

'He texted you?' Lissy looked delighted, as if this was playing into the sitcom she was living out in her head. Chloe nodded, deciding that was easier than explaining. 'Not busy, just having drinks with girls from my/our corridor. C x,' she texted back.

'Don't text back now!' yelped Lissy as she watched Chloe press send. 'You have to wait!'

'Too late,' smiled Chloe, taking a swig of her drink.

'You won't hear from him until at least tomorrow now,' said Samantha, her face solemn. As if in reply, Chloe's phone buzzed, spinning on the sticky table. Her body thudded as she picked it up. 'Want to come over? 29 Archer Crescent.'

The sickly lemonade taste of the Bacardi Breezer burned the back of Chloe's throat.

'What did he say?' Lissy pulled at Chloe's arm.

'Asked me over,' Chloe confessed. She wanted to share the excitement, even if she wasn't being exactly honest. 'Where's Archer Crescent?'

Both girls raised their eyebrows, almost in unison. 'He lives on Archer Crescent?' Chloe nodded and pretended to listen while Samantha gave her directions and Lissy explained how much houses on Archer Crescent cost.

Chloe got to her feet, grabbing her bag. 'I have to go,' she said. 'Drinks on me tomorrow, okay?'

The girls smiled at her back as she turned for the door. Chloe knew they'd spend the evening talking about what a mistake she was making, about how easy she was. But she quite literally could not have cared less.

Archer Crescent was a half-moon of yellow stone houses set on a hill. They looked down over the river and sat a few hundred metres away from the boathouse. Number 29 was at the furthest end. Chloe looked down at her feet as they moved over the cobbled street and pulled her coat closer around her. It was cheap acrylic and the wind seemed to find its way up the sleeves and down the neck. She sniffed, hoping the cold wouldn't have made her face too pink. Her nail varnish was chipped, she realized, as she pressed her finger to the porcelain doorbell.

She heard the bell, shrill and old-fashioned, sound inside and after a few minutes feet on the stairs. The door swung open and standing in the warm yellow light was Zadie.

Her feet were bare on the stone floor, her hair piled up on top of her head. She wore a pair of pyjama shorts, a man's jumper and an excited expression.

'Chloe!' she cried, throwing her arms around her. 'You're freezing! Come in, come in.'

Stepping over the threshold, Chloe tried to keep her face expressionless. There were bunches of flowers in vases on every surface. Art on the walls. The hall led down to a huge kitchen with a dining table and sixteen chairs.

How could a bunch of students afford to live here? How could anyone afford to live here?

'Come upstairs,' said Zadie, taking the steps two at a time. 'I'm still getting ready.'

'Ready?' said Chloe to Zadie's back. 'For what?'

Zadie stopped, throwing open the door to an enormous bedroom. She turned, looking surprised. 'I didn't tell you? We're having a party.' She went to the wardrobe, which ran almost the length of the room, and pulled open the doors. It was stuffed full of garments on hangers. Dresses, T-shirts, jackets, and jumpers Chloe didn't need to touch to know they were cashmere.

'This place is amazing,' she said, taking it all in. 'No wonder you don't want to live in our room.'

Zadie laughed. 'Isn't it obscene? Max's parents bought it when they found out he was coming here, so that he could be close to the gym. They're loaded, and he's their little prince. Can't do wrong, nothing ever good enough. You know the type.'

Chloe didn't know the type, but she didn't say that. 'Does Max play rugby?'

Zadie rolled her eyes. 'Yes, but do *not* ask him about it, otherwise he'll want to talk about it and, honestly, the only thing more boring than watching rugby is listening to people talk about it. He only came to uni here because it's so good for sport. And then I came here because I'm pathetic and I missed him.'

Chloe sat down on the bed, sinking into its heavy covers, her head spinning at the idea that you could get into

a university like this one just because you wanted to be
with your boyfriend.

Zadie started to pull things off hangers. 'I am so useless. I can't believe I didn't warn you about the party. Do
you want to borrow something? You've probably got
stuff back at college that you'd rather wear, but seeing as
you're here already, this would be great on you.' She held
up a short black silk dress.

Chloe knew she should at least protest that she didn't
want to wear it, that she was happy in her jeans and top.
In her head her mother's voice was scolding her about
taking things from people, asking why anyone like Zadie
would want to lend someone like Chloe a dress. But in
spite of all that, before she'd even realized what she was
doing, she was stripping her clothes off with a kind of
abandon that didn't belong to her, her jeans and top were
shoved into her rucksack and she was looking into the
mirror at a girl in a beautiful dress.

Zadie gave a dramatic sigh when Chloe turned around
to show her. 'Fuck, you look great. Do you want shoes?'
She turned back to the dressing table, where she was
doing her make-up in front of a huge antique mirror.
'What size are you?'

'Five.'

'Oh, I'm a seven. Annoying. Never mind, just go
barefoot.'

'You're sure you don't mind?'

Zadie looked at her in the mirror, their eyes meeting
in the glass. 'Mind?'

'The dress, and everything.' She shifted from one foot to the other, not sure where to put herself.

Zadie put her lipstick down and turned to look at her properly. Did she sense Chloe's discomfort? 'D'you want to go and get us both a drink before everyone gets here?' she said. 'Glasses are in a cabinet by the back door, and there are loads of bottles in the fridge. Just open one. Max should be around somewhere.'

Relieved by the idea of having something to do, Chloe padded down the stairs and into the kitchen. It was warm in the house, the kind of indulgent warmth that came from having the heating on all the time. People like Max and Zadie didn't worry about bills. They probably had someone to sort things like that out. Chloe couldn't imagine someone as sparkly as Zadie having to deal with the dullness of paperwork.

How was it possible that the people who lived here were in their teens and twenties? The kitchen looked like something her mother would cut out of an interior-design magazine. Marble floor, pale grey walls, a huge island in the middle with a marble top and stools all around it. It was also, strangely, empty. Enjoying the feeling of being in the room, as if she were on the set of a film, she took two glasses from the cabinet then pulled open the door of the American-style fridge. A girl she had known at school had a fridge like that, with a door which made ice. She'd always made a point of letting them have a go with it at sleepovers.

The fridge was full of mineral water, champagne and

Diet Coke, nothing as pedestrian as food. She pulled out a bottle of champagne and as she pulled off the foil around the top of the bottle she was grateful, for the first time in her life, that she'd spent two years working at the Sun and Mitre on the high road and so knew how to open it. Expertly, she twisted the cork from the bottle. It gave a low hiss as it came cleanly off, not a drop spilled over the neck.

A voice came from behind her. 'Impressive.' Startled, Chloe spun around, catching the bottle with her wrist and tipping it over on the counter. 'Fuck!' she yelped.

The boy was tall and broad-shouldered and had dark hair. His eyes were somewhere between green and brown and he looked – Chloe couldn't find a better way to explain it – like a grown-up. The boys she had met so far, with their fleeces and trainers and stubby fingernails, had all seemed like children. But everything about this boy screamed adult, despite the fact that he couldn't have been any older than twenty-one.

Smiling at her distress, he took a cloth from the side and threw it to her. 'Usual house rules say that if you spill it, you have to lick it up. But seeing as you're new here, I think we'll make an exception.'

Chloe raised one eyebrow, trying to think of something smart to say, trying to ignore the fact that every single cliché from every book she had ever read was taking place underneath her ribcage. She put the cloth on top of the pool of champagne that was fizzing on the counter.

'You're very kind,' she said, smiling up into his face and parting her lips to tell him her name, but as she did so Zadie entered the room. Her long hair trailed over her bare shoulders and her skin glowed. She grinned at Chloe. 'Oh, good. You two found each other. I wanted you to meet.' She pulled her lithe body up on to tiptoes and kissed the boy on the lips. The realization of who he was came crashing down around Chloe's shoulders. It was as if someone had dropped an ice cube down her back. She fixed her face into a smile, horrified at her own reaction.

'We just met,' said Max, crossing the room to get another champagne glass. He set it on the marble countertop with a clink and took Chloe's hand in his.

'I'm Chloe,' she said.

'It's nice to meet you, Chloe. I heard you came to Zadie's rescue the other day.'

He picked up the bottle, filled three glasses and handed one to each of the girls. His eyes were locked into Zadie's. How could a gesture that innocent feel so intimate? 'Here's to Chloe,' he said, raising his glass. 'Our saviour.'

'Our saviour,' repeated Zadie, with a grin.

6
NOW

'We're late,' said Rav, sighing and looking at his phone. He'd been putting it back into his jacket pocket then taking it out again for the last twenty minutes, as if staring at the time had any influence on how late it was or how slowly the traffic crawled.

'Not very,' Chloe replied. She looked to the front seat of the car, searching for the time on the dashboard, hoping it disputed the numbers on Rav's screen. The driver was playing Magic FM, the 'Greatest Hits of the Eighties', but he'd turned the volume down so low she could hardly hear it. She never understood why people did that.

'Half an hour late,' said Rav. He sounded genuinely worried. Something about the rawness in his voice pulled at her, making her want to comfort him.

'I thought he said seven thirty for eight?' Her voice was bright and cheerful, though she wasn't sure why. How had it become her responsibility to cheer Rav up about going to a dinner she had tried to refuse to attend?

Rav looked away, staring out of the window at the

bumper-to-bumper cars. Chloe could have told him they'd have made better time getting from north London to south-west London if they'd taken the Tube. But there was no point. He already knew that. He'd probably be ashamed of himself for thinking that getting a taxi across London was an impressive way to arrive, as if Max gave a shit how they got there, as if he would even notice. She didn't need to say any of it. Rav would already be bullying himself internally about it.

The closer they got to Max's house, the more she wanted to ease the tension. If they fought now, they'd still put on a good show when they arrived, of course. But Max had always had a nose for these things – a strange character trait for someone so jocular. Chloe pushed the button to open the window. It squealed as it did so, raspingly dry against the frame of the door. The air outside was warm and laden with petrol fumes.

'Thank you for doing this,' said Rav, looking out of the window on his side of the car. 'I know you didn't want to.'

Chloe cocked her head, surprised. 'I know it's important to you. And that you want the work.'

'Like I said, it might be fun. It's been a while.'

Chloe made a non-committal noise.

'I know you still think Max was partially responsible,' Rav said. His voice was gentle and his thumb softly stroked her arm. 'For what happened with Zadie. But it was a long time ago. We've all changed so much since then.'

Halfway through swallowing, Chloe's throat stuck together. It had been years since she'd heard Rav say Zadie's name.

Rav had no idea what he was talking about. Sure, he knew that Zadie had disappeared from university and that Zadie and Max had been a couple. But he had never really been in the inner circle, never seen Max and Zadie unguarded, up close. And he hadn't seen Max's face the morning that Zadie vanished. His skin – usually an even dark olive – had been waxy and somehow grey. By the time Rav saw them, Max was composed. Calm. The worried, long-suffering boyfriend with the highly strung, complicated girlfriend. Rav had swallowed Max's lies about loving Zadie and missing her but respecting her need for space. Which was all very convenient. Space meant that Zadie couldn't say anything. Couldn't bring his beautifully designed artifice crashing down.

'We're pretty close now,' she said, putting her hand on Rav's thigh and inclining her head towards the driver's satnav. There was no point revisiting the conversation about Zadie. Nothing she could say to convince him that Max was guilty as sin. Rav had chosen what he believed, the version of the story that best suited him. His muscles felt tight under her hand. Not desperately so, but tighter than usual. The kind of thing you only notice when you've touched the same person's leg in the same way for fifteen years.

The car turned off the slow, busy road and on to a quieter one. Suddenly the trees either side were green and the buildings pretty. They must be nearly there. Eventually, the taxi came to a stop outside a modern glass house that stood, almost comically mismatched, at the end of a terrace of pretty Victorian buildings.

'No prizes for guessing which one's his,' Chloe breathed as she got out of the car. Her skirt clung to the back of her thighs, sticky from the pleather seats. Rav rang the doorbell and Chloe counted inside her head, trying to stay calm. She was about to see Max for the first time in a decade and a half, the first time since . . . She stopped herself. She was not going to be dragged back there, even for a moment, even inside her own head.

Moments later, there he was, framed by the doorway. His feet were tanned and bare, his legs clad in dark, expensive jeans. His linen shirt was untucked and he'd not done up anywhere near enough buttons. The belt was Gucci, the watch Breitling. It pained her to note that he was still exceptionally handsome – almost more than he had been, in that irritating way some men had of improving with age. She detected, as she allowed him to kiss her on each cheek, that he had changed his scent. At uni it had been CK One. Presumably, he wouldn't wear anything quite so passé now.

'Coco. You look stunning.' Was there a hint of an Australian accent, after all those years there?

Her shoulders raised a quarter of an inch at the old nickname, the name Max had dubbed her with so many years ago. At the time, it had felt like being anointed, as if she belonged to some new and brilliant world. Most of their posh friends had nicknames. Girls named Georgia who everyone called Winky, or boys called Josh who everyone called Wank. Coco was the kind of silly, pretty, sexy name your parents gave you if they didn't have to worry about you being taken seriously, if your life was destined to be parties and lunches, laughing and shopping.

Chloe pushed the bunch of flowers into his chest rather than saying anything and looked around. It was all so desperately Max – lots of glass and chrome, everything brand new. But there was another force at work, too, something undeniably feminine. There were candles flickering on most of the surfaces and cut flowers in several vases. It was almost eerily like Archer Crescent.

'It's a great place,' she heard Rav say as he followed Max down a staircase. 'Have you had a lot done?' She moved after them, her hand on the cool banister, feet on glass stairs, unable to quite believe that Rav had talked her into this, that she hadn't put up more of a fight.

Rav was right about the house. It *was* great. Chic, and tastefully done. The hall was high-ceilinged and had wooden floorboards. The staircase gave on to an open-plan basement kitchen, sparklingly clean and magazine-modern, looking out over a wide green garden. How much would all of this have cost? Millions. Several millions. Clearly, things were going well for Max. But then that couldn't come as any kind of surprise.

'We redecorated a lot of it,' Max was saying as he busied himself in the kitchen. 'Structurally, it was fine, but the previous lot were some awful internet celebrities, after every interiors trend going. We wanted it to be a bit more timeless.'

Max had always been a 'we', as long as Chloe had known him. In fact, this was all almost exactly how she had imagined it would be when they got older. Her and Rav, dinner at Max's incredible house. The only thing wrong was the woman who slid open the French doors and came in from the garden, a pair of secateurs in one hand and a bunch of herbs in the other.

'This,' said Max, striding across the kitchen and wrapping his arms around the waist of the tiny woman, 'is Verity.'

As they bumped cheeks and exchanged pleasantries, Chloe drank Verity in. Her limbs had the kind of thinness that made clothes look expensive even when they weren't – though hers clearly were. She wore a cream silk blouse tucked into high-waisted jeans cinched in with a Gucci belt. His 'n' hers, thought Chloe, snidely. Verity's hair was long and wavy, just dark enough blonde that it might be natural. Chloe pulled the strap of her dress on to her shoulder, feeling overdressed and far too tall in her heels.

'What can I get you to drink?' asked Verity, her voice sweet, and with a hint of an accent.

'White wine,' said Chloe.

'Whatever's open,' said Rav at the same time. Chloe tried not to roll her eyes. Rav's deference was exhausting.

'We've got a bottle of this on the go,' said Max, holding up a bottle of Taittinger. 'Will that do, Coco?'

Chloe didn't like champagne any more; she found it too sharp and acrid. Perhaps she'd drunk too much of it in the year that she and Max had been friends. But she didn't want to be rude. 'Sure,' she said, shifting her weight from one foot to the other.

'I gather congratulations are in order,' Chloe said, for lack of anything better to say.

Verity looked up from the chopping board and smiled. 'Thank you,' she said. 'It was quite a surprise.'

'You've had a busy time of it, mate.' Rav nudged Max's arm. 'New house, new fiancée. You're turning into a real grown-up.'

'Don't remind me.' Max sighed. 'Though I think it's worth it for this one.' He looked across the room at Verity, an expression of rapture on his face. 'I still can't quite believe she said yes.'

Chloe looked at Verity's left ring finger, white against the dark red ruby flanked by two square diamonds on a gold band. With anyone else, she'd have squealed and demanded to be told all the details of the proposal, but now she just couldn't. Her stomach was churning, bile tickling the softness at the back of her throat. She had seen that ring before.

It had looked better on Zadie. Mind you, everything always did. She had had this way about her, this way of injecting life into anything she touched.

Verity must have seen where Chloe was looking because she lifted her hand and said, 'Lovely, isn't it?'

Chloe murmured her agreement, forcing her words

out. 'Is it antique?' she asked, knowing what the answer would be.

'It's a family ring,' said Verity. 'One of a kind. It's been in the bank since Max's great-grandmother died.'

Chloe took a sip of the champagne, trying to forget herself and Zadie, nineteen years old and high as kites, finding the ring in Max's room and screaming as Zadie tried it on, jumping up and down and yelling the words 'bride' and 'bridesmaid'. But as she pushed that memory away it was replaced by another one. The same ring on Zadie's bloodied finger, as she lay on the bedroom floor.

Chloe felt herself burn with an anger she had spent fifteen years trying to extinguish.

He really thought he had got away with it.

7
THEN

Chloe had been to parties before of course. She hadn't been especially beloved at school, but she hadn't been reviled either and had always been invited along even if no one would really have noticed if she didn't turn up. But parties at home had been bottles of cheap fizzy wine, lukewarm, in someone's parents' garden, before summoning the local taxi driver to take them to a club in town, and the driver then warning them several times that he always enforced the soiling charge. Chloe had usually stood on the outside of these gatherings, sitting in the front of the taxi, talking to the parents during the pre-drinks, never entirely sure where to put herself. This party was different. It belonged in an American TV show. The house might have looked grown-up earlier, but now it reeked of student. The garden was full of boys in T-shirts, despite the chill in the air. There were pretty girls with long hair and lace-edged vest tops sitting on every surface, cigarettes hanging from their delicate fingers.

In the living room someone had set up a speaker and sickly dance music pumped into the rooms. The house was detached and ancient, but the music still travelled. Chloe wondered how angry the neighbours must be and then immediately hated herself for it. The kitchen, where she had been standing for longer than she wanted to admit to herself, had been transformed, drowned in students drinking from plastic cups, every surface littered with bottles.

The party might have been different, but the feeling that she had no idea where to put herself was exactly the same as it had been back in Surrey. She couldn't see Zadie or Max, both of whom had disappeared into the crowd an hour or so earlier. They'd pointed at a few people and shouted their names at her before they'd gone, clearly assuming that Chloe had a far better grasp of herself than she did. Term had only been going for a few weeks. How did all these people already know each other so well? She took a long slug from her drink and steeled herself.

'Hey,' she said to a pretty girl with auburn hair who was pressing her back against the fridge.

The girl raised an eyebrow. 'Hello.'

'How do you know Max and Zadie?' she heard herself ask. As if this were one of Greg's golf-club mixers. The girl cocked her head. Perhaps she would think it was a satirical remark. Maybe it was such a pathetic thing to have asked that it would seem funny.

'I went to school with Max,' she replied, still seemingly uncertain. 'I have to pee.'

She had left a cigarette – a rollie – on the counter next to where she had been standing. Chloe picked it up. Really, she shouldn't take it, but it was only a cigarette, and the girl had been unfriendly enough that Chloe sort of hated her. Plus, she knew from watching people at school that smoking was the quickest and easiest way to make friends. She put the cigarette between her lips and went into the garden, looking for someone with a lighter. A group of boys were gathered, watching the tallest of them down a giant bottle of Magners. 'Have you got a light?' she asked one of them. He turned and she drank in his dark hair, dark eyes, dark blue polo shirt.

'Sure,' he said.

She took a long, heavy drag as he flicked the flame, grateful that, if nothing else, she did at least know how to smoke properly. The thought evaporated as the acrid stream filled her lungs, and she coughed, an embarrassing, hacking cough.

'You might want to go easy on that,' the boy said, smiling. 'It smells fucking lethal.'

Chloe held the cigarette out, looking at it sideways, as the realization dawned on her.

'I think this might be a spliff,' she said, breathing in the familiar smell, which took her back to pretending to inhale in the school car park.

'I think it might be.'

'Do you want to share it with me?' she blurted, trying to recover.

He cast a glance back at the group. 'Go on, then. I'm Rav, by the way.'

'Chloe.'

'Nice to meet you.'

They sat on the wall at the bottom of the garden, taking turns to drag on the spliff while watching the scene unfold in front of them. Chloe could feel the dampness of the stone soak slowly through the thin material of Zadie's dress. Her mother would have told her she was bound to get piles. She giggled, thinking about it, then looked at Rav's profile, trying to see whether he had noticed her laughing. Chloe hadn't ever given much thought to a person's profile before, but now she studied Rav's in the half-light. His jaw was a perfect right angle and his nose had clearly been broken, presumably playing rugby, like Max did, but somehow it only added to the symmetry of his face. He had the slightest hint of stubble – proper adult, not the sad, downy stuff that so many boys his age seemed inexplicably proud of.

'It's like a play,' said Chloe. 'All lit up, all of them playing, us sitting here, watching.'

'Do you like plays?'

Chloe nodded. 'I wanted to go to drama school. But Greg said I didn't stand a chance, and my mum does whatever he says. So I'm here. Studying English. Sorry. *Reading* English. Why do they say that? *Reading?* What if you're doing a course like Maths or Engineering, where there isn't any reading?'

'I'm doing Engineering. Trust me, there's reading. Who's Greg? He sounds like a twat.'

'Greg *is* a twat, you are so totally right. He's my step-father. Well, he's my mum's boyfriend. My mum had me when she was nineteen. That's like us having a baby right now.'

'I think I should at least take your number first.'

Chloe dictated her number, and then, giddy with the excitement of how well this was all going, almost slipped backwards off the wall. Rav caught her around the waist. 'Careful!'

'You saved me.'

'I did.'

'That's quite romantic.'

'It is, isn't it?'

Chloe blushed and avoided making eye contact. But when she looked up Rav was staring straight ahead at a pretty girl standing a few metres away with a group of friends.

'That's her!' shouted the girl. 'That's the bitch who stole my spliff.'

'Finish it, quickly,' said Rav. Chloe looked down at the spliff, which was still just glowing at the tip, then up at the girl, then at Rav. He hopped down off the wall. 'Don't think so, Corinne. That one's mine, and Chloe only just got here.'

The girl looked disbelieving. She threw Chloe a dirty look then turned her back on them. Chloe took another deep drag from the spliff as Rav offered her his hand so she could jump down from the wall. Her head spun. Cold blood rushed from her feet to the back of her neck. 'Rav, I don't feel—' she started, but before she could stop her words were interrupted by a stream of vomit, which splattered all over Rav's feet and legs.

ZADIE

Sometimes Zadie liked to wait until a party was in full flow and then retreat. Max called it her 'Gatsby act', though she was absolutely sure that he hadn't read the book. It wasn't that she didn't like parties. She loved them. But they were like paintings. Something lovely to create, and then to step back and look at.

Max was having fun. Laughing, joking, drinking. And he had told her how glad he was to see Chloe there. She had ticked a box. Made a friend. Now he didn't have to feel guilty that she had come here to be with him. It was still completely true, but he could enjoy plausible deniability. And, to her surprise, she liked Chloe. It had been a very long time since she had got ready with another girl. And while she knew that it was probably awful, she liked how impressed Chloe was with the house, with her clothes, with all of it. It made her feel less like a pathetic little hanger-on. Chloe didn't seem to regard her as Max's girlfriend, someone who just followed him around. And she was so brave. She had just walked off into the party, apparently without a second thought. It must be wonderful to be able to do that.

She pushed open the door to find a boy in her bedroom. A beautiful, tall boy with dark skin and dark hair, and no trousers on. He was crouched down, going through Max's chest of drawers. She smiled as she watched him catch sight of her and panic. 'I'm not stealing!' he said. 'The guy whose party this is said I could borrow some trousers.'

Zadie laughed. 'Ah. That was nice of him. What's wrong with your own ones?'

'A girl was sick on me.'

'Oh. Gross.'

'I was trying to find some jeans.'

'They're in here.' Zadie opened the bottom drawer and pulled some out. They were neatly ironed, probably by Max's precious mother, who'd ironed his clothes before packing them, with more enjoyment than Zadie considered normal. His family had a housekeeper, but his mother still liked doing things for her little prince.

'Thanks,' said the boy. 'How did you know that?'

'I live here.'

The boy seemed even more embarrassed now. Zadie sat on the bed, enjoying his sweet bashfulness. 'Why was this girl sick on you?'

'She was smoking a spliff. It was really strong. She kind of whiteyed.'

'Is she okay?'

'Not sure. I sort of legged it to wash myself off.'

'What a gentleman. I'm assuming she's not a girlfriend?'

'No, no. I don't have a girlfriend. I just met her tonight.'

'Poor girl.'

A pause settled between them, and the boy seemed to realize all over again that he wasn't wearing any trousers. He coughed. 'I should probably . . .' He trailed off and started pulling the jeans on. Zadie turned away obligingly, but not before she caught a glimpse of his tanned, toned thighs.

'Okay, I'm decent,' he said a few seconds later, awkwardly wiping his palms on the denim.

She looked over her shoulder. 'Shall we go back to the party?'

So they did. And when they reached the bottom of the stairs they turned in different directions. She watched as the boy walked through the party and stood on the edge of a conversation, listening to someone else speak. Then a pair of arms came from behind, twisting around her waist. 'Hello, gorgeous.'

'I'm sorry, do I know you?'

'I certainly bloody hope so,' Max replied. 'Shall we go upstairs and fuck? I'm bored of everyone who isn't you.'

'Absolutely.'

8
NOW

Verity could cook, Chloe had to give her that. She'd served
them bruschetta, which Max had proudly announced
was home-made. He said it like he was telling everyone
that she'd won a Nobel Prize. But then, Chloe supposed,
to Max, splitting the atom and making bread were probably equally miraculous. He'd never been able to cook.
She had vague memories of him drinking pints of protein shake or loading up on plain chicken breasts when
they were younger, determined to become bigger and
bigger. He'd told her once that he took after his father,
who had owned – perhaps still owned – a chain of Italian
restaurants but didn't really like food.

The bruschetta was crisp on the outside and soft in the
middle, tangy with oil and sharp with garlic and rose-
mary. The tomatoes were bright and fat, clearly bought
from some organic farmers' market rather than the local
supermarket. It even smelled vibrant, but it was impossible to eat. The boys laughed as they picked it up, spilling
tomatoes on to the plate. Verity busied herself, flitting

around, clearly not intending to let a morsel of bread pass her bee-stung lips. Chloe pushed bits of tomato around with her fork, not wanting to risk an oil spill down the front of her dress, unwilling to look messy as well as overdressed next to Verity. She broke off a piece of bread and carefully placed it in her mouth. She needed to eat something; her head was swimming. Two glasses of champagne already down, despite the fact she didn't like it, and she was now part way through a glass of buttery white wine.

'So, Rav, where are you from?' Verity asked him, smiling over the candles. People did this to Rav a lot – assumed that because of his name and the colour of his skin he had a huge family straight out of central casting hidden in some terraced house in west London, full of laughter and women in saris making roti.

Chloe had often wished that were the case. She had indulged in fantasies of how that might be, of being welcomed into the middle of a loud, loving rabble. But not a chance.

Rav's mother hadn't been to Pakistan since the seventies. She and his father lived in a pristine apartment in Zurich, where she and Rav visited them twice a year, under extreme sufferance. Photos of Rav, their favourite son, lined the surfaces and the entire place smelled like Dettol.

On their first visit, nearly a decade ago now, Chloe had got her period on the sheets of the bed in the enormous white guest room. Horrified, she'd crept down the corridor to Rav's room, woken him up and whimpered what had happened. He had kissed her forehead, sneaked the sheets into the laundry and sent Chloe back to bed. 'I'll fix it. Go back to sleep,' he'd said.

'I'll fix it' was Rav's mantra. He took care of everything. Labours of love – Chloe knew that. He did it to make her life easier, happier, better. But just occasionally, when she realized that all the morning's post had been opened, dealt with and all the bills paid before she'd even looked at it, she wondered if there was any harm, any danger, in letting Rav do all of it. How would she manage if a day came when she had to do it by herself?

To this day, Rav insisted that his mother had no idea what had happened, but the look in her eyes over breakfast the next morning had told Chloe that she did know.

'Switzerland,' Rav said now, pulling Chloe's focus back to the table.

Chloe loved these exchanges. Or rather, she loved how Rav handled himself in them.

'Oh.' Verity looked confused. 'But originally?'

'I went to school in England, grew up in Switzerland, but my grandparents were from Pakistan. Where's your family from? Verity is a French name, isn't it?'

Chloe looked up from her plate. That wasn't like him. Generally, Rav would say, 'Ohh, you meant *originally*. My parents are *originally* from Zurich,' and then laugh. He never usually felt the need to explain his skin colour. Back at university, he and Max were occasionally mistaken for brothers or cousins, and he loved the joke.

At the time, Chloe had assumed it was because it amused him that people couldn't tell the difference between Max, Italian and Greek, and him, Swiss-Pakistani. But she wondered now if his reaction might have been more about the delight of being conflated with the coolest person on campus.

Chloe watched a blush creep up Verity's white neck. 'Yes,' she replied. 'My mother is French.'

Rav smiled and started to ask her what part of France, whether she had grown up there, if she spoke French, if she was going to teach Max. A pleasant, fluent stream of questions that allowed Verity to talk about herself. She seemed to be unwinding under Rav's attention. Had she been nervous about this evening? How many of Max's friends had she been expected to cook for and entertain since they'd got engaged?

Max's shoulder brushed hers. He smelled expensive and clean. His aftershave had changed, but the real smell of him was just the same. He tipped the rest of the bottle of white wine into her glass. 'Isn't she gorgeous?' he asked, quietly enough that only she could hear.

'Sure,' she said, dropping her gaze as if she had been caught looking at something she shouldn't have been. 'If you like that sort of thing.'

Max laughed. 'Beautiful, clever, sweet. That sort of thing?' Then, seeing her expression, he stopped. 'She's really great. You just need to get to know her a bit.'

'How old is she?' Chloe looked down into the bottom of her glass.

'Twenty-three.'

Only a few years older than they had been last time they saw each other.

Chloe said nothing. Max would delight in her disapproval and ignore any advice. She would gain absolutely nothing by opening her mouth. Instead she pulled herself up, correcting her posture and painting a smile across her face.

'She's the best thing that's ever happened to me,' Max went on. 'No drama, no tantrums, no getting drunk and turning into a nightmare.'

Was this deliberate? Her back teeth locked together, tensing her neck.

'She's just – I mean, don't get me wrong, I don't want to sound like a prick, but she's a nice girl. No mess, no fuss. No skeletons in the closet. Just straightforward, down to earth.'

Chloe tried to catch Rav's eye from across the room, to send him a Mayday signal, to drag the conversation back to all four of them, to break open this weirdly intimate trap Max had pulled her into.

'I guess what I'm saying' – Max smiled down at her, his dark curls shining – 'is that she's nothing like Zadie.'

Chloe opened her mouth to reply, but Max went on. 'Look, I know you probably don't want to talk about it, and after what happened we're not supposed to say it, but she was awful. Remember how she used to get? My God, she was such a burden on you. She practically made you fail your first year.'

'What?' Rav asked, drawn away from his conversation with Verity.

'Nothing,' Chloe said hurriedly.

'We were exchanging memories. Like the time that Chloe nearly got kicked out of uni in her first year.'

'You what?'

She hadn't ever told Rav about that. He would have blamed Zadie. Claimed she was a 'bad influence', that Chloe's lack of dedication to her university work was somehow Zadie's responsibility. Even now, she couldn't bear the idea of him blaming Zadie. She wanted to remember Zadie as her beloved best friend, not as the tornado she could sometimes be.

'He's exaggerating. I got a formal warning for missing some work. Like a lot of people did in their first year. It wasn't a big deal.'

Rav raised his eyebrows. 'More than fifteen years together, and I'm still learning new things about you. I guess that's something to be pleased about.'

'I'm not sure learning new things about our other halves is always ideal,' laughed Max. 'Verity and I have a nice amnesty about anything I did before I was twenty-one.'

I bet you do, thought Chloe. She took another long drink from her glass. She looked around the table. Everyone was staring at her. Had she said that out loud?

'Has everyone finished their starter?' asked Verity as a hush settled across the table. There was a general murmur of agreement and she took the plates away to the kitchen. Chloe got up to help, starting to open cupboards, looking for a dishwasher.

'Oh, you don't need to do that,' said Verity. 'I've got someone coming in tomorrow. She's wonderful, but she gets upset with me if I try and clear up. She has her own ways of doing things.'

How could someone so young be so completely at ease in a home like this? Chloe still got up an hour early on the day their cleaner came and wiped down all the surfaces, hid her vibrator under a nest of tights in her underwear drawer and gave the bathroom a quick bleach. She had to be at school by eight, so it usually meant getting up before six. Rav couldn't understand why she did it. To him, having a cleaner meant that a person who didn't really exist would arrive at their house while they weren't there and they would return to a neat and tidy living space. To Chloe, the cleaner was completely and utterly real, having a painfully unvarnished view into their life, seeing what they ate and how much they drank, whether Rav had slept on the sofa after a row or if she had bothered cooking something elaborate. She still pretended to her mother that she didn't have a cleaner. The prospect of explaining why – that they were both so busy – was too much. She couldn't face the inevitable 'But, darling, you've got lots of time, you're only a teacher.'

'So, how long have you lived together?' Chloe asked as Verity took vegetables from the fridge and set about making a salad.

Verity shook her head. 'We don't.' The little gold dia-mond hoops which punctured her ear lobes caught the light as they moved. She had only one hole in each ear. Zadie had had loads. Her first had been done at Selfridges in London, something which Chloe had been blown away by. The rest of them had been done by friends at school, copying *The Parent Trap*, people on beaches in Bali or hostels in Berlin. Zadie had done Chloe's second set, drunk at Archer Crescent one night. She'd flicked a lighter over a needle while Chloe lay on the bed hoping she was drunk enough not to feel it and pretending she wasn't worried about her mother's reaction. She hadn't wanted the piercing, really. Just something permanent on her body which came from Zadie.

'My family are very traditional. I have a little place in Notting Hill. Of course, I stay here often, but I won't live here until we're married.'

'My mum was horrified when I moved in with Rav. Said something about men not buying the cow if you give out the milk for free.'

Verity laughed. It was the first time Chloe had seen her do so in an unguarded fashion. She looked even younger. 'I think my grandmother had a similar expres-sion. Though, clearly, it's not true. How long have you been married?'

'Six years. We'd been together for nearly a decade before that, though. When I told my mother he'd pro-posed she said "Finally" so much she forgot to say "Congratulations".'

Verity laughed again, then turned to look through the kitchen, down to the dining room. It was open plan, but Max and Rav were far enough away that, with the music on, they couldn't quite make out what they were talking about.

'They look very intense,' said Verity. 'I hope they're not talking about business.'

'They will be. Rav thinks Max is some kind of genius.'

'You don't?'

Chloe looked apologetic. Verity was not Zadie. She wouldn't laugh at Max in the same way. In the way he needed to be laughed at. 'I'm sure he's very good at what he does.'

'He is.' Verity's prim manner had returned. 'Shall we go through?'

Rav wasn't drunk, not properly. But he wore the expression he always got after a few glasses of wine, when he was in a really good mood and wanted to throw love out on to the people around him. If Chloe was the only one around when it happened, he would shower her with praise, telling her that she was making a difference to young people's lives with her job, that she was more beautiful in her mid-thirties than she had been in her twenties, that she was funny and clever and would inevitably write an award-winning play one day. But tonight his megawatt love was aimed at Max.

'So, go on,' he said. 'Tell us everything that's happened since we last saw each other. I want to hear the Max Trentino success story.'

'Oh, it's not such a success. Plenty of cock-ups along the way.'

'Go on, tell us. How'd you go from a rugby bum to' – Rav spread his hands out, gesturing around the room – 'all this?'

Max adopted a falsely modest expression, clearly looking forward to dominating the conversation. 'So, I went off to play rugby in Oz – you knew that. Was there for a while. Dad's dad was from Melbourne so I was able to play properly. Looked like it might go all the way, but then I bust my shoulder.'

'You two don't know any of this?' Verity looked confused. 'You've been friends for so long.'

There was a brief, tense silence. How was it possible that Max hadn't explained anything before they got here? Perhaps he had assumed that Verity would be so uninterested she wouldn't ask.

Chloe waited to see who would break the silence, determined that she wasn't going to be the one to make things less awkward. She hadn't wanted to come here in the first place, so she was damned if she was going to do anything to make Max's life easier. Eventually, he said, 'We lost touch when I went to Oz and we only reconnected recently. You have to remember, my love, we're ancient. There wasn't any Instagram when we were at university.'

Verity pursed her lips. What had she been told? Had Max led her to believe that they were all still best friends?

'Anyway,' Max went on, topping up everyone's glass,

Verity's especially full, 'one of the blokes I played with was in construction, and he brought me in for a bit of work. I got on with his old man, who ran the company, and we did rather well together. But my folks are getting on a bit and living over there seemed a bit much, so I told him that I wanted to move home and he asked me to set up the UK branch of the business.'

'Bloody great for you,' said Rav. 'And how did you two meet?'

'I'm an assistant to an interior designer. Max was speaking to my boss about working on one of his projects and I came to take notes in the meeting. He dropped his phone number into my lap when she wasn't looking.'

'Very smooth,' said Rav.

'Or sexual harassment, depending on how you look at it.' Chloe heard herself say the words, and then tried to feel remorseful when Verity looked horrified.

'I didn't feel harassed at all. He picked me up from my flat in his beautiful car, and then on the way to dinner it ground to a halt. He pulled over and started fixing the engine right then and there, oil on his shirt and everything. I fell for him hook, line and sinker. He was just so together, so grown-up. All the boys I knew were such children compared to Max.' Verity was the most animated Chloe had seen her all evening, lit up from the inside. Her stomach twisted in sympathy. The poor girl, so excited to tie her life to someone like Max.

'The food is delicious,' Chloe said, in lieu of something more meaningful. She wasn't lying; it really was. There were roast aubergines with miso, butterflied leg of lamb and a huge, fresh salad.

'It really is. We'll have to get the recipe from you,' said Rav.

Chloe snorted. 'Oh, you're going to cook this?'

'No,' said Rav. 'I mean, I could try.'

'That would be a first.'

Rav looked hurt. Chloe shifted in her seat and tried to get a grip on herself. She could sense that being around Max was putting her in a terrible mood, bringing back all the anger all over again.

'Sorry.' Chloe smiled at Verity. 'Bit of a running joke between Rav and me. He's a really terrible cook.'

It was true. Rav was one of the worst cooks Chloe had ever encountered. His family had a maid when he was a child and he was at boarding school throughout his teens, so at no point had he learned to do anything other than wrap a chicken breast covered in packet spice mix in tin foil and bake it in the oven. He called it chicken à la Rav. Once, when they'd gone to Zurich to stay with his family, Chloe had made a joke about Rav's cooking, or rather the lack of it. 'I suppose we didn't equip Ravinder with cooking skills. An oversight,' his mother had said. Chloe had burned with shame for hours.

'Excuse me,' said Max, getting up from the table and laying his napkin over the dining chair. 'The glasses are getting worryingly empty.' Chloe watched him as he went to the far side of the kitchen.

'I'll go and get some more water,' she said, picking up the jug.

'I can do that,' offered Verity.

'No, no. You've been running around all evening. I'll do it.' This was Chloe's chance to speak to Max alone and to find out how the hell he got that ring.

9
THEN

A week after Max and Zadie's party, Chloe was sitting at her desk in her room, rereading the same passage of *Love's Labour's Lost* for the third time. Zadie hadn't been back since the day her parents had visited. All that remained of her was a trail of detritus from the bottom of her handbag – tobacco strands, glitter and dust – still strewn over the otherwise empty bedside table. Chloe couldn't quite bring herself to clean it up. She stretched in her seat, wondering what time it was. It had to be at least ten. Maybe eleven. The spiteful clock on her bedside table claimed that it wasn't even quite nine. Still at least another hour until she could reasonably go to bed, and nothing to distract her but her own cramped blue handwriting in the margins of her least favourite Shakespeare play. She could go downstairs to the bar; she knew that. Staying here was cutting off her nose to spite her face, as her mother would have so enjoyed saying. But after what had happened at Max and Zadie's house she had entered a sort of self-imposed isolation. She'd turned her phone off, not checked her college email address and pretended not to be in when Lissy and the other girls from her corridor banged on the door and tried to tempt her to pizza and rom-coms in the common room.

She wasn't entirely sure what she was trying to achieve by going into hiding. It wasn't as if she would bump into anyone from the party in such a pedestrian location as the common room or the college bar. But still, the idea of seeing anyone again, let alone risking making a fool of herself all over again, was too much to bear. She wished she had someone to phone, someone close enough who could make her feel better about what had happened. But when she went through her mental Rolodex of people, no one seemed right. All her friends from home existed in a chain. In a group, they made sense. But she felt that none of them seemed close enough individually for it to seem right to pick up the phone.

She would go to bed. There was nothing wrong with getting an early night. Then she could have an early start in the morning in order to . . . what? Work on her essay? Go for a run? She sighed as she pulled on her pyjamas, cleansed her face, brushed her teeth and tied her hair into a neat bun, just as her mother had taught her to do.

'Chloe?' A voice came from outside the door, accompanied by a knock that sounded more like a slam.

Chloe froze, feeling as if she had been caught doing something unspeakable. 'Yes?' she replied, hating the shake in her voice.

'Can I come in?' The door opened alongside the words

and in half fell Zadie. 'Oh, no,' she said, looking horrified. 'You were going to bed.' Her voice was thick and her
lips were tinted with dried red wine. 'I've interrupted
you going to bed. I'm so, so sorry. What time is it?'

Chloe pushed her alarm clock face down. 'About ten,'
she lied. 'What's wrong? Come in.'

Zadie flopped on to her bed, still wearing her shoes
and coat, and looked at the ceiling. 'Can I stay here
tonight?'

'It's your room, too. Of course you can.'

'Thank goodness for you.'

'What happened?'

Zadie got up and started stripping off her clothes. She
shimmied off her heavy fur coat and dropped it on to the
floor. Then she pulled off the dress she was wearing, a
flimsy pink thing which couldn't have been much pro-
tection against the late-November winds outside. Her
skin was pink with cold. She unhooked her bra and
dropped it on the floor. Much to Chloe's surprise, she
was wearing a suspender belt, which she deftly started
unhooking. 'Max and I had a fight.'

'Oh, no,' Chloe said, trying desperately not to stare at
Zadie's near-naked body. She was ballerina thin, with
long, lean muscles. Her breasts were so perfect Chloe
couldn't help wondering whether they might have had
some assistance. It was something of a relief when Zadie
got under the duvet, leaving her clothes in a pool on the
floor.

'What kind of fight?'

Zadie sighed. 'Have you got anything to drink?'

To her joy, Chloe did. Most of a bottle of red wine she had bought at a supermarket, because it felt like a grown-up thing to do. She had imagined she would drink it while reading some French poetry, but she'd actually had a glass while she watched *The X Factor*. Would it be the kind of thing Zadie would drink? She seemed like she had had quite a few already. Perhaps she wouldn't notice how cheap it was. She poured two mugfuls and handed one to Zadie, who wrapped herself in the duvet and lit a cigarette, using one of Chloe's candles as an ashtray. 'Thank you.' She smiled. 'I think this might be the best glass of wine I've ever had.'

Chloe looked up nervously at the smoke alarm. Surely one cigarette wasn't enough to set it off? 'It's only from Tesco.'

'It's perfect. Don't you hate people who know lots about wine? All that swirling and sniffing, it's such a sign of being a wanker.'

Chloe had never met anyone who knew lots about wine. 'Yes, such a wanky thing to do.'

A pause fell between them. Should she ask again about the fight with Max? Or had Zadie not responded before because she didn't want to talk about it? She settled on asking, 'Are you okay?'

'Yes, fine. I shouldn't moan. A fight with your boy-friend is hardly losing a limb in a terrible accident, is it?'

'If it upsets you, it upsets you. If we're only allowed to

complain about things which compare to limb loss, then we'd never say much.'

'What a nice thing to say.' Zadie sat up straighter. 'But, honestly, it was mostly my fault. He said he'd be back at six. I got all dressed up – the whole lingerie-clad seduction, you know?'

She paused, apparently waiting for Chloe to nod, like this was something she had done before as well. Only it wasn't, because she'd never had sex, let alone dressed up in expensive lingerie to seduce someone. She shook her head weakly.

'No?' said Zadie. 'Good for you. You're clearly far less of a sap than I am. So anyway, I waited for him to come back, and he was two hours late. Didn't call or anything. Then he came back, happy as Larry, and told me he's been picked to go and play rugby for an Australian university next year. Can you imagine? I'm there in all this complicated underwear and he's talking about whether the change in climate will affect his sprinting speed. I started crying, he said I wasn't being supportive, I said of course I'm not supportive, I don't want you to move to Australia, and then he got angry, and he can be so awful when he's cross, so then I stormed out and realized that I didn't have anywhere to go. So I came and spoilt your lovely quiet evening.'

Back at home, when someone had a fight with a boy-friend Chloe usually knew what to say. Her mother had lined most of the shelves in their house with self-help books, books about how to find love, books about how to keep love, books about how to cope with lost love. Chloe could recite chunks of *Men are from Mars, Women are from Venus* and *He's Just Not That Into You* like some children knew nursery rhymes. But this was entirely outside her area of expertise. How could anyone who was party to Zadie's obscene beauty want to do anything other than be with her? How could Max want to move to the other side of the world?

'Why was he late?' she settled on.

'Rugby. It's always rugby. Until the spring, when things ease off a little bit, and then, before you know it, it's pre-season and all about rugby again. He loves it more than he loves me.'

'I'm sure that's not true. Maybe he's just worried about being successful at it.'

Zadie snorted. 'Max doesn't worry about anything. He knows he's the best. And even if he wasn't, his father has dozens of restaurants.'

'Restaurants?'

'Yeah. His father started Mangiamo.'

There was a Mangiamo in almost every town. Enough of a treat that it was exciting to visit, but not so prohibitively expensive that it was beyond the likes of Chloe's family. Mangiamo was where Chloe had been taken for her eighteenth-birthday dinner. Greg had made a big deal about how they could order anything they wanted, even though he and her mother had entirely joint finances. Her mother had liked it, playing the little wife, as if she didn't work five days a week at a call centre and pour all her money into their shared bank account, which Greg without any compunction used to buy golf clubs and rounds for his mates. She couldn't decide what to say. She wasn't gauche enough to express that she was impressed, though she was, undeniably.

'My parents hate his parents,' Zadie went on. 'That's why they don't want us to live together. They think Max is spoilt and his parents are nouveau riche, which, as far as they're concerned, is the greatest sin a person can commit.'

This comment wasn't any more use. Chloe still wasn't sure what to say. Admittedly, she wasn't nouveau riche, because she wasn't riche, but she couldn't imagine that Astrid or Bob would have much time for her parents. Or her. But that was okay. Even if the single benefit of their friendship, in the eyes of Zadie's parents, would be that she was a 'good influence', that would be all right. She'd spent her entire teenage years with other people's parents saying, 'Why don't you spend time with that nice Chloe girl?', rendering her as unappealing as it was possible to be. So perhaps she was going to have to be here tonight to make sure Zadie didn't choke on her own vomit. Was that really who she wanted to be? The sensible friend who stood in the background making sure nothing serious happened? She shook her head, trying to stop thinking about it. She was making friends with her room-mate. Nothing more complicated than that.

'How was the rest of the party?'

'Oh, it was fine. The same as always, really.'

'Did, um—' She broke off. But she'd started the question

now. She would have to finish it. 'Did your friend Rav say anything about me?'

Zadie finished her wine. 'Are we out? And who's Rav?'

'No, there's still a little bit left.' She went to tip the remainder into Zadie's mug but stopped herself half-way, saving a good glug for herself. She watched the dark red splash into the white mug and felt a little thrill of pride.

'Tall. Handsome. Plays rugby with Max.'

'Could be any of them.'

'He's—' She stopped, trying to work out whether she was about to say the wrong thing. 'His parents are Pakistani. He studies Engineering.'

If she had accidentally sounded like a small-town racist, then Zadie didn't seem to have noticed. 'I don't know him,' she said. 'But I can ask Max. Did you like him?'

'I did, but I fucked it up.'

'How?'

She weighed the possible answers in her head. It was a funny story, really, however much it made her burn with shame. And it made her sound interesting, or, at least, it didn't make her sound boring. 'I accidentally stole someone's spliff, and then I smoked it too fast and threw up on his shoes.'

Zadie laughed a surprisingly inelegant laugh and twisted her hair up into a cloud of a bun. The duvet slipped down, re-exposing her left breast and a small tattoo of three stars on her ribs. She followed Chloe's gaze. 'Oh, don't. I got it on holiday in Turkey when I was fourteen, then had to wear a plaster over it every time we went on a family holiday. Max says it's hideous.'

'I like it.'

'Do you have any?'

Chloe shook her head. 'My parents take a similar view to yours.'

'Parents are the worst. So, does he have your number?'

'Rav?'

'Yes, Rav. If he's any kind of interesting person, he'll be desperate to go out with you and see what you do next.'

'I gave it to him when we were talking, but I don't think he's been in touch.'

'Don't think?'

'I turned my phone off after the party.'

Zadie put her head to one side. 'Shame is an entirely pointless emotion, and is almost exclusively experienced by women. It was a party. At least fifteen people vomited. Trust me, I know. It's my house. We've had to start paying the cleaners double. Also, turn your phone on. I texted you and you didn't reply. I was devastated.' She took a long breath and stretched. 'I'm exhausted. Literally can't remember the last time I went to bed at a sensible time. Can I borrow your toothbrush?'

Chloe thought Zadie was joking initially. Then, 'Yes, of course,' she said weakly as Zadie went to the sink in the corner of the room.

'You're an angel. No matter how wasted I am, I can't sleep without doing my teeth. Can you?' Zadie climbed into bed. She turned her light off, turned to face the wall and, within moments, was breathing in a slow, even pattern.

Chloe took her phone from the top drawer of her desk and held down the 'on' button. It took a few minutes to wake up. She watched as the screen began to buzz. Two messages from her mother, telling her to call. A text from Lissy asking if she wanted to take part in a charity netball match. And two messages from Zadie. 'Did you have fun last night? So hung over I wish I was dead,' read the first one. 'Come over tonight if you're not busy. Having another bloody party,' read the other. It was a confusing feeling, the delight of Zadie's attention mixed with the bitter disappointment that there was nothing from Rav.

10
NOW

Chloe placed the glass jug carefully in the sink. It was heavy and intricately designed, probably worth hundreds of pounds, so she really mustn't drop it. Rav would inevitably insist on replacing it if she broke it. She felt Max's breath on her bare shoulder.

'Having fun?'

'Where the hell did you get that ring?'

Max looked confused. She didn't believe it for a second. 'It was my grandmother's. Verity told you that.'

'Don't play games. You know exactly what I'm asking.'

'On the contrary, I've got no idea why you're so upset about my fiancée's engagement ring. Jealous?' He grinned and Chloe bit into the inside of her lip, trying to contain her rage.

'Zadie was wearing that ring the night of your twenty-first. She was wearing it when I found her.'

Max went to the fridge. 'Was she? I don't remember. Let's not do this again, Coco. If you still think I'm guilty of something, why the hell did you come here?'

'It was important to Rav. When you love someone, you make sacrifices for them. Hopefully, you'll work that out at some point before you take that poor girl down the aisle.'

She had promised herself she wouldn't do this. She had promised that she would say as little as possible; get in, get out. But the sight of the ring had knocked her off her axis. Chloe started moving towards the table. She would sit down. Play nicely. Pretend none of this had ever happened, then tell Rav on the way home that they were never, ever doing this again.

'So I take it you haven't heard from her?'

She stopped, turning on the spot, almost in a pirou-ette. 'Who?'

'You know who.'

Chloe's heart was flickering, her blood suddenly hot-ter. Was Max about to tell her that he knew something about Zadie? Where she was? How was it possible that he could know? Chloe had spent hours – probably days – looking her up on the internet. She had scoured every social networking website, trying to find a profile for her. She'd searched the Births, Deaths and Marriages regis-ter. She'd read the comments sections of articles she thought Zadie would like, looked out for her in crowds on the street and searched the backgrounds of TV programmes. She'd even considered hiring a private investigator and had only been prevented from doing so because she couldn't find the money to do it without Rav noticing.

'Have you?'

'I asked first,' Max said, a challenging note in his voice. 'This isn't funny.'

'It's not supposed to be.'

'Have you heard from her?'

Max shook his head. 'Nothing, not since the night she left. Have you?'

Chloe hesitated. She wanted to tell him yes. She wanted to tell him that Zadie had called her, told her the truth about everything that had ever happened between them, confirmed every suspicion that Chloe had ever had. But it wasn't true. Zadie had cut both of them out of her life in the exact same moment.

'No,' she said. 'Nothing.'

She walked through and put the jug back down on the table, and Max reappeared beside her with a bottle of white wine. He kissed Verity on the neck. 'Your favourite bottle, my darling.'

'You took your time,' said Rav. 'Everything okay?'

Chloe nodded. 'Everything's perfect.'

Verity produced a pudding, which no one seemed very interested in eating. Rav eventually asked if he could have a cigarette in the garden, which prompted Chloe to realize that he'd clearly been desperate for one, but holding back, for most of the evening. God, he really did want Max to like him. She watched his face light up when Verity said she would join him and took a packet of French cigarettes and an engraved lighter from a drawer. Max and Chloe sat at the dining table, looking into the garden. Verity even smoked elegantly, and Rav's shoulders seemed to drop several inches from his first drag.

'She's not perfect, then,' Chloe couldn't resist saying.

'No?'

'You complained about Zadie smoking all the time.'

Zadie's name felt good on her lips. She could almost pretend that things hadn't come crashing down, that all three of them had remained friends and that here they were, adults, sitting together while their friend Zadie was in the next room, or unable to attend this evening because she was at home with a baby or busy at work. It was a nice little fantasy. It felt safe.

'Did I?'

'Yes. You said it was like kissing an ashtray, which was really unimaginative, but probably true. I don't like it on Rav.'

'It's worth it for Verity.'

Chloe felt stung. Was he trying to antagonize her? For a moment she had allowed herself to slip back into friendship, forgetting why she hated him.

He had tried to get in touch before. Not many times. A text after their fight, the day after his birthday. Chloe had saved it for years, transferring it from new phone to new phone. 'Call me. Let's chat. I don't want to fight. M x.'

Weeks later, another text, this time angrier. 'If you know where she is, you have to tell me. This isn't funny any more.'

A year later there was an email from Australia. Long and unwieldy, clearly written while he was drunk. It had started calmly, telling her that he missed what the three of them had had, detailing his life in Melbourne. But it had descended into accusations and anger, ranting about how selfish Zadie had been. Chloe had printed it out, put it in her diary and hadn't replied. Creating a wall of silence between herself and Max felt like a scrap of control, like she was subjecting him to the same punishment to which Zadie had sentenced Chloe.

Chloe stood up. 'We should get going. It'll take us ages to get back.'

'It's late. I'll call you a car.'

'That's not necessary. We'll get the Tube.'

'Suit yourself.' He stood up and gazed down at her. He was uncomfortably close. 'You know, I was really hoping that we could start again. We were such good mates.'

Chloe picked up the water jug to pour herself a glass. 'I was Zadie's friend, really.'

'Maybe. But I was the one who told her to keep you around, to have you over when she wanted someone to play with. Because I fancied you so much.'

Chloe froze, giving Max enough time to catch up to her. There were beads of condensation sliding down the outside of the jug, because their 'drinking water' tap was so perfectly cold. What a Max thing to have.

'You didn't,' she breathed, hating herself for not telling him to fuck off.

'Still do,' he whispered, his breath on her neck. The strap of Chloe's dress slipped off her shoulder, on to her arm. She watched as Max reached out, picked it up, slipped it back on to her shoulder, then paused for a quarter of a second, looking into her eyes. He cocked his head and moved towards her another tiny fraction of an inch. She felt the jug slip from between her hands, slick with the moisturizer she had slid over her arms and legs earlier that evening. She watched almost in slow motion as it slammed into the ground, shattering on the stone floor, flooding her shoes.

'Oh dear, Coco,' Max smirked.

'All okay?' asked Rav, coming in through the French doors. He wiped his feet then reclaimed his wine glass. 'I heard a noise?'

'Chloe had a little accident,' said Max, who had picked up the pieces of the jug and thrown a fancy-looking towel down.

'I'm so sorry,' said Rav, as if he had had anything to do with it. 'We'll replace whatever it was, of course. Maybe we should head off before we destroy anything else.'

There was an edge to Rav's voice, as if he knew something had happened while he was outside, that there was more to this accident. Verity seemed happy enough, putting things away in the fridge. But then, she had been a little girl when Max and Chloe had been running around together, their lives so completely entangled. Rav, on the other hand, had been a spectator. He knew exactly how much history he was up against.

In some ways, it was a relief that Rav was bothered, that he was willing to be even the tiniest bit territorial towards Max. Chloe had sort of assumed that Rav would let Max say, do or have anything he wanted. Including Chloe.

The Tube on the way home was, blessedly, packed. Usually when they went out for dinner with friends, they loved the post-mortem. How had the food been? Who seemed happy and who seemed like they might be destined for a break-up? Gossiping about their friends was one of their closest shared hobbies. But Rav didn't want to talk about how young Verity was, or to get the property app up on his phone so they could speculate how much the house was worth. They rode along in silence. By the time they got home Chloe's mascara had seeped under her eyes, the straps of her dress had made red marks in her shoulders and her feet ached. She didn't have to pretend very hard that she wanted to go to bed.

The flat felt even smaller than usual. She could see Rav looking at it, working out how many times it would fit in Max's basement. The windows had been shut all evening and the air was oppressively warm, like standing over a radiator, which made it feel yet smaller. Chloe threw open the windows, but the evening was so still it did almost nothing to cool the room.

She made a half-hearted attempt at taking off her make-up and clambered into bed.

'You're wearing pyjamas,' said Rav as he pulled back the sheet they were sleeping under.

'Yes,' said Chloe sleepily.

'It's so hot.'

'Mm-hmm.'

'So why the pyjamas? You usually sleep naked when it's like this.'

The last thing in the world Chloe wanted was to have a discussion about why she wanted to cover her body with an oversized T-shirt and a pair of pyjama shorts. He was right. She did usually sleep naked, and he was right, there was a reason she didn't want to tonight. The whole evening had felt so exposing, like she was being stripped, that she wanted to cover her body up. Perhaps it didn't make much sense. Rav would almost certainly think it didn't.

'I think I'm getting my period,' she said, her face pressed into the pillow.

'Oh. Okay.'

They lay in silence, the fuzzy blackness getting lighter as Chloe's eyes adjusted to the darkness and the orange lights from the world outside lit the room away from peaceful dark.

'Max thinks he might have some work for me,' said Rav, facing away from her.

Chloe's stomach churned. The oil and acid from the meal crept up her throat, stinging her soft palate. 'That's great. I know that's what you were hoping would happen.'

Rav turned over and landed a kiss on Chloe's neck. 'I love you.'

Chloe swallowed. 'I love you, too.'

11

THEN

The morning after Zadie slept in their room Chloe woke up to find her gone. The bed had been made, which made her a little sad, a sign that Zadie clearly didn't consider this to be home. But she had left a note – 'Thank you for the wine, you are the biggest babe!!' – on the back of an envelope, with lots of kisses and a wonky heart. Chloe smiled at it, then inwardly scolded herself for being weird. She was acting as if Zadie was a boy she had a crush on, not a new friend. She'd known girls at school who would get 'girl crushes' on sixth-formers, usually someone sporty or big into drama. But she'd never been like that. She didn't want to be like that. Zadie wasn't a sixth-former who was impressive because she had a car and a boyfriend, she told herself. She was a friend. An equal.

It was almost a month before she saw Zadie again. December had arrived, with all its usual trappings, trees in the lecture buildings, kindly academics wearing Santa hats for their final tutorials of the year. Chloe found herself homesick, which was an enormous surprise to her. But the string in her chest seemed to tug when she thought about how the previous year she and her mother had brought the tree down from the loft, opened the boxes of decorations, laughed about all the silly ornaments she had made as a child and listened to a cheesy jazz album while they put it all together. Her mother loved Christmas. There would be a nativity scene on the windowsill of the living room, tinsel on the banisters, presents under the tree wrapped with military precision, almost impossible to open. These weren't things she had ever really relished or enjoyed at the time. The memories felt like burns, raw to the touch. The university had made all the right noises, of course. Put a Christmas tree in the entrance to each college. Carol services and parties.

The Thursday evening before the end of term, Lissy knocked on Chloe's door wearing Christmas-tree deelyboppers and a pair of jeans so low slung they were almost indecent. 'Come out,' she instructed. 'We're going to the pub and then, when we're drunk enough not to realize what we're doing, we'll go to Koolerz.'

For a moment Chloe reached for an excuse. But really, what was there? Another evening sitting here on her own, working on an essay which was already perfectly fine? Lissy had knocked on her door once a week for an entire term and had almost always been told to go away. Why not say yes this time?

'Okay,' she said. 'Give me a sec to get changed.'

The disbelief from Lissy was palpable. 'Really?' she shrieked. 'Really?'

'Yes, really,' laughed Chloe. 'Give me a minute.' She pulled Zadie's black dress from the cupboard, peeled off her jeans and shoved her feet into a pair of heels. She thought about the dress for a moment. She had meant to give it back. Really she had. But it was the most flattering garment she'd ever worn in her life, and while she'd rather shave her head than admit it to anyone, wearing the dress made her feel like a little bit of Zadie was rubbing off on her.

'You're going to freeze,' said Lissy as she reappeared at the door.

'I don't care. Can I borrow a lip gloss?'

The pub was boiling, sticky and heavy with the scent of mulled wine. Bodies were pressed against bodies, winter coats strewn over every chair, and it seemed that no one in that room was willing to go home without a Christmas snog under the mistletoe. Lissy was dancing to Slade with a boy from her course, the rest of the girls from their corridor were, inexplicably, doing the Macarena, and Chloe felt an unwelcome wave of homesickness washing over her. She stumbled outside into the cold air, scrabbling in her bag to find a packet of cigarettes. The warmth from inside didn't last long, and by her fourth drag she was shivering.

'Can I borrow a light?' said a voice next to her. She turned to see Rav standing, looking unfairly warm in a Puffa jacket. 'Oh! It's you.'

TWO WRONGS

Did he seem panicked? He certainly didn't seem pleased. 'Chloe,' she said, sparing them both the embarrassment of him not remembering her name. 'Rav, right?'

'I remembered your name.'

She handed him her lighter. 'Sure.'

'I'm sorry I didn't text you.'

'Oh God, don't be. I had actually forgotten I gave you my number. It probably wasn't even the right number. I was pretty wasted, I don't know if you remember.'

'I remember.'

'Yeah. I'm sorry about that.'

Unsure what to do with her hands, Chloe pulled her phone out. To her relief, she had a message from Zadie. 'Max insisted on renting out the basement at the Lounge this evening, which is beyond unimaginative but it does at least have decent cocktails. Come?'

'I've got to go,' she said to Rav. 'Another party.'

'Koolerz?'

'No, actually. The Lounge.'

There was no question by the expression on Rav's face that he was impressed. 'You're going to Max and Zadie's thing? Any chance you've got a plus one?'

For the first time in her life, she was delighted that her mother had owned every single book about dating ever published. She knew exactly what she needed to do. 'Sorry,' she smiled, pushing the pub door open. 'I'm taking someone else.'

'Who is that guy?' Lissy yelled over the music. 'He's delish.'

'He's a wanker,' Chloe replied. 'Want to go to a private party at the Lounge?'

Lissy looked at Chloe as if she were a newly descended angel. 'Are you serious? Absolutely, let's go. Are you sure we'll get in? Am I wearing the right outfit? Do they let people in in jeans? I know these are smart jeans, but they're still jeans . . . Or we could go back to our room and change and then go out? But then we might be too late . . .'

Chloe smiled, feeling the guilt of months of rebuffing Lissy's attempts to be friendly begin to evaporate. Admittedly, entrance to a swanky bar and a few free Piña Coladas didn't put them on an entirely even footing, but it was something.

The Lounge was on the other side of town, so Lissy and Chloe flagged down a taxi. Lissy's enthusiasm was contagious. 'Have you been here before?' she asked Chloe as she undid her seatbelt when the driver pulled up.

'No, of course not,' Chloe muttered, handing the driver a £5 note. 'Have you got a quid?'

Lissy stood on the pavement fumbling with her purse then readjusted her jeans. 'Can you see my bum crack?'

'No,' Chloe lied. 'Come on, let's go.'

The Lounge was in a tall Georgian house in the shopping street. It would have been impossible to find if it weren't for a tall bald man in a suit standing outside. Chloe looked to her left, where Lissy was hanging behind her, starting to look a bit green. She was going to have to pretend she knew how to handle this. She walked to the door and moved to open it.

'It's a private party, ladies,' said the bouncer, not unkindly.

'We're here for Zadie Lister's . . . thing.'

'Name?'

'Chloe Sanders.'

'And your friend?'

Lissy was swaying slightly. 'I'm her plush one,' she told the bouncer, smiling with red-wine-stained teeth.

'I think you've had enough for this evening, love,' said the bouncer. 'Come back another time, when you haven't had a skinful.' He turned to Chloe. 'Are you going in?'

She looked at Lissy, whose last pint of red wine seemed to be catching up with her. She couldn't very well abandon her in the street. 'No, I'll take my friend home.'

She took Lissy by the arm and stood on the corner, looking for a taxi. Her coat felt especially inefficient against the wind stripping down the pretty Georgian street.

'Why aren't we going in?' asked Lissy.

'It's closed. Look, a taxi.' She stuck out her hand. 'Please try to seem sober.'

To her great relief, the taxi slowed down, and Lissy clambered in. 'Market Gardens, please,' she slurred. 'Are you coming, Chlo?'

Chloe looked at Lissy, pale and drunk under the yellow light of the taxi. Lissy needed to go to bed. It wouldn't make any difference to her whether Chloe went home or not. She would be asleep in an hour or two.

'Would you mind if I stayed?'

*

'Back again,' smiled the bouncer.

'My friend wanted to go home.'

If he disapproved of what she had done, he certainly didn't show it. He simply opened a heavy wooden door and let her inside, to a long stone corridor at the end of which was a desk. Behind it stood a good-looking woman with dark hair wearing a white polo neck. 'Welcome to the Lounge.' She smiled a smile that didn't reach the rest of her face.

Chloe followed a winding staircase which led to a huge, low-ceilinged room full of sofas. It was dimly lit, and thumping, lyricless music played. People lay over the sofas, stroking each other, smiling. She wasn't naïve enough to think that this was just the result of a couple of glasses of wine. A PSHE lesson from school about teenagers dying after taking an E for the first time, or drowning because they drank so much water, flashed into her mind. She tried to wave it away. Those were stories made up to scare people into behaving like boring, responsible members of society, just like fairy tales were created to teach children about morality. She wouldn't die if she took a pill. And where would she even get one? She twisted her head, trying to work out where the bar was, worrying that someone would notice her not knowing where the bar was and automatically deduce that she didn't belong here. In the midst of all this, she heard her name being called. She turned and saw Max lying on a sofa, holding a glass. Gratefully, she went to join him. There were two blonde girls lying next to him. Not quite on him, not close enough that she wanted to find Zadie and tell her. But close enough that it registered; that it seemed not quite right.

'Have a drink.' He smiled, pouring a drink for her. 'So glad you came.'

Chloe took it and tried to think of something to say. She settled on 'Cheers!'

'To your victory,' added one of the blonde girls lying on the sofa.

'Victory?' asked Chloe.

The girls laughed, as if it was funny to think anyone might not know what they were talking about.

'We had a good match this afternoon.' Max smiled.

'He completely destroyed them,' said one of the girls. 'He's far too modest.'

'Well done, you,' said Chloe, internally admonishing herself for sounding like a grandparent. 'Where's Zadie?'

'Probably in the bathroom,' laughed the other blonde, touching her nose. The first girl laughed along with her. Chloe studied Max's face, watching to see whether he would defend his girlfriend. Instead he smiled, showing the kind of perfect, even white teeth that Chloe had only previously seen on American TV. 'Why don't you go and join her?' he said to them. 'I think we all know she's not the only one who likes a bit of the old Colombian marching powder.'

Both of the blonde girls got up, tugging their skirts down over their tanned thighs. Chloe felt suddenly aware of the space between her and Max on the sofa. He slid towards her, offering to top up her drink, though she had only taken a couple of sips. 'Thanks,' she said, too quietly for it to travel over the thumping music.

'So,' Max said. 'Long time no see.'

'I've been revising. I've got exams before the holidays.'

'What are you reading?'

'English Literature.'

'Cute. I'm glad you came. I thought Zadie and I had scared you off.'

Was Chloe imagining it, or was Max flirting with her? Not for the first time, she cursed the fact that she'd been to an all-girls school. Other people seemed to know the difference between boys being friendly and trying it on, but her mother was so obsessed with her avoiding teen pregnancy that Chloe had barely spoken to a boy until sixth form, and even then it was nothing significant. Surely he wouldn't be flirting with her? He was Zadie's boyfriend. No one who was going out with Zadie could fancy someone else. Only, he was leaning forward and his eyelashes kept dipping, touching his cheeks, as his eyes sought her chest.

'I've seen Zadie recently,' she said, testing the waters. 'She stayed at our room the other night.'

Max raised an eyebrow. 'Ah, so that's where she went. Interesting.'

'We had fun.'

'I think she wanted me to think she'd gone somewhere far more scandalous.' She must have looked worried because he added, 'Don't worry, I'll keep our little secret. I'm good at doing that.'

He wasn't touching her. No part of his body was in any contact with hers. And yet the warmth of him, the smell of his jumper, his hair, his skin. The way his eyes were so unashamedly resting on her face, her neck, her chest, her legs. All of it felt wrong. Wrong, and delicious in a way that was beyond confusing.

'Did you bring anyone?' he asked. Chloe shook her head.

'No boyfriend? I presume there's a bloke back at home crying into a pint because he let you get away.'

'No, no boyfriend.'

Max smiled. His hand brushed her arm, his skin olive against her whiteness. 'Why not? You're fucking beautiful.'

A flock of questions swirled in Chloe's mind. Was this how people like Max and Zadie spoke to each other? All the books she had read about rich people seemed to involve a certain amount of bed-hopping and loose morals, but did that mean this was okay? And the loudest question of all: why didn't she want Max to stop looking at her like that?

Finding her resolve, she got to her feet. 'I'm going to . . .' She tailed off and the blonde girls tumbled back from the bathroom, laughing and sniffing. They sat either side of Max, even closer than before, and picked up their glasses. Either Max assumed he had missed the end of her sentence or he didn't care where she was going. Either way, he had turned his face from her and it felt like the moment when the warm sun which was on your back moved behind a cloud and your skin seemed to glow with cold. She could see what it was that Zadie found so deeply compelling about him.

She danced. Met more of Max's friends. Drank more. Pretended she wasn't frustrated that Zadie had invited her and now was nowhere to be seen. Told herself that she was having fun. All the way home, putting one numb foot in front of the other and walking through the freezing wind because she didn't have any more money for a taxi, she tried to shake off the desire that had settled into the pit of her stomach, but she couldn't.

When she got back to her room her feet were so cold she couldn't move her toes. She stood, her back against the door, and to her own shock put her hand between her legs, thinking of Rav's smirk outside the bar, of Max's eyes on her bare legs at the club. She came sharply, moments later, then stood, dazed and scandalized by her own behaviour. She hung up her dress, washed her face and hands in the little sink at the corner of the room, rubbing her fingers until they were red. Then she put on a pair of sensible pyjamas, turned off the light and tried desperately to convince herself that what she had just done meant nothing.

The next day Chloe woke to find that she had four texts. Her stomach flipped, and before she could tell herself not to think it she had brewed a fantasy about a message from Rav. Or Zadie. Which would be better? Which would make her happier? She tried to quash the voice in the back of her mind that was whispering Max's name.

She needn't have worried. The first one was from the phone company. The second was from Lissy: 'i'm so sorry I was such a mess last night, thank you SO SO SO MUCH for taking me to the lounge!' It seemed she couldn't remember that she didn't get in, which was a relief. Chloe could pretend that she hadn't ditched her and sent her home alone, drunk in a taxi, and Lissy could believe that she had gone to the most exclusive club for miles around.

The next was from her mother, reminding her that she needed to ask Greg nicely if he would come and collect her from the train station, and to give him plenty of notice (as if he was ever busy).

The last one was from a number she didn't recognize. 'Hey, good to see you last night. Fancy a drink before the end of term? Rav.'

She sat up, wishing someone – wishing Zadie – were here to talk about it. Why had he texted her now? The butterflies over Rav's message replaced the guilt about her flirtation with Max. She didn't fancy Max. She fancied Rav. And it seemed like Rav might actually feel the same way – despite the vomit incident. Maybe, in time, it would become a funny story, one they told people. She imagined them both sitting around a long glass table in a house in London, laughing with their friends. Max and Zadie would be married, she and Rav wouldn't be, but they'd have kids, eventually. She'd be a celebrated playwright, Zadie would be an artist, Max would be whatever people were when they got too old to play rugby. The fantasy teetered in her mind for a moment before reality set in. Rav had had her number for weeks. He hadn't texted her after the party, hadn't shown any interest at all until he realized that she was going to some private party he hadn't been invited to. She'd heard her mum say it enough times to know that if someone is interested in you, they make it clear. She held her finger over the delete button, then forced herself to press it.

12

NOW

The week after dinner at Max's was strange. It had been stickily warm all week, but when Chloe woke one morning she felt her skin puckering with goose pimples and pulled the sheet, swapped for the oppressively hot duvet a couple of weeks ago, over her body. The sky outside was blue-grey and the sun non-existent. Summer felt like a hallucination, rather than a reality that had been entirely normal the day before. When she got up none of the summer dresses she favoured during the school holidays, strappy cotton things in various ice-cream shades, afforded the warmth she wanted. She had planned to enjoy the warm weather, to sit outside reading a book and, finally, having finished sorting out everything she had neglected in the rush of report writing and end-of-term excitement, to make use of the 'long holidays' everyone was so convinced she got. It was the favourite comment of Rav's friends. 'Three reasons to be a teacher,' they would smirk at dinner parties or barbecues. 'Easter, summer, Christmas.' It was an unfair joke because it only left two options – to laugh along at her profession's expense, or to take offence and be seen as a humourless bore. She almost always opted for the former, but it rankled. She made half what Rav did by turning ugly houses into slightly less ugly houses, and yet he seemed to have near-infinite time to chat on WhatsApp all day or to pore over online listings for houses they couldn't afford.

Sitting outside wasn't going to be an option, so Chloe benched the idea of enjoying herself and did several loads of laundry, washed the floors, sewed buttons back on to shirts and dresses that had been sitting in a pile for weeks or, in some cases, months. She dusted, hoovered, put some clothes in a bag to take to the charity shop, and by six thirty she was feeling practically saintly. A chink of sunlight had broken through the clouds, warming their tiny garden. Delighted with her timing, Chloe poured herself a gin and tonic and sat outside, presenting her face to the sun, feeling it soaking into her skin. Of course, the moment she relaxed, feeling her shoulders drop, Rav came bounding through the door.

'All right for some!' He laughed. 'You're making the most of the break.'

She could explain that she'd done nine hours of almost unbroken cleaning, but it just didn't seem worth it. He should notice, but he wouldn't. Chloe had realized that when you grew up having everything done for you you didn't question things being perfect. You only noticed if your shirt wasn't clean or if the sheets hadn't been changed.

'Good day?' she asked instead.

'Actually, yes. Very good.'

'Very good?'

'I've been asked to do a trip.'

Chloe sat up straighter. 'Really? Where to?'

'Max is interested in putting some work our way and he needs me to go to Australia for a few days. Ten days, in fact.'

'Isn't that quite a long way to go?' Chloe heard the words coming out of her mouth and realized she had said the wrong thing, focused on the negative and the prosaic when Rav needed to hear praise. He looked a little wounded.

'I guess,' he said.

'I'm sorry.' Chloe meant it. 'I was being selfish because I'm going to miss you. Tell me about the project, what you're going to do out there. Are your bosses pleased?'

'It's gone down beyond well with the firm that I've brought Max in. He's such a great guy. He made sure they knew he'd come in via me and he asked for me specifically to go on this trip. It's done wonders for my rep. I reckon I might be able to get a promotion out of this.'

Chloe searched into the recesses of her being to find some positivity for him. 'That's really great,' she tried. 'How exciting.'

Clearly, Rav wanted to believe that she was happy for him, because he disappeared and came back with a beer, brimming with enthusiasm to talk about the project, the office he'd go to, the hotel that was being booked for him. He showed her pictures of the places he would be visiting, read her the LinkedIn biographies of the people he was going to meet, and all the while she fixed a smile on her face. He deserved that. He deserved to feel happy. None of this mess was his fault, after all.

She wished this could have happened without Max, that much was true. But, she reasoned, Rav had had a shit deal with his company for years, and while neither of them had ever said it out loud they both knew it had more than a little to do with the fact that he wasn't white. The big bosses who ran the place still talked a little more slowly when they took meetings with Rav, or mentioned that they'd had a lovely curry recently. Meanwhile, his contemporaries were starting to move past him. Asked to lunches he wasn't invited to, or 'impromptu' meetings. So, while the idea of Max helping Rav made her toes curl, the idea of trying to take this away from him, or ruin the happy glow seeping off him, felt just too wrong. So, she listened and made all the right noises. And every time he said something like 'I know you don't really like Max, but he's really helping us out. He's doing us a favour. He's really sorting us out,' Chloe smiled and didn't say what was really on her mind. There would, of course, be a reason Max was doing this. There would be something in it for him. Max had never done anything unselfish in his entire life, at least not as far as Chloe could see, and it seemed unlikely that he was about to start now.

The following week passed, Rav fizzing with excitement about everything he was going to achieve when he was in Australia, Chloe quietly anticipating having ten days of the house entirely to herself. The smallness of the flat was becoming increasingly difficult to cope with. A couple of glasses or plates left lying around and one wet towel on the floor and the entire place looked like a tip. The school holidays were always difficult, she reminded herself. She and Rav got out of sync; he left for work while she was still asleep and wanted to go to bed before she was tired. She was left without much to tell him, no anecdotes from a day of work, which meant she ended up listening far more than she talked. It was hard not to spend money every day if you went out, which inevitably meant she stayed at home. Occasionally, she would go over the road to see Lissy, but Lissy's single focus was Claudia, who was cute, but still a baby and therefore a limited source of entertainment.

The morning Rav left, his taxi arrived just before five. He kissed Chloe's forehead and then slipped away, so when Chloe woke, hours later, from a blissfully deep, uninterrupted sleep, he was already in the air. The next ten days lay out in front of her, a sea of possibilities. She could do anything she wanted. She lay on her back, staring up at the ceiling, trying on option after option in her mind. She could cook the various vegetarian dishes that Rav thought were boring. Rewatch old episodes of *Friends*. Tumble-dry clothes that could easily be put on the washing line, just to feel them all warm and static from the machine. But first of all, she felt an old desire swelling in her stomach. Her fingers itched. But there was no one here to judge her. So she put on her robe, opened up her laptop and typed 'Zadie Lister' into Google.

She tried to leave it at least two weeks between sessions, telling herself that you couldn't really be addicted to something you only did once a fortnight. There had been a time when it was a daily activity, back when Zadie had first disappeared. She used to cycle to the library or pay an internet café for half an hour of uninterrupted browsing. Of course, the internet had been different, then. Emptier. It would have been easier to find results there, if any had existed. Privacy settings on social media had been more lax, too. It had been far simpler to trawl through Zadie's friends' photo albums, searching for a glimpse of her in the background at balls, birthday bashes and barbecues.

A year after Zadie disappeared, Rav had asked her to stop looking. 'This isn't healthy. She knows that you're looking for her,' he had reasoned. 'If she wants to find you, she knows where to look. But if she doesn't want to be found, then you have to allow her that.'

Chloe had agreed, at least on the face of it, and had confined her searches to when she was alone. Making it into a secret habit had made it more exciting. As her phones had become smarter, she'd been able to search whenever she wanted to, clearing her history afterwards as if she had been looking at hard-core porn. Eventually, she had started limiting herself, treating these searches like a binge when she was on a diet. A treat. Something to be permitted, but not encouraged.

She'd never found anything. Not in all the years she had been searching. No engagement announcement. No wedding. No children. No mention of Zadie on a corporate website, no personal page selling art. No books, no articles, no Facebook, no Instagram, no Twitter. Nothing.

Until today. An announcement in the *Telegraph*. Right at the top of her search page, in black and white. All the years of trying to find her on the deepest, darkest fringes of the internet, and here she was. As Chloe wrestled with the enormity of the fact that something had come up, she stared at the screen, not really taking the words in. Then she blinked, and focused. All the letters made sense, but in conjunction they meant nothing.

Chloe sat up. Refreshed the page. But it was still there.

Zadie Elizabeth Henrietta Barber Lister, died, 19 August. 1985–2020.

ZADIE

'I'll wash up,' said Zadie, getting up from the dining table.

Her parents both looked up, seeming surprised. 'That's very nice of you, darling,' said her mother. Their apparent shock at her willingness to help rankled. She had been home for two weeks now, and every day she had tried harder to convince them that she was 'doing well', as they called it. Walking the dogs. Doing the laundry. On Christmas Day she had even consented to let her mother serve the food on her plate, no counting, no weighing, no checking. She had made a fuss about wanting the green Quality Street, played Charades with her little brothers and let her moody teenage sister, Louella, borrow her clothes. She had chattered away about the friends she was making at university, about the work she was doing, about how hard she had found her first essay, and how the library was the fourth biggest in the whole of the UK. In short, she had been the model child.

'I was wondering,' she said now, picking one of the serving bowls off the table, 'whether Max could come for the New Year's Eve party?'

She took the bowls into the kitchen. It was a good way to ask for things, she had found over the years. The journey from dining room to kitchen and back took about a minute and a half, giving them time to talk across the table about her request but not long enough to really think of a reason to say no.

When she came back her mother was folding her napkin and putting it back in the silver napkin ring she always used.

'I thought his parents liked to go away for Christmas?' She made 'go away' sound like 'murder puppies'.

'They went to Thailand. But they're back in a few days, and we haven't seen each other for ages. I could go to his, I suppose, but I thought it would be nice for him to come here. He's never been to the New Year party.'

Her father refilled his wine glass. 'I don't see why not.'

'Really?' Zadie put her arms around him. 'Thank you.'

'And why don't you invite some other friends as well?'

Zadie froze. 'Other friends?'

'The girl you share the room with, for instance?' said her mother. 'She seemed so sweet.'

Did they know? It was impossible to tell whether they were fully aware that she was lying to them, that she barely knew her pretty, studious room-mate. Or did they genuinely want her to invite friends to join them?

'She might be busy.'

'You should ask her. Or some of your other friends. The people from your course you've been talking about. But it would be nice if you invited Chloe. We thought she seemed a lovely girl.'

Zadie finished the washing-up then trudged upstairs to her

bedroom. *It was a beautiful room and she was lucky to have it. She knew that. But the views from the windows still reminded her of furious weekends of arguments, of hiding in here from her family, determined not to speak to any of them. At her worst, she had traced every corner of the room, walking in circle after circle, determined to burn off whatever they had forced her to eat over an enormous row.*

She turned on her phone. A new one, given as one of her Christmas presents. Since she had been away they had installed a phone mast in the village and now, rather than hanging out of a window or walking up the drive, she could send messages from her bed. She would have to message Chloe. Not that having her here would be a bad thing, but wouldn't it seem odd to Chloe to get an invitation like that, out of the blue? She probably wouldn't want to come all that way and leave her family on New Year's Eve. Chloe probably had parents who adored her, who were proud of her and thought she was brilliant. No mother could disapprove of anyone that diligent or neat. And she probably had loads of friends from school, too. But she would ask. And on the off chance that Chloe didn't have a hundred better things to do, it would be nice to see her. And it would make her parents more welcoming of Max.

She sent a text: 'What are you doing for new year? MY PARENTS ARE DRIVING ME FUCKING BONKERS xxxxx.'

13

THEN

Chloe arrived home for the Christmas holidays and found herself surprised at how grateful she was to be back. The house was completely unchanged. Still perfect in its boring, semi-detached way. Cleaner than clean, scented with fabric softener and air freshener. For the first two weeks, she revelled in it all, sitting in the back of the Ford Jazz while her mother, who was an uncharacteristically brilliant driver, sat in the passenger seat and Greg drove badly. She folded laundry with her mother, followed her round the supermarket, filling the trolley with uninspiring things. It felt safe and necessary. They ate a slightly dry turkey crown on Christmas Day, exchanged practical, thoughtful gifts. Chloe and her mother shared smiles over Greg's bald head while he snored in front of the afternoon film on BBC2. It was exactly as it always had been. But as the holiday wore on her mother seemed to grow frustrated with her. The house felt small, even though, as her mother regularly stated, it was the biggest in the cul de sac. Chloe hid in her room, claiming to have lots of work to do, but then procrastinated, reading the books she'd loved as a teenager, poring over her old diaries and staring at her phone, waiting for a message.

Her mother had always told her that waiting for someone to call was the surest way to make sure they didn't. But in this case, she was wrong. A few days after Christmas Chloe woke, turned on her phone and, just as she had secretly hoped, there was a text from Zadie. 'What are you doing for new year? MY PARENTS ARE DRIVING ME FUCKING BONKERS xxxxx.'

What was the right reply? If she said she had no plans, she might get an invitation, which was obviously the ideal. But it would be slightly mortifying to admit that all her friends from home had made arrangements with other people. She'd told her mother that she wanted a quiet one after so much partying at uni, but she wasn't sure that she had believed her.

'Not sure yet,' she typed. 'You? X.'

The reply came almost immediately. 'My parents always have a big thing at home. Wanna come?'

Chloe wanted to pinch herself – not in a 'pinch me, I'm dreaming' way, but to punish herself for how pathetically excited she was. But there was no point trying to suffocate this kind of excitement. A party at Zadie's parents' house would inevitably be something out of Evelyn Waugh.

'I think I might go to a friend's for New Year's Eve,' Chloe ventured to her mother later, twisting a tea towel between her fingers. She and her mother were washing up after supper while Greg watched television, just as they had every evening since he had moved in.

'Zadie's?'

'Yes,' said Chloe, surprised. 'How did you know?'

Her mother sighed. 'She's all you talk about, love. Ever since you got back, Zadie this, Zadie that. Zadie went to boarding school where you wore your own clothes, Zadie has four brothers and sisters; Zadie, Zadie, Zadie. Apart from sometimes, when it's Max, Max, Max.'

'Oh.' Chloe felt stung. What was she supposed to say to that?

'I'm not having a go at you, my love, it's all right. I just don't want you to get too attached to a couple of people and miss out on making other friends.'

'I am making other friends.'

'Your own friends? Or their friends?' Her mother was polishing the glasses before putting them away, her favourite part of the cleaning ritual. 'Because if things go sour with them you want to still have other friends to spend time with.'

'Why would it go sour with them?'

Her mother seemed to consider her next words carefully. 'I might not know what I'm talking about. Maybe it won't happen. It's just that people like them, people from money, they can see people like us as . . .' She paused. Chloe looked at the plate in her hand and imagined just how it would feel to smash it against the countertop. 'Disposable,' her mother finished.

'Max and Zadie aren't like that.'

'Hopefully not.'

Her mother's hands were pink against the white tea towel, patterned with blue veins. Her wrists were twig-like, tiny. 'I am making other friends as well,' she repeated, after a little while.

'Oh?'

'The girls on my corridor are really sweet. Lissy, she's one of my good friends. We go to the pub together, and we went out clubbing before the end of term. She's from a couple of miles down the road.'

Her mother looked as if a weight had been lifted from her shoulders, which made Chloe feel simultaneously furious and comforted.

A few days later Chloe found herself on a train to Zadie's parents' house. Or rather, one of Zadie's parents' houses – the country pile where the party was going to take place was where they spent weekends and holidays, but there was an apartment in London and a tumble-down cottage in the south of France. Chloe knew this because in the days between Boxing Day and New Year she and Zadie had fallen into the habit of talking on the phone, like teenagers. Every night at nine o'clock, as her parents were thinking about going to bed, the phone would ring. Zadie would be in the bath or smoking on the roof, always something extraordinary, always with a glass of wine in her hand, and they would talk in a way that Chloe hadn't talked since she was fifteen. About what they wanted to do next week, next month, next decade.

About people they disliked, people they admired, books they had read – it was here that Chloe outshone Zadie – and films and plays they had seen, which Zadie knew far more about than Chloe, and current affairs, where they were both cheerfully ill informed.

The train slowed into the station. It was the kind of place they filmed period dramas. Standing on the platform in jeans and a jumper was Max. Chloe's relief that someone had come to collect her and that she hadn't been forgotten was swallowed by her nerves. Why had Zadie sent Max? Memories of his finger on her bare arm at the Lounge flickered through her mind.

Max took Chloe's suitcase and swung it from one hand, even though it had wheels. 'You've packed light.'

'It's only one night.'

'You should see what Zadie takes when we go anywhere. Despite the fact that none of her clothes are more than about an inch big.'

Chloe laughed politely, but then felt disloyal. 'Where is Zadie?'

Max beeped his keys at an Audi and slung her suitcase in the back. 'She's at home, bit of a family drama over lunch. Plus, she can't drive, so she's not much use on the station runs.'

'It's nice of you to pick me up.'

'I'm bloody delighted to get out of that house.'

Max drove exactly as Chloe would have imagined – fast but accurate, taking corners with alarming speed and astonishing control. He casually ignored speed restrictions and yet somehow Chloe felt safe. He only slowed down when they reached the brow of a hill, at which point he momentarily flicked the indicator and swung on to a long, cream-pebbled drive. At the bottom of it stood a breathtakingly pretty house made of yellow stone covered in snaky green ivy.

'Woah,' she said, under her breath.

Max stuck the car between a battered Land Rover and an even more battered Polo. 'I know. It's ridiculous. It's Hogwarts.'

Chloe lowered her brow. 'I thought you'd be . . .' She stopped, unable to think of a polite way to finish her sentence.

Max seemed unperturbed. 'My parents have a nice four-bed in London. This is a different fucking league. As far as they're concerned, I'm the Artful Dodger.' He pulled his keys from the ignition. 'Are you okay?'

There was no point in lying. 'I'm nervous.'

'I'm not surprised. But it's fine. We go in, they tell you where your room is, you unpack, even if you're only staying one night. Then you go back downstairs at four thirty, there'll be tea, we'll all stand around talking, then you'll get ready, and then we'll all get so drunk that we won't remember what happened, only they'll call it getting "blotto" and it's such expensive booze that you'll actually feel okay tomorrow. As long as you call it a loo not a toilet and you're nice to the dogs, they'll like you.' He opened the car door. 'Now come on. Otherwise they'll try to convince Zadie we're having a dalliance so that she'll dump me.'

Chloe laughed a little too loud.

It was just as Max had described. He had opened the huge front door and pointed her up some stairs to a pretty little bedroom at the far end of the first-floor corridor. It had twin beds, a proper dressing table with a stool, and an en suite bathroom that contained the kind of claw-foot bath that her mother would have given a kidney for. It was almost dark outside now, but she could see the outline of a swimming pool, all tucked away for winter. The house sat in the middle of two wide, square lawns which gave way into woodlands. Was all of this theirs? What a place to have grown up.

She put her clothes into the wardrobe, remembering Max's words about unpacking even though she wasn't staying long. He had been more helpful than perhaps he realized in his induction to how the Listers lived.

The clock on the mantelpiece said four thirty so, haltingly, she made her way downstairs, first to the hall, then, following a hum of conversation, she opened a door into a warm orange room filled with people, adults milling around in jeans and sensible jumpers, teenagers splayed on sofas in hoodies and denim mini-skirts, various dogs lying in front of a roaring fire. Max was standing by the farthest window. A group of children were piled up on a sofa, their shoes on the cushions, hands filled with cake.

'Chloe!' said a slender woman. It took Chloe a moment to realize that it was Zadie's mother. She was less made up than she had been the first time Chloe had met her, and her hair was pulled back. She looked years younger, and much softer. 'I'm so glad you could come. Would you like some tea?'

On a table at the side of the room there was sort of afternoon tea set up, pretty pink-and-gold tea cups with saucers, several slightly wonky home-made-looking cakes and a variety of sandwiches curling at the edges. 'Yes, please,' she said.

Mrs Lister pulled her away to the tea table and started piling up a plate with things to eat. 'I'm not just saying this, but you really must eat up now, we won't have supper until ridiculously late because we've got thirty people coming and I'm very disorganized.'

'Gosh, you're doing all the cooking?' Chloe hadn't ever said 'gosh' before in her life.

Mrs Lister laughed. 'It's only beef bourguignon, nothing very exciting. I did most of it yesterday. The hardest bit has been keeping the dogs out of the larder. I'm terrified they'll get in and eat all the cheese, then we'll have a revolt on our hands.' She pressed the plate and a tea cup into Chloe's hands. 'Have you got everything you need?'

'Absolutely, yes,' Chloe said. 'I haven't seen Zadie, though.'

'Zadie is having one of her moods. You know how she gets.'

'How she gets?' Chloe realized too late that, as Zadie's

room-mate, she would have seen every single one of her moods for the last ten weeks, not just intermittent flashes of her. 'Oh, yes, of course.'

'But she does seem to be better since she's been living with you,' Mrs Lister added. 'At least some of the time. She said you really cheered her up recently, after a fight with Max.' The change in her tone when she spoke Max's name was almost inaudible. But not quite.

'She's great to me, too,' Chloe said. 'It's a two-way street.'

Somehow, Chloe had said the perfect thing. Mrs Lister smiled a huge, genuine smile. 'I really am so glad that you came—' It sounded as if she had been going to continue her sentence, but before she could there was a wail from the sofa as a child who looked about five – Chloe assumed it was Zadie's youngest brother, William – slid on to the floor and banged his elbow. Mrs Lister was there in a moment. She looked down at her hands, one taken up with the plate of food and the other with a cup of Earl Grey. There wasn't anywhere obvious to sit, certainly nowhere she would be able to balance the cup and the plate. Max was still standing by the window, looking out into the dark. She went over to join him.

'I think the expression is usually "Penny for them?"'

Max jerked up, as if her voice had pulled him back from wherever he had been.

'Fuck me, you're hungry.' He looked at her plate.

'I didn't fill it, Zadie's mum did.'

Max raised one eyebrow. 'Really? She must like you.'

133

'I think she does, yeah. Remember, Zadie and I live together.'

'Ah, yes, of course, the grand housing deception.' His voice was soaked with contempt.

'She told me that they wouldn't pay her fees if she told them the truth.'

He scoffed. 'Bollocks. They'd have one brief argument and then get over it. You think they want to tell all their nice friends that their bonkers daughter dropped out of university? Zadie's all better now – that's their story and they're sticking to it.'

'All better?'

Max shook his head and Chloe wasn't bold enough to press him. 'Where is Zadie?'

'Sleeping, I think. She likes a disco nap before a late night.' He took a sandwich off Chloe's plate. 'You should eat some of that. Astrid never serves dinner before about ten – you can starve to death in this house. Or drink yourself to death. Whichever comes first.'

Mrs Lister clinked a teaspoon against her cup and addressed the room. 'Don't worry, I'm not going to sing. I only wanted to say that we'll expect you all downstairs dressed to the nines at half past seven. Last one down doesn't get a drink.'

'Do you really think she likes me?' Chloe asked, sotto voce.

'Trust me,' replied Max. 'If they didn't, you'd know about it.'

14

NOW

There was no obituary. Chloe had spent the rest of the day searching for one. She signed up to service after service, not even bothering to cover her tracks on the joint account, hoping that someone, somewhere, would be able to tell her what had happened to Zadie. She would be thirty-five. The same age as Chloe. A year and a half younger than Max. What did people die of in their mid-thirties? Childbirth. Cancer. Car accidents. Suicide. She searched for the statistics to back her assumption up. Car accidents and suicide. Then she searched for car accidents on and around Zadie's death date. There were dozens. None of them fitted her description. She hadn't had a driving licence back then. And she didn't exactly seem the type to study for her theory test or learn to reverse around a corner.

There was one weapon in Chloe's arsenal, one that she had been keeping for years, telling herself she would never use.

She had a phone number for Zadie's younger sister,

Louella, who had been an awkward, moody teenager when they had met all those years ago.

A few years ago, Chloe had found a Facebook post from someone in their local area. This person had lost her phone and had asked all her friends to post their numbers on the page so that she could put them all in her new one. And there, on the page, had been Louella Lister – usually so careful, with her profile locked down – her number in blue and white on the screen.

Chloe had written it down, agonizingly careful not to make a mistake, and kept a copy. If she was honest with herself, she probably knew the number off by heart. Very occasionally, she allowed herself to call it from a with-held number, to make sure that it was still in service. But she had never spoken to Louella. She had never known what to say.

Chloe dialled the number now, her whole body vibrat-ing with excitement, fear and horror at what she was about to do. And on the third ring, a voice, one that sounded less like Zadie's than Chloe had hoped, answered.

'Hello?'

Chloe swallowed. She had planned what she was going to say. But now all the words had dried up.

'Hello?'

'Hi,' she forced out. 'Hi, Louella. It's Chloe here. I was a friend of' – she swallowed – 'Zadie's. We lived together at university.'

Would her family know that had been a lie? That they hadn't really lived together?

Louella's voice was guarded. Hostile. 'I remember,' she said. 'Can I help?' If she was confused about how Chloe had got hold of her number, she wasn't saying anything. Maybe her phone had been ringing a lot recently.

'I heard what happened. I read about it. I just wanted to call – I just wanted to tell you how sorry I am for your loss. That I'm thinking of you all – that . . .'

Louella's breathing was audible. 'That's very kind,' she said. Her voice was tight and clipped.

'I wish I could have done something,' Chloe ventured, deviating from the script she had written herself. 'I wish I could have helped.'

'We all do,' Louella said, softening. 'But there's no one to blame. Apart from that psycho she was seeing at university.'

Chloe's blood stopped in her veins. 'What?'

'Nothing.' Louella clearly regretted having said anything. She must think Chloe had no idea about any of it. 'You're very kind to call. I'll pass your condolences on to the rest of the family. Goodbye.'

For the first time, perhaps, in her life, Chloe knew exactly what she needed to do.

It was dark now. When had that happened? She remembered getting up to go inside when her hands started to cramp around her phone, thinking that the laptop would be easier to work on. And then a couple of hours later she must have got up to plug in her charger. Had she eaten anything? Not for a while. She searched for some sense of hunger, but it didn't come. Her mouth felt dry and sticky, her tongue sealed to the roof of her mouth, her lips sealed together.

There was only one person who might have the answers she needed. She watched her finger shake as she dialled the phone.

Max picked up on the third ring.

'Hello?'

'It's Chloe.'

He paused. 'Hey, Coco.'

'Zadie's dead.'

There was a shuffling of papers and the noise of a door being closed gently. 'I know.'

'You saw the announcement?'

Another pause. Chloe's stomach twisted while she waited. 'Max?' she said, unable to bear the wait.

'I spoke to her father.'

Chloe tried to compose herself. She tried to swallow the bile in the back of her throat.

'What did he say?'

'Very little. He thanked me for getting in touch, said that it hadn't been unexpected and that he and Astrid were coping as best they could. Her brothers and sisters are devastated, of course. They're having a very small family funeral. They don't want flowers.'

'Hadn't been unexpected? What does that mean?'

Max sighed. 'Come on, Coco. You knew her. You know what it means.'

'Say it.'

'She killed herself.'

Chloe shook her head, as if she were trying to shake the knowledge out of her ears. 'Why?'

'I don't think there was a reason.'

'You didn't ask?'

'Why would he tell me that?'

'You're her ex-boyfriend. You were together for six years.'

'A long time ago. It's not my business. It's got nothing to do with either of us, or anything that happened back then. People don't kill themselves because of a falling-out they had fifteen years earlier. She was ill then and, clearly, she was still ill. That's it.'

Chloe paused. She traced her finger in a circle on the cheap Ikea kitchen table. Of course he wanted to claim it wasn't their fault. Of course he wasn't going to allow even the tiniest hint of guilt to creep in. That way would lie ruin.

She knew what she had to do.

'What are you doing now?' she asked.

'I'm about to head to Verity's. She's cooking supper.'

'Does she know?'

'Of course not.'

Why would he have told her? Their life was going to carry on unchanged. He would be greeted with a kiss from Verity and drink a glass of wine and compliment whatever pretentious dish she had cooked up, not caring that, somewhere, Zadie's body was lying in a morgue, waiting to be buried or burned.

Chloe swallowed, pulling herself together.

'I don't want to be alone,' she said in a small voice.

'Where's Rav?' Max said after a slight pause.

'Australia. You sent him there, remember?'

'Ah, yes.' Silence fell between them again and she forced herself to wait for him to break it first. 'Want to come over?'

She breathed a silent sigh of relief. 'What about Verity?'

'I'll tell her I've got to work. She'll understand. I'll send a car for half an hour's time.'

'Thanks, Max. I really appreciate it. See you soon,' she made herself say, then hung up, her hands starting to tremble.

15
THEN

Chloe was ready too early. She had left plenty of time to get ready, wanting to luxuriate in a bath, take care over her make-up and make the whole thing as much like a country-house weekend in a novel as she could manage. Only, with her legs and underarms already shaved and her hair already clean, her bath didn't take long. Neither did a bit of foundation, some eyeliner, mascara and lipstick. Plus, she'd only packed one suitable outfit, a pale pink dress – a surprisingly successful Christmas present from her mother. So, with half an hour until the party was supposed to start, she sat on the bed, watching the hands on the clock move, thinking up things to say to her fellow party guests then hating herself for trying so hard. Finally, the spindly black hands pointed at the six and the seven.

The room they had been in earlier was transformed. The fire was low and there were candles everywhere. The rugs had been magicked away and the sofas placed against the walls, leaving a wide, open space. A table groaned with champagne flutes, fizzing in expectation of guests. Chloe flushed when she realized that she was the first person downstairs.

'I think you may be the only one of Zadie's friends who has ever been on time,' came a voice behind her. Chloe turned to see Zadie's father smiling, in black tie. 'Drink?'

Chloe nodded. 'Yes, please.'

Mr Lister handed her a glass and tapped it lightly with his own.

'Happy New Year,' she said politely.

'And to you, my dear. We were so glad that Zadie invited you. She usually ignores anything we suggest, on principle.'

She spluttered a little as his meaning hit her. His words stung, of course. But Chloe tried very hard to let them bounce off her, as if she had always been aware that her invitation came from Mr and Mrs Lister, not Zadie herself.

'What are your hopes for the coming year?' Mr Lister asked.

It struck Chloe as a surprisingly personal question. 'I'm not sure,' she said. 'I'd like to pass my exams.'

'I can see why Zadie calls you a good influence.'

'Does she?' *Is that why you made her invite me* is what she really wanted to say.

'The way he says it makes it sound boring,' said Zadie, coming through the door at the far side of the room, 'but it's meant as a compliment.' She threw her arms around Chloe. Her dress was bright green, contrasting beautifully with her very unlikely tan.

'Hello, darling, you look lovely – are you feeling better? Chloe here was all on her own.'

Zadie cocked her head. 'What do you mean? I've been fine all day.'

Mr Lister looked as if he was going to say something, but then stopped. 'I'm going to go and chivvy your mother. She can't be the last down at her own party.'

Zadie topped up a champagne glass right to the rim, then sipped from it to stop it from spilling. 'I'm so glad you're here.'

'Thank you for inviting me. Are you okay?'

'Why do people keep asking me that?'

'Your mother said you weren't having a good day, then Max said you were asleep, so I was just—'

'I'm fine,' snapped Zadie. It was the first time she'd ever been anything even approaching sharp with Chloe. 'Where's Max?'

Chloe sensed that being confused, or suggesting that Zadie should know where Zadie's boyfriend was, might go down badly. 'I'm not sure,' she said. 'I saw him a bit earlier, when we were having tea.'

'Did he behave himself? Make an effort to talk to people?'

'Yes,' Chloe lied. 'He looked like he was having a good time.'

Not long after Chloe and Zadie had come downstairs the room was heaving, loud with chatter and the clink of glasses. Chloe's parents didn't have parties, not really.

Sometimes they had a few friends over and sat in the garden with the 'girls', who drank sweet rosé, and the 'boys' (everyone was in their late forties), who drank beer. But this kind of party, where people with interesting jobs and interesting lives milled around talking to each other, flirting, laughing, and would all fall into their various bedrooms upstairs afterwards, this was an entirely different thing. There was pretty French music on in the background and the children had been allowed to stay up on the proviso that they passed around tray after tray of blinis. Chloe had found herself embroiled in a long conversation with an attractive middle-aged literary agent when Zadie came up behind her and placed her cold hand on the naked portion of her back. Chloe jumped, then laughed. The man excused himself.

'He's a complete pervert,' Zadie whispered in her ear. 'Honestly, tell him the worst idea for a book ever and he'll swear blind he could get it published, all while looking down your top. No follow-through, though. I tried to kiss him once when I was sixteen and he looked like he was going to cry.'

'Who did you try to kiss?' asked Max, sliding behind Zadie and wrapping his arms around her torso. 'Was this a recent development?'

'Obviously not. I only have eyes for you.' She twisted her neck to kiss him. Chloe shifted her weight between her feet, unsure where to look.

'Shall we?'

Zadie nodded. 'Come on, Chlo. Nearly midnight.'

Chloe followed them upstairs, Zadie and Max both carrying bottles of champagne, then up some more stairs, then up another smaller flight to a glass door which opened out on to the roof. The cold stole the air from Chloe's body.

'Look up!' said Zadie, her teeth chattering. The stars above them were unlike anything Chloe had ever seen before. She searched for the right metaphor, something devoid of cliché, but failed. Her head was heavy as she tipped it back, as if it were filled with the champagne she had been drinking all evening. Zadie tipped some between her lips from the bottle she was holding and walked towards the edge.

'Careful,' said Max, who had taken a spot sitting on a chimneypot. 'You're off your tits. I don't want to start the New Year by telling your parents they've only got four kids left.'

Zadie laughed too loud, and drank again. Max held his bottle out to Chloe, who took it gratefully.

'Cold?'

'Fucking freezing.'

Max shrugged off his jacket and gave it to her.

'I can't.'

'Yes, you can. If you don't, then I'm a prick.'

She wrapped the jacket around her, feeling the warmness he had left in it seep into her skin. It smelled of CK One and cigarette smoke.

'Chloe, come and look over the side!' shouted Zadie, who was still standing perilously close to the edge.

'I don't like heights,' Chloe lied. She didn't dislike heights if it was a skyscraper or a roller coaster. She disliked heights which were genuinely dangerous.

'Come on! It's amazing, it makes you feel all tiny.'

'I can feel tiny from over here.'

'Come onnnn.'

Chloe stood up. Max put his hand on her forearm. 'You are allowed to say no to her, you know. She needs it.'

Zadie turned. 'You're talking about me.'

'No, we're not. I'm just telling Chloe she doesn't have to risk her neck to entertain you. You need to play nicely with your toys. Any memory of any previous ones?'

Zadie pouted. 'She's my friend. Not yours.'

Max snorted. 'Is that true? Chloe?'

She should object to being used as a toy, she knew that. But the feeling that both Zadie and Max cared who she preferred was more intoxicating than the champagne.

'I'm Zadie's first,' she smiled. 'She is my room-mate, after all.' It was supposed to sound playful, but it hadn't quite landed. Max considered her, then stood, pulled Zadie back then ran his hands over her shoulders, down her arms, and kissed her, lightly at first but then harder, more insistently. Zadie seemed to like it, melting her body into his.

Chloe stood, pulling Max's jacket around her, trying to work out what to do. Should she go inside? Max's hands were on Zadie's ribs, breasts, legs now. She didn't want to watch it; she didn't want to look. Was he doing this because she had said she was on Zadie's side? Was it some kind of punishment? Or were they just drunk and in love? She took a step towards the door and then stopped. If she went downstairs, she'd have to answer questions about where Zadie was and why she wasn't with her. She stopped, rooted to the spot. Zadie pulled away from Max.

'Max, you're being gross. Chloe doesn't want to watch a live sex show.'

'Oh, I don't know. People pay a lot of money for that sort of stuff in some places.'

'Chloe, do you want to watch me and Max have sex?'

The question was rhetorical. She knew that. But in asking it Zadie had made it seem like a genuine invitation. Max looked slowly between them, and something in the atmosphere became charged. The idea of watching his body, his huge shoulders and thick arms, his narrow torso, on top of Zadie's bird-like nakedness was undeniably thrilling. It wasn't as if she wanted to see it because it would turn her on, more that the idea of seeing the two people she was so fascinated by doing something so private and so intimate would be so completely remarkable.

'No,' she said. 'A very kind offer, but no.'

Zadie giggled. 'Of course, a threesome would probably be a bit much for your first time.'

Chloe tensed, knowing what was about to happen yet praying it wouldn't.

'You're not?' asked Max, his eyes wide.

Chloe could feel herself turning crimson. Maybe she had enough make-up on to cover it.

'You're a virgin?' Max exclaimed. 'But you're hot?!'

The embarrassment was so acute Chloe couldn't bring herself to enjoy the compliment. Before she could think of an appropriate response a huge pink-and-blue explosion above made her jump.

The three of them settled on the freezing roof, the awkwardness of the moment forgotten. Chloe and Zadie were sharing Max's jacket, all of them wearing champagne for warmth, as overhead the sky burst into colour after colour after colour.

'Happy New Year!' said Chloe as the fireworks finally finished and the smoke hung in the inky air.

'Cheers,' said Max, tilting his glass against hers.

'Happy New Year, my two favourite people,' said Zadie.

After a while, even the drink couldn't keep them warm, so the three of them descended the stairs. 'This is my room,' said Max. 'Right next door to Mummy and Daddy, so there's no corridor-creeping to be had, as if their darling daughter was still *virgo intacta*.' A smile played across his lips as he directed those last words at Chloe.

Chloe resolved that the moment – no, the second – she had the chance to have sex, she was going to do it. And then she would make sure that Zadie told Max, so that the word 'virgin' couldn't haunt her any longer.

Chloe followed behind Zadie. As they reached her

room Chloe paused, one hand steadying her on the door frame.

'Can I ask something?'

'Of course.'

'Your dad said that he and your mum told you to invite me.'

Zadie didn't look flustered. Or embarrassed. What must it be like to be that cool, all the time? 'They did. They think you're brilliant. Apparently, you're a good influence, which I know sounds boring but is actually very nice from them, because they do pretty much hate everyone.'

'You didn't invite anyone else.'

'I invited Max.'

'But no one else. Did you want me to come? Or was this just to keep convincing them you're living in our room?'

Zadie picked up Chloe's hands and gripped them with her long fingers. Her skin was still freezing cold, even with the warmth of the house. 'I literally never do anything because my parents want me to. I asked you because I wanted you to come. You're my best friend.'

16

NOW

A few minutes later a text pinged, telling her that her driver would arrive in fifteen minutes. So predictable of Max to have a luxury car service on tap. She stood under the lukewarm water of the shower, wondering if she could really go through with the evening. She scrubbed crudely between her legs, under her arms, along her neck. Then she covered herself with an expensive oil Rav's mother had given her for Christmas. It had a heavy, sexy scent which always felt wrong to wear to work and too grown-up for her.

She pulled a white dress from the wardrobe, which she didn't wear often because the front needed safety-pinning. The lace of her orange-pink bra peeped out, rude against the white broderie anglaise. She didn't pin it.

Tinted moisturizer. Mascara. Creamy pink lipstick. Blusher. The freckles had come out across the bridge of her nose in the last few days, making her look younger than she was. Her phone rang just as she was buckling her sandals. She didn't take a bag – putting her keys in her pocket and her credit card in her phone case, she slammed the door behind her, thankful for the anonymity that living here provided. None of her neighbours knew her, or Rav. They didn't know that he was away, or that she was going out, and even if they did they wouldn't care. It was the polar opposite of the cliquey, gossipy cul de sac where her mother and Greg still lived, becoming more obsessed with other people's comings and goings every single day.

The journey was smooth. Perhaps Max's driver knew a better route, or it was late enough that the roads were empty, but it took half the time it had when she and Rav had taken a cab together. She rested her head against the car door, the open window wafting cool air over her face, marinating in the surprising calm she felt about what she was about to do.

Max came to the door before she even rang the bell. He must have had an alert that she was coming.

'Drink?' he asked as she walked in.

She nodded and kicked off her shoes. They went down to the basement kitchen and he poured her a large glass of rosé, the palest pink a rosé could be, then pointed towards the open doors.

The garden was clearly managed by someone who wasn't Max or Verity. It was on two levels, the first an ordered, perfect lawn with uniform-length grass. Steps led down to a second lawn. Chloe felt the soft grass under her feet as she padded towards it.

'I like that.' She pointed at a double swing seat.

Max had followed her, his feet also bare, the bottle of rosé in his hand. 'Verity can't stand it. Says it's suburban and tacky.'

They sat down. It was comfortable, still warm from the day. The seat faced back to the house, perfect in its glassy arrogance. 'Does that mean I'm suburban and tacky?'

'If you are, I am, too.'

Zadie's parents had always thought so. Chloe smiled to herself, remembering how incredibly impressed she had been on discovering that his father owned Mangi-amo, branches of which still dotted high streets today, clinging on in a world of sourdough pizza and artisanal burrata. They swung back and forward in companion-able silence for a while, looking into the light, inky evening, warmed by all the lights from the house.

'I can't believe she's dead,' said Chloe eventually.

Max seemed to think about it for a while. Then: 'I can.'

Chloe took a long drink from her glass. 'Don't say that.'

'It's true.'

'She was the most alive person I'd ever known.'

'Some of the time.'

'What do you mean?'

'She adored you, Chloe, but she only showed you some things. She didn't show you what she was like in between bouts of being wonderful. She'd lie in bed for days, smash things up, break things. Shoplift for fun. Drink until she threw up. Threaten to kill herself if I did anything that upset her.'

Chloe shook her head. 'You're exaggerating.'

Max said nothing.

'You really hadn't spoken to her?'

'No. The first person I've spoken to who had anything to do with her was her father, yesterday.'

'Do they still hate you?'

'I don't think so. Not sure they were thinking about anything other than her.'

'Zadie said they didn't like you because they were snobs. Because your parents were "trade".'

'They didn't like me because they were worried about her, and because I helped her hide things from them. She liked to believe it was about snobbery, but it was about trying to keep her safe. That's all they ever tried to do.'

Chloe tried to dismiss a vision in her mind of Astrid and Bob, older, Zadie's siblings, now adults, standing around in the hall of their enormous house, dressed in black, waiting for the cars to arrive to take them to the church. Cars which would never have needed to arrive if she had done things differently, or if Max had. They could have saved her, if it hadn't been for everything that had happened at Max's party. Chloe was sure of that.

'Was it you?'

Max turned to look at her, noticed that her glass was almost empty and refilled it. 'Was what me?'

'The night of your birthday. I found her bleeding and

bruised. Her dress was all ripped up. Someone had beaten the living hell out of her. Did you hurt her?'

He put the bottle down heavily. 'Are we really doing this again?'

'We were so young. You'd have been scared. I know she could be horrible to you. I know she tried to wind you up and needled you.'

Max shook his head.

'It's okay. You can tell me. It's been fifteen years. But you should tell me.' Chloe could hear her tone getting shriller. She stopped, trying to calm herself. She must not lose her temper. She must not lose her cool. This entire evening depended on her ability to keep her calm. To make Max feel safe.

'I only feel guilty about one thing that happened that night – and you know what it was.' Chloe tried to shake the picture from behind her eyes: Max's white shirt, his lips tasting of red wine, her party dress around her waist.

'I still feel guilty about that, too,' she replied, trying to keep her voice light. At least that was true. She had felt guilty then, and every single day since. But she was here now. And she was finally going to make it right. She had given him every single chance to confess to what he had done, and he had chosen not to.

She took a gulp from her glass of wine. This was for Zadie. It didn't matter if it was shameful, or embarrass-ing. For Zadie. For Zadie. For Zadie. 'But I think about it a lot,' she said. 'When I'm alone.'

Max looked at her and a smug smile stole across his face. She had his interest now.

'What's Verity like in bed?' she asked.

'Coco, I'm shocked,' said Max, sounding anything but. This was just the kind of pseudo-forbidden conversation he had always liked.

'So?'

'I'm not going to tell you that.'

'I'll tell you what Rav's like if you tell me what Verity is like.'

Max put his arm along the back of the seat, just above Chloe's shoulders. She could feel the warmth radiating through his linen shirt.

'Verity is . . .' He hesitated. 'Innocent. She'd only ever slept with one boyfriend before me. She's a little mouse. Badly wants to be good at it, but not much technique. And not a huge amount of enthusiasm for the actual deed, if I'm honest.' He paused. 'How honest are we being?'

'Brutally.'

'I don't think she's ever had an orgasm.'

'I think that's more about you than it is about her, to be fair.'

'I've never had any other complaints in that department, thanks very much. Go on, then. Your turn.'

Chloe thought about it for a moment. She knew what Max would want to hear, what would make him want to prove himself. 'Rav's . . . sweet.'

Max laughed. 'Oh dear. That bad?'

'Not bad, just . . . Not very adventurous, I suppose.

I've asked him to be a bit more . . . no holds barred. But he can't seem to manage it.'

'He can't manage it?' Max smiled, eyebrows raised.

'No, no, he can do that part. But anything more exotic than "love-making" seems to freak him out. I'd occasionally like him to be a bit more . . . full on.'

'Full on how?'

There was no doubt that the conversation had captivated Max. He was leaning forward and his eyes were focused on Chloe's lips.

'I asked if he'd knock me about a bit. Nothing awful, just a little slap. Maybe some hair-pulling. Choking. That sort of thing. Lots of people like it. It's not a big deal.'

Max whistled. 'It's always the quiet ones.'

'Lots of people like that sort of thing! Remember *Fifty Shades*?'

'But Rav can't manage the Christian Grey thing.'

'No.'

'And you feel hard done by?'

'Yes. I do.' Chloe traced her finger round the rim of her wine glass. It was now or never. 'You remember what you said to me the other night. Before I dropped the jug?'

'That I fancied you, back at uni?'

Chloe nodded. 'Did you mean it, or were you just trying to wind me up?'

'Of course I meant it.'

Chloe forced herself to smile. 'I want to tell you something. But I'm worried it will come out the wrong way. That it will sound awful.'

Max's smile was easy as ever. 'Try me.'

'I feel' – she sipped her wine – 'I feel like things are different. Now that she's gone. Is that terrible? You were always hers. But now that she isn't here any more, I don't feel like I have to fight my feelings. Like it wouldn't be disloyal to act on them.'

'Feelings?'

She held his gaze, then dropped her eyes down. 'Feelings. For you.'

Max breathed out slowly. 'I get it. And you know what, in some strange way I think she would get it, too. She knew there was chemistry between us. And you can say a lot about Zadie, but God knows she wasn't a prude.'

The smile on Chloe's lips was hurting her cheeks. 'I think you're right,' she whispered. And then she leaned forward, brushing her lips softly against his.

He grasped the back of her neck and pulled her against him, deepening the kiss. 'I've waited a long time to do that,' he said in a low voice.

The back of Chloe's throat was burning. She wanted a cigarette for the first time in about a decade. 'I don't think I can wait any more.'

'Me neither.' He took her by the hand and led her inside.

17

THEN

The last week of the holidays dragged, but eventually Chloe was packing up her suitcase and taking another train, this time back to university. Greg's offer of a lift only seemed to have applied to her first day. Her mother did a tearful, performative goodbye on the doorstep of the house, Greg said something about getting out of the car quickly so he didn't get a fine for parking in the wrong place, and a few hours later she was standing back in her cold bedroom. To her surprise, there was a note on her pillow.

'First party of the new term – see you at 9, Z xx.'

When Chloe arrived at Archer Crescent there was no one but Zadie in the house. She answered the door in a silk dressing gown, clearly already several drinks down. 'Where's Max?' Chloe asked, following Zadie up the stairs to her bedroom. Every surface was strewn with make-up and products and the floor was covered in clothing.

'On some rugby camp until next week, which is a blessing, because he's pre-season.'

'Pre-season?'

'Rugby gets super-serious this term, so he stops eating anything apart from steak and chicken breasts, and he goes off the drink, which makes him enormously grumpy.'

'You're having a welcome-back party without him?'

'Just a little one.' She knelt down, pulling things out of a suitcase. 'I can't find anything.'

'Maybe if you unpacked?'

'I know, I know, but Max's parents don't send anyone to clean unless he's here, and I'm basically a human manifestation of chaos. How about these?' She picked up a pair of wide-legged velvet trousers. 'Nice?'

'Great,' Chloe said, bemused. 'Does your cleaner put your clothes away?'

Zadie zipped up the trousers. 'Yes, I know, I'm a hideous brat. I quite like these with just a bra.'

'You'll be freezing.'

'You're being very' – she paused – 'motherly this evening.'

'Sorry. I've been at home too long. Come on, let's have a drink.'

The party unfolded as Chloe had come to realize Zadie's parties often did. They drank, someone cranked up the music in the living room, people lay around on sofas getting high, ran around the garden playing complicated drinking games, disappeared into bedrooms to fuck. Chloe moved from room to room, trying to decide what she was in the mood for. A nagging voice at the back of her head kept reminding her that she had exams coming up, set texts to read, notes to revise. Before she had come here, when she was doing her school exams, she had woken every day at seven, run for an hour, studied until her mother brought her a sandwich, and then studied until seven at night. Not to make herself suffer, not even because she had to, but because she wanted to. This was what was going to change her life. This was what was going to get her out.

But then, she was out now. This was the 'out' she had dreamed of, the world she had wanted to reach. She'd got through the door, behind the curtain – whatever metaphor you wanted to use. She'd dreamed of leaving her town, finding people who also wanted to live in a different time and to have adventures. That was what she was doing right now. So if she couldn't wake up tomorrow to re-read *Great Expectations*, or her notes on *Beowulf* went untouched, did it really matter? Was she really missing anything?

She needed another drink to silence the nag, to let herself believe that she deserved to have some fun, to enjoy what it was she had worked so hard to achieve. The kitchen was filled with ten, twenty people, setting up a game of Beer Pong. Chloe took a bottle from the fridge and tipped it up into her glass, filling it to the lip.

'If you ever get a bar job, tell me, so I can bring everyone I know,' said a voice close to her ear. Without looking up, she knew who it was going to be.

'Happy New Year,' she said, before putting the cold glass to her lips, numbing them.

'And to you. You didn't text me back.' Rav pouted.

'I was busy.'

'I see.'

Chloe looked him up and down. It irritated her how attractive he was. 'You're not on rugby camp?'

He shook his head. 'Didn't make the cut. Only the first six go on camp. The rest of us stay here and hope someone breaks a leg so we get to play at some point.'

Chloe must have looked horrified because he added, 'Or sprains an ankle, at least. You look great, by the way. Different.'

'Different?'

'Not that you didn't look good before. You did. You just look – I'm not sure. Is something different? Should I stop talking? Or maybe just top myself?'

'I'm not wearing any of Zadie's clothes, for a change. That might be it.'

'You usually wear her stuff?'

'She's got the kind of wardrobe that most Hollywood starlets would kill for.'

'Really? I'm not sure Max notices what anyone's wearing unless it's a rugby shirt.'

'They're quite different from each other. I guess that's part of what makes them work. It's so loud in here. Do you want to go upstairs?' she suggested. As they climbed the stairs and opened doors, looking for an empty room, she listened to herself talking about how Zadie bought vintage and borrowed things from her grandmother and great-grandmother's old clothing collections, and, while she had seen her own mother getting bored of the topic, waiting for a chance to change the subject, Rav seemed genuinely interested. It was as if he wanted to hear the things Chloe was thinking about and wondering about. She'd spent the last three weeks trying to steer the conversation back to Max or Zadie, without meaning to, hating herself for it, wanting to talk about them and wanting to not want to talk to them. By the time she finished her monologue she found that they were sitting either side of each other on the bed of the spare room.

'You're very, very pretty.'

'Thank you.'

'No, really. The longer I look at you, the more I see it.'

Chloe leaned forward and pressed her lips to Rav's. It was the first time she had ever kissed someone. She'd been kissed, of course. Dry lips pressed to hers during parties, wet snogs on dance floors, games of Spin the Bottle, half-hearted attempts at deriving some kind of pleasure from intimacy. She'd even acquiesced to a kiss from a girl at her school, wondering if her lack of enjoyment might have been caused by an interest in an entirely different type of person. That hadn't been any better. But this was the first time she had made the first move. Rav parted his lips, gently met her tongue and ran his hand along the side of her torso. She shivered slightly.

His hands were all over her body, running inside her top, unzipping her jeans, pulling them off with surprising deftness. He'd clearly done this many times before.

'Do you have a condom?' she asked as his crotch pushed against her, leaving her in no doubt of his desire for her.

He pulled one from his wallet. 'You're sure that you want to?'

'Yes,' she said. 'But I haven't exactly done this before.'

Rav froze. 'You're a virgin?'

Why had she told him? What if he didn't want to do it now? 'Yeah,' she said breezily. 'But it's okay. I'm nearly nineteen – it's not exactly something I'm clinging to at this point.'

He looked uneasy. 'Are you sure? I thought people liked their first time to be something special, with some-one they loved, and all that.'

'You mean . . . you're not in love with me?' Chloe's attempt at a serious expression quickly cracked as panic flitted across Rav's face. 'Yes, I'm sure. I want to. I like you. I want to have sex. It's not a big deal.'

So Rav kissed her, and after a long while he knelt between her legs and eased himself inside her. 'You okay?' he asked as her legs tensed around his torso.

She nodded, breathing through the initial pain.

They moved together slowly while Chloe got used to the sensation. It felt strange, foreign more than anything else. Odd to have someone else invade her body. Then Rav gave a shuddering sigh and finished. 'That was amazing,' he said.

'Really?'

'You're one for ego boosts, are you?'

'Sorry, I didn't mean it like that. I just don't have anything to compare it to. Obviously.'

'You're a natural.' He smiled, wrapping his arm around her. 'Let's stay here for a bit.'

Chloe's hair splayed over Rav's chest and the rhythmic movement as it rose and fell rocked her. He was warm, and their bodies seemed to fit together in a way she couldn't understand. He gently stroked her hair, twisting long strands of it around his fingers. For the first time in a long time the monologue inside her head went quiet.

When she woke up, the house was quiet. Chloe was surprised to see it was morning – and that Rav hadn't sneaked out in the night. He left for a lecture at about eight o'clock, kissing Chloe's forehead and grumbling about not having time to go back and get his notes.

'Entirely your own fault,' said Chloe, pulling the duvet up around her chest.

'Entirely worth it,' he said, winking before shutting the door behind him.

She lay back, a warm feeling spreading through her. She'd finally done it. She couldn't wait to tell Zadie.

The house was, predictably, a mess. The kitchen was covered in plastic cups and cigarette butts, and freezing cold because the back door had been left open all night. Chloe made a cafetière of coffee, the kitchen now as familiar to her as her own, then went to Zadie's bedroom.

'Wake up,' she said, knocking on the door. 'We have to clean up before Max gets back, or he'll murder us.'

Zadie moaned dramatically. 'I can't.'

'You're hung over.'

'No, I know what a hangover feels like. This is something entirely different. This is something fatal. I know it. Can you ring my tutor and tell him I'll need at least a week off?'

Chloe tugged open the curtains and handed Zadie a cup of coffee. 'Nope. But I did bring coffee, because I am a very good person. And I have gossip.'

Zadie hitched up the strap of the negligee she was wearing and propped herself up on one of the dozens of pillows that dressed her bed. 'Well, if there's gossip, then I suppose I won't exile you for waking me up before noon. What happened?'

Chloe left a dramatic pause and then said proudly, 'I had sex.' She jumped on to the bed.

Zadie's face lit up. 'You didn't just have sex, you lost your virginity! I mean, obviously, virginity is a construct made up to subjugate women and all that, but *you had sex!*'

'I did.' Chloe sipped her coffee and looked out at the clear blue sky. Shards of sunlight were falling on the white duvet cover and the day felt exciting. New.

'Tell me everything. What happened? Who with? How was it?'

'It was . . . good. Weird? Good weird, though. I don't know. I'd done other stuff before, of course, so I wasn't expecting it to feel so different. But it was nice. He was nice.'

'Who was he?'

'Max's friend Rav.'

The excitement drained from Zadie's face. 'Oh.'

'What?'

'No, nothing.'

'Zadie, I can read your face like a book. Everyone can read your face like a book – you're the worst liar in the history of the world.'

'It's just . . . Didn't he take your number and then not text you last term?'

'Yeah. He did.'

'And then he only got interested when you started playing hard to get?'

'Yeah. I guess . . .' Chloe said, suddenly feeling less confident.

Zadie pursed her lips for a moment then rubbed Chloe's knee kindly. 'But you had fun, that's what matters. And it's not like you're thinking you're going to marry him.'

'No. That's true,' Chloe said, and gave a small smile in return.

Zadie drained her coffee cup and readjusted herself. 'Oh, I've made you sad. I'm sorry. I didn't mean to. The last thing I want is to take the shine off it. If it helps, I lost mine to one of the grounds staff at school – no, don't look horrified, he was only a year older than me – but then it got around and the school found out and fired him. I felt awful, he was sad, my parents were informed. The whole thing was horrible and I was furious that they'd all stolen the loveliness of it away. And now I've done the same thing to you. I'm so sorry.'

Her earnestness would have seemed false on anyone else, but something about the way Zadie spoke made it impossible not to believe every word she said.

'No, no, not sad. I guess I was just still in my little bubble. I wasn't thinking about that stuff.'

Zadie wrapped her arms around Chloe, wobbling her coffee cup on the pristine white duvet cover. 'Think about it. It would have been a disaster if you'd ended up loving him for ever. Who wants to marry the only person they've ever slept with?'

ZADIE

Max was never around in January. Even when he was at school, he had chosen to go back early so that he could run round the muddy fields, punishing his body for the excess of Christmas. And now that he had the peak of his career in touching distance, he was even worse. Every morning when she woke up he would be long gone, across town at rugby camp, back late and covered in dirt, interested only in a protein shake or, if he was feeling truly punishing, an ice bath. Zadie had been back at uni for a week, but they'd barely spent a waking hour together.

It shouldn't matter, she knew that. But she hated January. It always filled her with this sort of sadness, like a pendulum in her chest. Other people seemed to be able to accept that Christmas was over, packing away decorations, pulling on Lycra leggings and embarking on diets. But Zadie found the passing of time, the way that the national mood shifted from celebration to misery in a matter of hours, unbearable. She gazed at her feet as she tramped back up to her room. She had called Max to see when he'd be home, because she couldn't face another afternoon at home alone, but he wasn't picking up. So she had time to kill here.

To her surprise, Chloe was sitting at the desk in their room, books spread out in front of her.

'You're already working?' asked Zadie.

Chloe looked startled. Embarrassed, even. 'Yeah,' she said. 'I got my marks back for the end-of-term exams, and I didn't do well. Plus, I missed a whole load of lectures last term, too hung over to go. I've got some make-up essays to write, otherwise they're going to get properly stressy with me. I have to send this piece of work in by midnight.'

Zadie looked sadly at all Chloe's books and felt guilty, not for the first time, that she only had three hours of lectures a week, and that she had a note from her psychologist saying that she shouldn't be placed under undue pressure, lest it trigger a breakdown.

'Have you got lots left to do?' she asked, flopping on to her bed. 'I was thinking we could go out.'

She shouldn't tempt Chloe. She knew that. At school she had been moved from room-sharing with girl after girl when their parents had complained that Zadie was a distraction. And it was true. Just because she could dash off an essay in an hour and get a passing grade didn't mean that everyone else could. And she tried to be grown-up about that. But the idea of an afternoon sitting alone, waiting for Max, was too much.

'I shouldn't,' said Chloe.

'We could just go into town for a little bit of shopping. And then maybe a glass of wine. You'd be back here by, like, five. You could work all evening.'

★

Chloe hadn't wanted to go into Feight, the boutique on the high street with the whippet-thin assistants and the sofas for bored husbands. But Zadie had insisted. Then she had forced Chloe to try on dress after dress. As Chloe came out of the changing room and smiled at her reflection in the mirror, a warm feeling flooded Zadie's insides. It made her feel better. Bad people didn't get joy out of buying presents for their friends.

'You have to have that one. And the blue one, and the pink one.'

Chloe laughed. 'And then I'll have to move in with you and Max because I won't be able to afford to pay for halls.'

'I'll get them,' Zadie said, scooping all the garments up in her arms and lying them on the counter. 'Wrap them up, please,' she said to the woman behind the counter, who gave her a snooty smile.

Chloe was flustered. She made lots of noises about not wanting them, about it being wrong, how she couldn't accept them. Zadie pretended to listen, then swiped the card and handed Chloe the bags. 'Now,' she said, 'drinks.'

Chloe wasn't sure how they lost track of time so badly. But before long it was dark. And then it was late. Zadie checked her phone and there were lots of missed calls from Max, who sounded cross when she eventually picked up the phone. She hailed a taxi and pulled Chloe, also giggling and falling over, into it.

'What time is it?' Chloe slurred.

'I think, like, ten,' Zadie replied.

'It's 1 a.m.,' said the driver.

Chloe looked upset.

'What's wrong?'

'I was supposed to email in my essay before midnight.'

Zadie laughed. But Chloe didn't. Zadie watched her face in profile, orange under the street lights. Her stomach twisted and the lovely warm glow from the wine and the cocktails started to slip away as she watched a single tear slide down Chloe's cheek.

18
NOW

Chloe followed Max upstairs. Up more stairs. Past what looked like the master bedroom, to a smaller but no less hotel-like room at the top of the house. He pulled open the skylights, flooding the hot room with cooler air. Then he bent to kiss her neck, her chest, her cheeks and, finally, her lips.

'I'd like another glass of wine,' she said when he pulled away for a moment.

'Of course. I'll be back in a minute.'

Chloe took off her dress and surveyed herself in the mirror. As if it mattered what she looked like. Max wanted her because he wanted to give her what Rav couldn't. He wanted to triumph where another man had failed. And, as an added bonus, he got to fuck the only one of his female friends who hadn't opened her legs for him at university. She put her phone on the bedside table, swiped at it then lay down.

Max came over to the bed, twisted her hair in his hand and yanked her head back. 'I always wondered what you'd be like in bed. Ever since that night when I found out that you were a virgin,' he said into her ear.

His hands were everywhere, and his lips were everywhere else. He bit her neck and her breasts. 'Harder,' she whispered.

'I don't want to bruise you,' he said. 'When Rav gets back . . .'

'Let me worry about that,' she replied, pressing her almost naked body against his clothed one. So he bit her again. Harder this time. Harder still, after she writhed and told him how much she liked it.

'Slap me,' she asked, looking up at him through her eyelashes. He tapped her cheek gently. 'Is that the best you can do?' He did it again, harder. She moaned, encouraging him with her enthusiasm.

It came as no surprise to Chloe that Max was good at sex. She had always assumed that he would be. But he was seamless. He moved from action to action without a moment of hesitation. To her intense surprise, surprise soaked in guilt, when she closed her eyes and divorced herself from who it was she was in bed with, she found that she was almost enjoying herself. How many times had she lain in bed at Archer Crescent, listening to Max and Zadie going at it with the kind of aggressive lust that belongs only to people of that age, and wondered what it would be like to have Max's hands on her skin? She watched his fingers brush her leg and tried not to rejoice in being touched by someone who had touched Zadie.

Eventually, he came, and remembering his complaint

about Verity, Chloe gave an impressive performance, whimpering and clenching around him. He rolled off her and flopped back on the bed.

'Fucking hell, Coco. That was quite something.'

'It really was.'

'Maybe there's something to that delayed-gratification thing other people talk about.'

Chloe lay her head on Max's chest. 'Can I stay the night? Or will Verity be back in the morning?'

'No, she won't be here until tomorrow evening. You're welcome to stay.'

Max fell asleep quickly. It was so like him to be able to drift off into a peaceful sleep moments after he had betrayed his fiancée. She got up quietly, gathered her clothes and went into the bathroom. It would be safer to wait until he was deeply asleep, but time was of the essence. She closed the recording she had made on her phone without watching it back. She couldn't bring herself to just yet. Then she turned the bathroom lights on and took detailed photos, one by one, of every single mark on her body. The love bites on her neck, the flush on her cheeks, the bruise on her upper thigh where he had responded to her cajoling him to spank her. It had hurt, but she was glad of the livid red handprint it had left.

She took a deep breath. The last part. She went back to the bedroom and photographed Max. Slowly, determinedly. Then she photographed herself with him. She took his thumb and pressed it, moving so slowly and so gently she could hear her own heart beating, against his phone. It unlocked. Her chest untightened.

What should she write? What message would keep her options most open?

'I hope that was okay – it's been a while since I've done anything like that. Don't tell Rav, and I won't tell Verity.'

That was good. It sounded like him. Or at least it sounded enough like him that it would be believable. If it needed to be. She deleted the message from his phone as it flashed up on her own screen.

Then she called the car service Max had used earlier. She dropped her voice, low and sad. 'I need a car, as soon as you can,' she said. She whispered Max's address. The woman at the other end of the line sounded suitably worried about her and assured her the car would be there as soon as possible.

On the way to the front door she paused, then went to the kitchen drawer where Verity kept her cigarettes. Took a couple out. Moved the lighter. It was the kind of thing that someone like Verity was certain to notice. Good.

The day after her encounter with Max, Chloe woke up with a feeling that reminded her of her birthday. A mixture of excitement and the anticipation of being disappointed, heavily laced with the guilt of what she had done to Rav. But there was no reason he would ever have to know. And it wasn't as if she had acted out of lust. She had done what she had to do, for her friend. Any enjoyment she had derived from it was purely physical. Not her fault.

Her skin was raw from where she had scrubbed any trace of Max away, the water from the shower mixing with the tears streaming down her face. She checked her phone constantly, looking again and again at everything she had collected, reassuring herself that she had it all safe, weighing up all the options it gave her. The video of them together. The photographs of the marks on her body in the harsh light of the bathroom. The picture of Max, in bed, naked. The pictures of them together. Now she had to decide what to do next. How best to deploy her hard-won weapons.

Alongside the obsession with Max, with her treasure trove there was something else. A heavy, sticky feeling of grief, unlike the grief she had ever felt before when a grandparent or a much-loved pet 'passed away'. For the last fifteen years she had indulged in daydreams – not often; once, perhaps twice a month – about a time in the future when she and Zadie would be friends again. When she would be able to share everything she did with her, when Zadie would sprinkle her very special brand of magic over their lives. She had created a version of Zadie as an adult, all her selfish, frightening tendencies wiped away by age but the sparkle still entirely present.

As the years wore on and Zadie was a more and more distant memory, she knew that it was unlikely. More and more unlikely. Eventually, almost impossible. But now, it was actually impossible. Completely, really, truly impossible. Zadie had always been there in the back of her mind, like an imaginary friend. She would hear her voice when she was deciding whether or not to buy a dress she couldn't afford, or sitting next to someone painfully dull at a dinner party. The fact that Zadie was dead shouldn't matter, not really. Nothing in Chloe's life had changed. But somehow, despite the fact Zadie had been no more alive for Chloe last week than she was now, Zadie was gone for her. The wicked little laugh, the ideas, the naughtiness. She couldn't hear it any more. It was gone.

At some point in the years that Chloe and Rav had lived in the flat, they had decided that it was too much work to look for anything that wasn't immediately at hand and, besides, the flat was so tiny they couldn't afford to waste a single centimetre of space. Every single one of their belongings that wasn't used every day was stored in a tiny, dark room which the estate agent had optimistically called a 'storage nook'. But today was going to be different. Chloe took out box after box, more than a little pleased that she had been so methodical when she had packed it all away. She found the record player she had bought Rav for his thirtieth birthday, when they'd lived with Lissy and Guy in the much bigger flat, and another box, filled with records. For a while, records had filled a little cavity in their marriage. Record-buying had become an activity. They stopped at charity shops as they passed to see if they could add to their collection. Surprised each other with strange or funny records they'd seen.

There was almost no space in the living room. A little round table, two bookshelves, a fireplace, a sofa and a TV. But, she reasoned, they never ate at the table, preferring to sit on the sofa and watch something mindless during the winter, or in the little garden in the summer. So she put the record player back together, wiring up the speakers and feeling beyond smug when the scratchy, warm music began to play, pulling her back to a time five years ago when she was newly married, living with her best friends and still convinced that everything would somehow be okay.

19

THEN

Chloe tried to push open the door to her bedroom. The carpet seemed to be resisting her. Finally, she won the fight, shoving the door open and realizing that there was a wad of post on the carpet, acting like a sort of doorstop. She hadn't been back here for a week. Maybe two weeks. She'd taken to sleeping at Zadie's after they had people over. When Max was away, for whatever rugby-related activity he had gone off on, she would sleep in Zadie's bed. They'd fallen into a soft, comfortable way of sleeping, each on their own side but facing each other, talking until they fell asleep. Zadie said it made her feel safe – reminded her of school, where she'd slept in a dormitory full of other girls for years. Chloe supposed it probably did something similar for her. Reminded her of a time when she was little, before Greg, when her mother would crawl into her bed, read to her and sing to her until she fell asleep.

Most of the bits of paper weren't important. There was a letter from the library curtly demanding that some books be returned, a postcard from her mother and Greg, who had gone to the Lake District. But there was also a white envelope with a window that made her stomach twist. Nothing good ever came from an envelope with a window, her mother had always said. She slid her finger under the flap and tried not to throw up when, moments later, the words on the paper started to scream in her mind.

She had missed too many lectures. Too many deadlines. They wanted to see her for a formal meeting, and if she didn't go, she would be automatically unenrolled. She had, the accusatory piece of paper claimed, ignored their previous attempts at getting in touch. How else would they have tried? When did she last check her university email address? Heart thumping, ocean noises inside her ears, she called Zadie.

'Zaid,' she said, her voice almost a whisper, 'they're going to kick me out.'

Zadie sounded sleepy, which shouldn't have come as a surprise. When Chloe had left that morning the house was still full of people and Zadie had been lying perfectly still and entirely asleep.

'What?'

'I've got a letter. I have to go to a meeting. If I don't convince them that there are' – she fumbled with the letter, trying to find the words – ' "extenuating circumstances", then I'm going to get chucked out.'

She listened to the rustle of sheets as Zadie sat up. 'Calm down,' she said.

'I can't, Zadie. If I get kicked out, I don't know what I would do. I can't move back home. I won't be able to get a job. I basically spent my whole life trying to get here.'

Zadie shushed her gently. 'Coco, it's not going to happen. When is this meeting?'

'Thursday.'

'Okay, so you just turn up looking like shit, tell them that you've been struggling, that you need to stay enrolled otherwise you don't know what you'll do – make a big deal about that bit – and then look all teary. They'll make you get some counselling and check in with your tutor a bit, and you'll be fine.'

'How do you know all this?'

'Everyone does it, it's fine.'

Chloe did as she had been instructed. She fought every one of her instincts, which told her to arrive in a neatly ironed blouse with her hair in a ponytail, and turned up wearing a lumpy jumper and jeans, unwashed hair loose over her shoulders. Most of the work was done for her, if she was honest. As she finished getting dressed, she looked at herself in the plastic-rimmed mirror above her sink. She had to admit that what looked back at her wasn't good. The skin under her eyes was inky and the rest of her face was milk-pale. There were three livid red spots on her jaw line, and her hair had gone sort of floppy. She was thinner than she used to be, but not in a way she could feel pleased with. Her skin was soft and tissue-papery. When was the last time she'd eaten properly?

The halls of residence put on dinner every night, safe, school-style food like sausages and mash or pasta bake. In her first weeks she had diligently gone every day, filling up on carbohydrates, making polite conversation with the people on her table. But as she had grown closer and closer to Zadie, she'd stopped. Zadie didn't seem very interested in food. Coffee in the morning. Diet Coke in the afternoon. Whatever outlandish cocktail she'd decided to make any given evening. Olives, sometimes, a handful of crisps. The fridge was full of lean protein, cooked and eaten by Max. But food seemed too pedestrian, too prosaic for Zadie. But everyone did this at university. Everyone knew that students weren't supposed to eat much, that drinking every day and being permanently hung over was how it was supposed to be. She had the whole of the rest of her life to eat vegetables and get eight hours of sleep a night.

The panel at her meeting was made up of her academic tutor, a middle-aged woman who she had met a couple of times in the first weeks of term but hadn't seen since, another slightly younger woman from the university who said she was 'in HR' and wore a necklace that looked as if it was made from pasta, and Jules, the graduate student from her halls who had moved her in on her first day.

It seemed as if Zadie's advice had worked. As she sat down in the chair, intimidatingly placed on the other side of the desk to the three older women, she watched the expressions of concern on their faces.

'So, Chloe,' said her tutor in a gentle voice, 'tell me a bit about what's been going on.'

What was she supposed to say now? Zadie had coached her the night before. Say as little as possible, get them as worried as possible.

'I've been having a hard time,' she said slowly.

'Okay. Can you tell us a little more about that?'

'I'm not sleeping much.' That was true. A few hours a night. Never before 2 a.m. 'And then I don't make it to my lectures because I'm so tired.'

They all nodded. Good. This was going well.

'Have you felt overwhelmed academically?'

No. Not really. She'd dashed off most of the work that needed doing and handed it in; she was still just about passing. And the marks from the first year didn't count towards her final degree grade anyway, so everyone said that going for anything over a pass mark was a waste of time.

'Yes,' she said. 'A bit.'

They asked more questions. She answered as close to honestly as she could.

'Our other worry,' the tutor said, her voice even gentler now, 'is that Jules says she doesn't see you around the halls much any more.'

What was she supposed to say to that?

'I stay over with a friend sometimes,' she ventured, once the silence had grown too loud to ignore.

'A friend?'

'A couple of friends. They live off campus. On Archer

Crescent.' She wasn't sure why she was expecting them to look impressed; they were adults. They didn't care about Archer Crescent.

'And these friends, are they—' Her tutor paused. 'Do you feel safe with them?'

Chloe felt stung. 'Yes, of course I do.'

'And is this a platonic friendship?'

She mistook Chloe's silence for her not knowing what 'platonic' meant. 'I mean, is this a boyfriend?'

'No. Just friends.'

'It seems like you're gone for weeks at a time,' said Jules. 'The girls on your corridor say that they barely see you any more.'

'Well, maybe I don't want to see them because they're the kind of people who tell tales on other adults.' Her voice was sharper than she had intended. 'Sorry,' she added, regaining control. She couldn't lose their sympathy. She mustn't screw this up.

'Could you step outside please, Chloe?'

Chloe stood in the draughty hallway, counting the wooden tiles on the floor and gently banging the toes of her trainers against the wall. There was an exam clock on the wall. She watched the third hand trace each number. How was it possible that she and Zadie could lose hours, sometimes even days, when they were partying but she had been standing here in this wood-panelled purgatory for four minutes and it felt like nine hours?

Eventually, they called her back in.

'We've had a chat, Chloe,' said the tutor. 'And we all

agree that you're clearly having a very difficult time. The first year of university can be difficult. There are so many different influences on you, so many choices to make.'

Why was she going on like this? If she was going to say that she was being chucked out, then why couldn't she hurry up and do it quickly?

'We are all in agreement that you should be given another chance. So, you will do some additional essays during the holidays, in order to achieve a pass grade for the year. We would ask that, going forward, you try to spend more time in your own halls of residence, and that if you are struggling to keep up academically, you talk to us about it, rather than suffering in silence.'

Zadie hugged her when she recounted the story later and pulled a bottle of champagne from the fridge. Chloe wasn't sure she should be celebrating, but it felt churlish to refuse.

'Is that the champagne from the cellar?' asked Max, striding into the kitchen half an hour later.

Zadie looked at the label. 'Probably. I found it in the cellar.'

'It was a present, for winning the finals last year.'

'You'd better have a glass, then.' She smiled, clearly refusing to apologize. Max shook his head. 'Can't you buy your own booze?'

'Nope. Astrid and Bob have put me on short rations.'

'Why?'

'There was a credit-card bill. It all sounds far worse

than it is. Don't be boring – there's nothing worse than talking about money. What shall we do tonight?'

'I've got a wild idea,' said Max. 'Why don't we play a game?'

Zadie looked pleased. 'What kind of game?'

'It's called "I've got to get up at five tomorrow morning, so why don't we watch an episode of *Midsomer Murders* and get an early night?" '

Chloe got to her feet. 'Actually, I've got a lecture first thing, and I don't think I should push my luck.'

'See? Chloe feels the same way.'

Chloe picked up her bag and kissed Zadie on the cheek, an affectation she had copied originally but now seemed unable to avoid. She brushed her lips against Max's cheek, too, still cold from outside. 'It's not that,' she said as she left the room. 'It's just that I had this disciplinary thing earlier. If I don't get my act together, then they're going to chuck me out.'

She paused in the hall, straining to hear what, if anything, Zadie was saying.

'Stop pouting,' Max said. 'We've had what, ten, fifteen parties since the start of the year? You can handle one quiet night. What's so wrong with spending a bit of time with me?'

She didn't catch what Zadie said in response.

'Either you can spend an evening here without getting slaughtered and putting £20 notes up your nose, or you can go back to that nice room in halls that your parents are paying for.'

Someone said something, but Chloe couldn't work out which of them it was, and then a glass – several glasses – smashed on the ground. Chloe slipped out of the front door and gently pressed it closed, desperate to stay and find out what had happened but even more desperate not to get caught listening.

20
NOW

A buzzing noise from the other room caught Chloe's attention. She padded through and picked her phone up. Lissy was calling her. Why? She hovered her finger over the button to accept the call, but before she could decide what to do it stopped ringing. The display showed three missed calls. She tried to remember how long it had been since they had spoken. A couple of weeks? Maybe more?

Chloe's chest tightened. Why had Lissy rung her so many times? Something must be wrong. Fumbling, she called her back. 'Lissy? Are you okay?'

'Fine,' said Lissy, talking at a volume which suggested she was driving and the phone was on hands-free. 'Just wondering whether you needed a lift, but you didn't pick up so I had to leave. Are you getting a cab or taking the train?'

Chloe searched her mind, trying to work out what Lissy was talking about. 'Sorry,' she said, pulling everything out of her handbag to try to find her diary. 'You're breaking up. Can you say that again?'

Lissy repeated herself while Chloe tore through her diary and found the day. Fuck. Fucking fuck. She had absolutely sworn blind that she would meet Lissy in central London, to go for high tea with Claudia. They had booked it when Lissy was seven and a half months pregnant and told that she had to be on bed rest. She had been utterly furious to lose her independence and Chloe had spent dozens of afternoons in her bedroom, planning all the things they would do when she got her freedom back. And they had booked this what felt like a lifetime ago, as something to look forward to. A treat.

'I'm getting the train,' she said, her voice too cheerful. 'I'll see you soon.'

'Okay. Can't wait! Claudia is wearing her first grown-up dress for the occasion and she's dying to see you.'

Claudia's eyesight would only just be good enough by this point to see her if she was a metre or two away. But Chloe was in no position to correct Lissy. She hung up, frantically dialled for a cab and blanched at the figure they quoted. It was rush hour, and it was going to take forty-five minutes to get into central London, and cost a fortune. Never mind. She turned her attention to her appearance. The plan had been to wash her hair that morning. The roots were getting darker, which made it look even dirtier, and she had a spot on her chin. She swept her make-up off the dressing table into her handbag and pulled a pretty summer dress out of her wardrobe, jamming trainers on to her feet.

The traffic moved so slowly that every three minutes

Chloe thought about getting out and walking. She was late. The dashboard of the taxi viciously displayed the time, taunting her with every minute she was later and later. Lissy kept sending her messages. Their tea slot was only ninety minutes. The car crawled, her phone pinged and she vibrated with stress, and with anger at herself for being so stupid and at Lissy for being so obsessive. Why had they even booked this ruinously expensive tea? The hotel wouldn't be baby friendly and it was going to be stupidly overpriced, plus they would be pushed out the second their slot finished. How could anyone want to be so tied to times? Zadie never had been. She had woken up when she felt like it, turned up to lectures if they sounded interesting, arrived whenever seemed right.

Eventually, they reached the top of the road. Chloe abandoned the cab and legged it, realizing that the weather was actually freezing and the summer dress a huge mistake. She pushed her way through the huge wooden doors and saw Lissy sitting at the far end of the lobby. She waved, saturated with relief that she was only fifteen minutes late.

'Madam?' came a voice from behind her.

'Yes?'

'I'm afraid we have a dress code.'

It was all Chloe could do not to scream. 'I'm sorry?'

'Our dress code prohibits trainers.'

Lissy had a spare pair of ballet pumps in her car, but by the time Chloe had got them and come back they had missed almost half of their time slot. The baby started to cry, Lissy's single glass of champagne, the only one she could have, as she was driving, as she repeated four times, had gone flat and the entire afternoon was ruined.

It started to rain on the drive home and Claudia finally fell asleep in the back.

'I'm sorry,' Chloe said, watching the raindrops race down the car window.

The road noise didn't fill the silence.

'I forgot that we were supposed to be meeting.'

'Yes, I had worked that out,' Lissy snapped.

'I didn't mean to.'

'Obviously. You can't forget something on purpose.'

It struck Chloe that she wished you *could* forget things on purpose. That life would be far easier if you could.

'Are you okay?' Lissy softened. 'I haven't seen you like this since—'

She needn't have stopped. Chloe knew exactly what she meant. She hadn't seen her like this since Zadie, since the days of sleeping until 3 p.m. and having a glass of red wine as the first beverage of the day, the days of absolutely promising to turn up to something and then remembering three days later that she hadn't even texted her apologies when she forgot to go.

'I'm okay,' she said. It wasn't true. She wasn't okay. She felt dirty, no matter how many showers she had. She felt swollen, and on the edge of weeping at every moment. She looked at Lissy's profile, her neat hair and the little gold necklace with Claudia's birthstone in it. She had got prettier since university. Getting older suited her. She was far sexier in her mid-thirties than she had been in her late teens. Perhaps it was because she had so much more of a grasp of herself, of her life. Back then, she had allowed Chloe to get away with being such a terrible friend. She had never complained that Chloe was a complete flake, someone who viewed her as a back-up option. Or maybe she didn't realize it at the time.

Perhaps Lissy would know what to say. Perhaps it was unfair to assume she wouldn't be able to help.

'A friend of mine died recently. I'm just having a hard time with it.'

Lissy's concern was genuine and obvious. 'Oh, Chlo, I'm so sorry, that's awful. What happened?'

'She killed herself.'

'Fuck. That's awful.' Lissy took her hand off the steering wheel and placed it on Chloe's forearm, a demonstration of real love, given that she was an obsessively by-the-book driver even before having Claudia in the car with her. 'Were you close?'

How was she supposed to answer that? What possible explanation could she give to explain that they had been closer than two people could ever usually be and yet hadn't spoken for more than a decade? Her first instinct had been right. There was no point in trying to discuss this with Lissy. She was too normal ever to be able to understand.

Lissy looked across at Chloe. Their eyes met. 'Is there something else?' Lissy asked, uncharacteristically astute.

Chloe allowed herself a tiny moment to imagine

telling Lissy everything, the relief that would come from completely unburdening herself. Then she pulled herself together. That wasn't an option so there was no point fantasizing about it. 'Rav and I are having a bit of a hard time, too,' she said, knowing it would distract Lissy.

Lissy's face changed. She looked relieved that Chloe had given her a problem she was more equipped to deal with. 'Why?'

'Same old row,' she said. 'He wants to have children straight away. I'm not sure that I'm ready.'

'You're never ready,' said Lissy, turning off a round-about. 'But you should do it. It's the best thing that ever happened to me. You have no idea how selfish you are until you become a mother.'

She had no right to be hurt by Lissy's words, especially after how she had behaved that day. But they still stung. All that evening, as she cooked herself dinner, washed her hair and sat on the sofa thinking about the mess she had made, the words kept circling around in her head. You have no idea how selfish you are.

21

THEN

Chloe was frightened that her resolution would crumble, that she would find herself unable to resist going straight back to Max and Zadie's. But to her own enormous surprise she didn't. Instead she got up at seven thirty every morning, went to her lectures, washed her hair, ate in the common dining room, let Lissy tell her long stories about her new boyfriend, Guy, and allowed herself only little snatches of Zadie. A cup of coffee on the way back from a lecture, a chat on the phone while Chloe tidied her bedroom and Zadie luxuriated in the bath. A Saturday afternoon sitting outside in the spring sunshine pretending not to be cold. No parties. No sleepovers. And while she hated herself for it, she felt better. Her skin was less deathly, her body less weak.

The sun was starting to set later and later. A four o'clock lecture would let out into light rather than dark. One day, Chloe wandered slowly along the tree-lined avenue where the English department was based and decided that she could permit herself a visit to Archer

Crescent. Zadie had asked that morning whether she would come and spend the day with her. Chloe had dug deep and found the willpower to say no, to tell Zadie she had work to do but would come over later. There hadn't been any answer, but that wasn't surprising. Zadie was always sporadic in her communication.

When she arrived, the front door was open, swinging in the wind. The door slammed against the frame and the force threatened to smash every tiny pane of coloured glass. 'Zadie?' Chloe called. The skin at the back of her neck prickled. Something wasn't right. She took the stairs two at a time, and when she reached the bedroom she found Zadie lying in the bed, wearing one of her silk nightdresses, her face and hair pressed into a pile of vomit. Chloe panicked. She pulled Zadie into a sitting position, praying that she would be breathing. Zadie's eyes moved under her heavy lids. 'Zadie? Zadie? What did you do? Should I call an ambulance? Should I call your parents?'

Zadie shook her head. 'Max,' she murmured. Chloe dialled Max's number, but the phone rang out. 'He isn't answering. Zadie, what happened? What did you do? I think I have to call an ambulance.' Zadie shook her head again. 'Max,' she repeated.

'You want me to call Max?'

Zadie nodded, her head slopping forward as if it were too heavy for her neck.

Chloe dialled Max again, and again he didn't answer.

'Zadie, I'm going to call Rav, okay? He plays rugby with Max. He'll be able to get hold of him.'

Zadie shook her head, a little more alert. 'No.'

'It's okay,' Chloe said, calling up the number. 'I promise he won't tell anybody.'

As she waited for Rav to pick up, the inconvenient realization that this would be the first time they'd spoken since sleeping together intruded on her thoughts. She batted it away.

'Rav,' she gabbled, 'are you at rugby? I need Max to come home, right now. It's Zadie, I don't know if she's okay and she doesn't want me to call an ambulance.'

'Fuck, okay. We're on our way.'

Chloe held Zadie upright, trying not to gag at the smell of vomit as Zadie's damp, sick-sodden hair trailed over her. She held a glass of water from Max's side of the bed up to Zadie's lips, trying to get her to drink, but it was too difficult to balance her body and the glass. Zadie slipped and the water tipped down her front, staining the pale pink nightdress a darker pink.

It was impossible to tell how long it took Rav and Max to arrive, but they came bounding up the stairs, taking them two at a time. Max took Zadie in his arms, twisted her heavy sheet of dirty hair away from her face and put his face level with hers. 'Baby, it's me. Tell me everything you've eaten and drunk in the last six hours or I'm calling Astrid and Bob.'

Zadie shuddered into a waking state and Max gestured for Chloe and Rav to leave. They went single file down the stairs until they reached the kitchen, which was covered in used glasses and plates. Without saying anything, Rav ran a sink of hot, soapy water, found some washing-up gloves under the sink and began to clean the dishes. Chloe found a tea towel in a drawer, presumably laundered by their long-suffering cleaner, and started to dry.

For a while they worked in silence, but sometime around the twentieth glass, Rav broke the silence.

'You didn't text me.'

'The first time we met you didn't text me.'

'We didn't have sex the first time we met.'

'True.'

'Was I that bad of a shag?'

'I don't know. I haven't got anything to compare you to.'

Rav laughed. 'True.'

'Do you think she's going to be okay?'

'I don't know.'

It seemed surprising that Rav hadn't lied, hadn't said that of course she was going to be completely, totally, utterly fine.

'I wanted to call an ambulance, but she wouldn't let me.'

'From what Max says, I think it's quite a complicated situation.'

'Max talks to you about that stuff?'

Rav nodded, his eyes still on the washing-up bowl. 'A bit. Only lately. He's under lots of pressure with rugby and this Australia deal. I think he's having a tough time.'

'She is, too.'

Rav's face suggested that he wasn't convinced. Chloe

opened her mouth to argue but was distracted by Max's arrival in the kitchen. 'She's okay,' he said. 'Swears blind it was just drinking.'

'On her own? On a Wednesday afternoon?' said Rav. 'Mate, I don't think that sounds like good news.'

Max shrugged. 'If I tell her parents, she'll be straight back to rehab.'

Chloe's lips were moving to ask, *Back?*, but something stopped her. Zadie hadn't ever mentioned rehab. She'd said nothing about it in all of the hundreds of hours they had spent talking about their mothers and their families and the things they were going to do differently when they were adults. Why not? Why hadn't she trusted Chloe enough to tell her about it?

'I know you're not staying over so much,' said Max, 'but is there any chance you'd consider staying here this evening? She's asking for you.'

'Of course.'

Chloe took Zadie a cup of Earl Grey, gently tapping on the bedroom door before entering. She was propped up on a sea of pillows, her hair clean and damp, tied in a neat knot at the back of her head. She wore one of Max's long-sleeved T-shirts.

'Hey,' Chloe whispered, not sure why she was keeping her voice so low. 'How are you feeling?'

'I'm okay. You didn't need to bring me tea.'

'I'll drink it myself, then.'

'Don't you dare.'

Chloe sat at the far end of the bed, leaning her weight

on the baseboard and studying Zadie. Max had done an impressive job. Dirty sheets stripped, Zadie showered and changed, awake and fully responsive. It seemed as if he had probably done this before.

'Are you okay?' Chloe ventured after a little while. 'What happened?'

'It was stupid. I forgot that some of the pills they like me to take don't mix so well with drinking. I was bored, I had a few drinks, got all woozy, went to bed, got sick.'

'You gave me a scare.'

'I know. I'm sorry. I'm wretched like that.'

'It's okay.'

'Will you stay tonight? Max has to go to a rugby social. He can't miss it or he'll lose out on some captain thing. I don't want to be on my own.'

'Of course.'

'And maybe for a few days?'

Chloe did some quick mental arithmetic, sketching out her essay deadlines on an imaginary calendar. 'Of course I will,' she said. 'But we have to do some work as well has having fun, okay?'

That evening, Chloe found some pasta in the cupboard and a block of cheese in the fridge. She set about making them macaroni cheese. Apart from the ridiculous house and everything that had happened earlier that day, with the telly on in the background and the steam on the windows, it almost felt to Chloe as if she were living with normal housemates.

'I think you're the first person ever to use our oven,' said Max as he picked a generous pinch of cheese from her chopping board. 'I'm heading out now. Are you sure you're okay to stay with her?'

'I wish I could say that surprised me. We'll be fine – go, have fun.'

'Thanks for earlier, by the way.'

'It's okay.' She paused, unsure how to ask more questions without seeming as if she was asking more questions. 'It seemed like you'd done that before.'

Max rolled his eyes. 'Many, many times.'

'She does that a lot?'

'Yep.'

Chloe stirred the sauce, grateful for something to do with her hands. 'I hope you didn't mind that I called Rav. I couldn't think of any other way to get hold of you.'

'Not at all. He drove me here in about fifteen seconds. Probably got a ticket coming his way, poor bastard.'

'You like him?'

'Rav?'

'Yes.'

'He's a sound bloke. Why?'

'Oh, nothing. We had a bit of a thing. But Zadie seemed to think he wasn't a good guy. She didn't think we should see each other.'

Max caught her elbow. 'Well, if my opinion matters, you could do a lot worse than him. Don't listen to Zadie too much. The thing you need to remember about her is that she really doesn't like sharing her toys.'

ZADIE

'Is it bad,' asked Max as he threw his clothes into the laundry basket and celebrated making the shot, 'that I really enjoyed this evening?'

Every muscle in Zadie's body felt tight. She ran her finger-nails along her forearm, telling herself to be careful, to be gentle, not to scratch because, once she started scratching, it was hard to stop. 'You did?'

'I really did. The whole telly and food and not doing any-thing thing. It's nice to do that when you're not nursing a screaming hangover.'

Zadie curled underneath Max's arm and rested her head on his chest. 'I know what you mean. Kind of boring, but in a nice way.'

'A really nice way. I think Chloe liked it, too. I worry about her sometimes.'

'Oh?'

'You know, that we might be corrupting her. She was such a cute little thing when you first started hanging out, and now she's got that look that all your schoolfriends had, like she's probably packing a gram and would know where to buy a gun.'

Zadie laughed. 'She's still cute. She likes the parties, too.'

'We all like the parties. But there's a difference between throwing a party every now and again and drinking three bottles of champagne and smoking ten thousand fags on a school night. We need to slow down.'

'Totally.' Zadie raised the glass of water from her bedside table. 'Here's to a new era of clean living.'

Max always fell asleep perfectly, within moments of his head hitting the pillow. Maybe it was all the running around he did during the day. But Zadie waited anyway, watching his chest falling in the half-light, waiting until he was completely, totally still. Then she put her feet on the cold floor and moved downstairs silently, without putting on any of the lights.

She sat on the floor of the kitchen, her back against the island, so that even if Max came down he wouldn't see her with the bottle of wine gripped between her hands. She poured a glass carefully, almost to the top, telling herself that it was normal to struggle to sleep without a drink. Lots of people drank a glass of wine every evening. Two glasses. Three. Her parents drank most nights, and they were grown-ups. And it was wine. Not vodka or gin or something hard like that. She stared at the bottle for a little while, watching the beads of condensation slip down the glass.

Other people could do this. Other people didn't have a thread from their chest connecting them to the nearest alcoholic drink, yanking and pulling until the urge was satiated. She stared at the glass a little longer, thinking about Max sleeping upstairs, so proud of her for taking a night off. If he came down and saw her now, he would be so horrified. Disgusted. He still saw her as the teenage girl he had fallen in love with at school, the one all his friends had been jealous he was dating. But they both knew that living together, spending every second of every day together, had stripped away the air of mystery that had always hung between them. Without the enemy of their parents or their schools, without her secretive weekend trips to stay with him while pretending that she was with her girlfriends, it was different. The sort of different that some people probably liked. Quieter. Gentler. More normal. But it made Zadie feel as if the air was constricting around her. As if she couldn't really move.

Would Max be happier with someone else? Zadie had asked herself that question a lot recently. Whenever she went for a long, rainy walk or took a scalding-hot bath, she tried on the idea in her mind. Chloe and Max, as a couple. His parents would like Chloe. She would be impressed by them. And she would be able to sit next to him on the sofa and watch a film and enjoy being close to him without the constant screaming, pounding need for a drink, without feeling that the house was empty and flat and pointless without people inside it.

But Max didn't belong to Chloe. He belonged to her.

She stood up. The glass was still on the floor. Still untouched. She picked it up gingerly, as if it were hot, and tipped it into the sink. Then, elated with her own triumph, she ran the tap, washing away every last drop so that there was nothing left in the sink.

She had done it.

She got into bed with Max and wrapped herself around his limbs. He emitted an astonishing amount of body heat. She breathed in his smell and, for the first time in as long as she could remember, fell into a warm, heavy, sober slumber.

22
NOW

A few days later, Chloe woke up with a sense of purpose and realized that today was going to be the day.

She had been telling herself that she hadn't acted yet because she was thinking about what to do next. Because she was planning. But she knew it wasn't true. The truth was, she liked turning the plan over in her head. She liked the feeling that it was going to happen soon, but not quite yet. When she lay awake at night she had taken to planning it, trying on different scenarios, working out different outcomes. Again, she told herself she was just being careful. Thorough. Thoughtful. But it wasn't just that. She was allowing herself dozens of different types of revenge.

But Rav would be home in a couple of days. So it had to be soon. Or rather, it had to be now.

She pressed Max's name on her phone display. He didn't pick up. So she pressed it again. Once again, nothing. How predictable that his claims of wanting her back in his life only lasted until he got her knickers off. She googled his company and found his office number.

'Max Trentino's office,' said an efficient voice at the end of the line.

'Could I speak with Max, please?'

'May I ask who is calling?'

'It's Verity, his fiancée.'

'Of course. Thank you for holding.'

The line went muffled for a moment and then Max's voice sounded, distant, as if he were on speaker phone. 'Hello, trouble. Sorry I was so late last night. Did you miss me?'

'It's Chloe.'

The silence told Chloe everything she needed to know.

'Hi, hi. Sorry I didn't pick up before. I'm about to go into this huge meeting and I really can't afford to fuck it up. Everything all right?'

'Meet me for lunch.'

Max sighed. 'Oh, Coco, I'm so sorry. Look, I should have been far clearer the other night. I should have made you realize that it was only going to be a one-off thing. You love Rav, I love Verity – it was just two old friends having a bit of fun. Putting out an old flame. Finishing what we almost started. You get that, right?'

'I think you should meet me for lunch.'

Max went quiet for a moment. 'I've got a very busy day.'

'You're really, really, going to regret it if you don't.'

'Fine.' The warmth was gone from Max's voice, stripped

back to the tone she'd heard him use with bar staff back in the day. 'I've got half an hour.'

'That's all I need. Meet me at Alessandro's at one.'

One of Rav's rugby friends had made a joke once that a team mate's girlfriend was the 'type of girl you only took to Alessandro's', and when Chloe had asked Rav about it later he'd explained that it was a famous restaurant in the City where you took women who you weren't serious about, or didn't want to be seen with. It was adjacent to several rather seedy hotels, therefore perfect for a rapid lunch and fuck if you were the sort of man who really did love his wife and didn't want to get caught and lose the country house and the kids but couldn't resist sticking it to a twenty-two-year-old secretary. Chloe ordered a bottle of fizzy water.

Max arrived five minutes late, looking harassed.

'I'll have an espresso,' he said to the waiter, without looking at him.

Chloe could see why this place was popular. The booths were padded and high-backed, gloriously private.

'What's wrong?'

Chloe took a deep breath. Where was she supposed to start with this?

'I want you to admit what you did to Zadie on the night of your twenty-first birthday. And I want you to tell me why.'

Max started to get up. 'I am not sitting here to listen to this nonsense again.'

'Don't you want to hear what I'm proposing?'

'Proposing? What the fuck are you talking about?' He sat back down, looking increasingly angry. His coffee arrived and he snatched it off the saucer without thanking the girl who brought it.

'Admit that you did it. Tell me. Tell her parents. Tell anyone who asks you. Otherwise, I am going to make you sorry.'

Chloe had worried that she would feel foolish doing this, that she lacked the composure it would require. But she was wrong. She had everything she needed right here. Watching Max's face twist between worry and disbelief was gratifying beyond imagining.

'How are you planning to do that?' he asked. He sounded as if he was wrestling to keep his tone light.

'You're going to tell Zadie's family what you did, and apologize, and take all the consequences. Otherwise, I'm going to tell Verity that we slept together.'

Max smiled, and Chloe tried to hold her nerve. Why didn't he seem worried? When she had played this over and over in her head, he had been falling over himself to do as she asked. Instead, he was smirking. Refilling his water glass as if this really were a casual lunch between friends. 'She won't believe you. You don't think anyone else has tried this on me before?'

A deep breath. Of course he wasn't worried. He didn't realize she had proof. She took out her phone, forcing herself to seem like she was confident, like her heart wasn't thumping almost audibly.

'I'm sure she would believe me. Especially given that I have evidence.' She showed him the pictures, flicking through a little slideshow on her phone. She paused, trying to read his expression. 'And then there's the text you sent me that night.'

Max raised an eyebrow. 'I didn't text you.'

She showed him the text. 'You did. Or rather, I did, from your phone. While you were sleeping. But there's really no way to prove that, is there?'

Chloe held up her phone, close enough to Max's face that he could read what she had written. But still, he didn't look scared. He met her stare with a cool, detached, almost amused expression. 'Okay,' he said.

Chloe waited for him to say more, but nothing came. 'Okay?'

'Tell her.'

She choked on her water. The indignity of it burned. 'You don't care if your fiancée leaves you?'

Another infuriating, gut-twisting smirk from Max. 'She won't leave. She's French. She doesn't care about little side flings. Besides, we're not even married yet.'

Anger had made Chloe's blood so thick she could feel it moving around her body. His smile, his face, his whole demeanour. All she wanted was to take the fork on the table and sink it straight into the back of the hand he was so casually resting there. This wasn't what was supposed to happen. He was supposed to panic. He was supposed to see his engagement breaking up, Verity leaving him and his life crashing down, and fall to pieces. But, of course, he wasn't. How could she have been so stupid? That might be what a normal person would do, but Max wasn't normal. Max never lost anything. Max always had exactly what he wanted, whenever he wanted it. He had an unshakeable sense that things would work out his way, because they always did. She wanted to hurt him. She wanted to see him bleed.

'Fine,' she said, forcing her voice to sound calm. 'You're probably right.'

'Does that mean that this ridiculous charade is over? Because I meant what I said earlier. I really do have a busy day.'

'No,' said Chloe, rearranging the cutlery on the table. She wasn't sure who was speaking now. It didn't feel like her. It felt like the kind of person who knew how to make a threat. Like the kind of person who knew how to scare someone so privileged, so perfect, they had never felt fear in their life before. 'It means that I won't tell Verity. I think, rather than doing that, I'll tell the police.'

There it was. A sunrise of horror etched across his face.

She went on, revelling in his panic. She didn't know where any of this was coming from, but finally, years and years later, he was getting what he deserved. 'And I'll make it clear quite how rough you were with me. How you tried to hurt me. I'll tell them that I didn't want to. That you forced me.'

Max's water glass slipped out of his hand. It hit the table and soaked the blue paper napkin. Various staff members came rushing over to pat the table down and sympathize with him. He ignored all of them. When the table was dry and they had retreated, he glared at her. He looked like he was going to vomit. Like he was going to cry.

'What the hell is wrong with you? This is ancient history. Zadie is dead. What do you think you're going to achieve by pulling shit like this? You want to put her family through all this, while they're still mourning? And if I don't help you then – what? – you're going to ruin my life?'

'That's about the size of it,' Chloe said. She watched him try to wriggle his way out of the situation, the same way he'd worked his way out of every other tight corner he had ever found himself in. 'I'll give you until tomorrow to decide.'

'Why are you doing this?'

'Because I know what you did to my best friend. And I am so fucking sick of you getting away with it. If it weren't for what you did, she wouldn't have had to leave university. She could have stayed. She wouldn't be dead right now.'

'What's this really about? Revenge? "Closure?" Your sad little life doesn't satisfy you any more, so now you're trying to ruin mine over a crazy bitch who just saw you as a plaything?'

She leaned in and hissed, 'Call it whatever the fuck

you want. I've told you my terms. Either you confess to what you did, or I will use everything on my phone to make your life a living hell.'

She picked up her bag and walked away, praying he couldn't see how much she was shaking.

23
THEN

It would have been nice to believe that she missed the parties, but the truth was Chloe loved the new pattern that she, Max and Zadie fell into in the weeks after Zadie's 'incident', as Chloe had taken to calling it in her head. Max seemed to be around more, still playing rugby, but away less and almost never out of the house overnight. Zadie stopped inviting huge hordes of people over. Sometimes a few of her favourites, some girls from school, a few of the people she knew who were also studying History of Art, would mill around the kitchen drinking wine, but it had none of the nihilism of the previous parties, crowds of strangers wantonly destroying the house.

Rav hadn't been back. Every time Chloe heard people in the kitchen she both hoped it was him and prayed that it wasn't. But of course it never was. He had sent her a couple of texts. One straight after he had come to the house, asking if she and Zadie were okay, and another a week later, asking if she wanted to go for a drink. She hadn't replied to either, and she wasn't sure why. She liked seeing him. Loved seeing him. But Max's words were stamped on her brain. She knew that he had meant it as a warning against indulging Zadie, as a reminder that she needed to have other friends, other people in her life. But that wasn't how it felt. It felt like a reminder that if she chose someone else over Zadie, all this might go away. And anyway, their new pattern was perfect. It didn't need anyone else. Chloe would bring books over and work in the sitting room during the afternoon while Zadie painted or slept, and in the evening they would watch a film on the huge, comfortable sofa while Zadie lay on Max's chest at the other end and talked over every single line.

In short, it was all going so well, until Zadie remembered that it was almost Max's birthday. The realization seemed to reignite some restlessness inside her.

'Max,' she said one evening, sitting in the garden with a coloured cigarette between two fingers, 'you're going to be twenty-one.'

'We all are, eventually.'

'Yes, but you're going to be twenty-one next month, and we haven't planned anything.'

'Haven't we?'

'Have you?' She turned to Chloe. 'Has he? Do you know anything about this?'

Chloe shook her head. 'Nothing. What are you planning, Max?'

Max looked incredibly pleased with himself – more so than usual. 'Wait and see.'

'I hate waiting,' said Zadie. 'It's your birthday, we're supposed to surprise you.'

They didn't have to wait long. A few days later Chloe woke up to find another envelope had been posted under her door, only this time it was something exciting. A pale cream envelope made of heavy paper. Inside was a proper, stiff card invitation with 'Max's 21st Birthday' in gold calligraphy and a piece of paper with all the details. They were going to a house in the country for a weekend, and all they had to bring was black tie for Saturday night, swimwear and a bottle of champagne. Chloe smiled down at the invitation, glowing with pride at the fact that she'd been asked. How many other people had Max invited? Surely if they'd rented a house for the weekend, then it couldn't be more than a handful. She had been chosen as one of his closest friends. She placed the invitation on her windowsill then re-read the information on the paper. But her excitement was punctured when her phone bleeped. It was Zadie.

'I can't believe it. Have you seen it?'

'What?'

'The invitation. For his damn party.'

Chloe wanted to be on Zadie's side, but she was struggling to see the problem. 'I got mine this morning. What's wrong?'

'He didn't even ask me. He just did it. He didn't tell me, he didn't want my opinion. You know he's invited less than twenty people, including us? That's tiny. How is it going to feel like a party with such a small group?'

Chloe tried not to feel pleased. 'It is his birthday, Zaid, I think we probably have to do what he wants.'

'He's invited the worst people, too. People from rugby. Their boring girlfriends.'

'Maybe they won't be as boring as we think they are.'

'They're on the netball team.'

'Well, then, we can complain about them all weekend.'

An exasperated noise came down the phone. 'Stop being so reasonable. He knows I love parties. He knows I would have wanted to organize it.'

'Maybe he's trying to keep you on the straight and narrow. He likes this "new normal", where we have a glass of wine and don't invite everyone we've ever met to trash the house.' Chloe sensed that she had said the wrong thing. She could feel the tension prickling down the line. 'When it's your twenty-first I promise we'll have the party to end all parties,' she added, trying to row back, trying to bury her previous comment as deep as possible so that she could escape Zadie's disapproval. 'It'll be several days long. So much booze that no one leaves without throwing up. So loud that you can't hear anyone's name even if they're screaming it.'

'Promise?'

'Promise.'

Max was proving difficult to buy a birthday present for, and Chloe wasn't the only one who thought so. It was

Sunday morning, a week before the party. Zadie and Chloe were lying on the sofa, searching for inspiration.

'What about a rugby ball?'

'I think that's the worst suggestion so far.'

'Okay, but what if it was an old rugby ball. A vintage one.'

'Would that make it any better?'

Zadie sat up. 'This is impossible. I'm just going to give him a blow job and have done with it.'

'At least you've got that option.' Chloe had meant the words to sound like a joke, but they had sounded almost envious. Zadie looked bemused.

'I think we need more inspiration. Let's go and look at the stuff he's got, see if it makes us think of anything.'

They ran up the stairs to the second bedroom, which Max kept his stuff in because Zadie's astonishing wardrobe filled the master bedroom. Max was almost frighteningly tidy. His shirts were hung up with military precision, his physio equipment all laid out, weights stacked. Chloe had never spent any time in here, for obvious reasons. 'My God, he's tidy,' she said, admiring the pile of clearly unopened textbooks on his desk.

'I know. That's boarding school for you.'

'You went to boarding school.'

Zadie opened Max's wardrobe, flicking through it absent-mindedly. 'I went to a special kind of boarding school where they encourage you to find your inner self and you can wear whatever you want. Max went to one where they make you run around the rugby pitch in your shorts even when it's minus one, and all the teachers talk about how much they miss caning. He hated it.'

'Why didn't he leave?'

'His parents thought it was the way to give him a "better" life, or some nonsense like that. They grew up with nothing, wanted better for Max, all that stuff people do when they're trying to convince themselves it's okay for their kid to be miserable.'

'It was that bad?'

'Absolutely. We were only allowed to talk on the phone once a week. He'd be standing in some freezing-cold corridor, trying not to cry because he was so unhappy. I hated him knowing that I was having such a lovely time. Sometimes I used to lie in my letters.'

Chloe realized that she'd never asked Zadie, in all their talks, how she and Max had met.

'It's nothing very exciting,' Zadie told her now. 'My school was a few miles from his and they used to bring us in to do plays. I was drafted in to be Cordelia in *King Lear*.' Chloe listened to the story as she opened the drawers of Max's desk.

'Was Max in it, too?'

'God, no, you couldn't pay him to act. I saw him coming off the rugby pitch and he was the best-looking boy I had ever seen in my life so I ran over and gave him my phone number. Everyone else was horrified that I'd made the first move, but then here we are.'

'Zadie,' said Chloe, slowly. 'What's this?' She held up a small leather box.

Zadie looked stunned. It was the first time Chloe had ever seen her lost for words.

'Open it.'

Puncturing the velvet cushion was a ring with a square port-red ruby flanked by two blinding diamonds. Chloe gave a long, low sigh. 'Is this what I think it is?'

'It's a ring,' said Zadie, but her voice couldn't hide her excitement.

'It's an engagement ring . . .'

'He's not going to propose – we're still students!'

'Why is it in here, then? Try it on.'

Zadie looked as if she was going to say no, but clearly couldn't resist. She slid the ring on to her long finger. It was too big, the heavy stone swivelling around to the back of her hand. She twisted it back around, clamped her fingers together and held out her hand. The girls both squealed. 'Will you be my bridesmaid?' Zadie asked.

Chloe's heart swelled. 'Of course!'

They jumped up and down, staring at the ring, until the slamming of the front door punctured their revelling. Zadie slipped the ring back in the box, Chloe replaced it in the drawer and they went back downstairs, pretending that nothing had happened.

ZADIE

Max was splayed on the sofa, beautiful as he always was, but his face was twisted in an expression of complete concentration, a video-game controller between his hands. Zadie smacked a bottle down on the kitchen counter, hoping he would notice. He didn't. She did it again.

'If you want to have an argument, then you need to come in here!' Max called from the living room. Zadie almost laughed, teetering on the edge of being amused by him. She went through, watching her bare feet on the wooden floorboards as she walked. 'I don't want to fight.'

'Yes, you do. You always do that slamming-around thing when you're building up to a big row.' He sat up and held his arms out to her. 'How about we try this? You come here and tell me what's wrong.'

Zadie wanted to stay cross, but his body was so warm and firm. She rested her head on his chest and felt her shoulders unfurl as he stroked her hair, a gesture that always thawed her.

'What's wrong?' he asked. 'The party?'

'Yes.'

'You're upset that I didn't consult you about it?'

'No.'

'Really?'

'Well, maybe a bit. I'm good at parties. Parties are my thing. And you're my boyfriend. Isn't it my job to throw you a party?'

'You've thrown me a hundred parties. And they've all been wonderful. But I wanted to do something for myself. I should have talked to you about it first. I'm sorry.'

'It's okay. I'm sorry I lost my temper.'

'It's going to be great, though, I promise.'

Zadie made a non-committal noise.

'What's wrong?'

'Nothing.'

'Come on, tell me.'

'It's the guest list. It's so . . .'

'Full of people I actually know and like?'

'Those girls are so dull. And the boys are so – rugby.'

'I like rugby.'

'And you invited Rav.'

'What's wrong with Rav?'

'I can't stand him. The way he's always hanging around here, desperate to be near you. It's pathetic. And he completely fucked Chloe over.'

'What did he do to Chloe?'

'He's been messing her around for weeks. He slept with her. Took her virginity, actually.'

'Chloe lost her virginity to Rav?'

'Oh, what? Jealous you didn't get to do the deed yourself?'

'No. I'm just surprised. You wait that long, you'd think she would want to do it with someone special.'

'Maybe she thinks Rav is special.' Zadie paused. 'I don't know why she would. But she really liked him. And I'm pretty sure he's lost interest now they've slept together.'

'Really? I thought he seemed serious about her.'

Zadie tried to keep her voice calm. 'Why would you think that? When have you ever seen them together?'

'We talked about her the other day. Seemed like he had it bad. That's mostly why I invited him along, so Chloe would have someone. I feel bad for her being third wheel with us all the time, thought it might be nice if she got a boyfriend of her own.'

'Max, what the fuck? I've been trying to talk her out of seeing Rav for weeks, because he treats her like shit, and you've just undone all my work. This is why we're supposed to plan this stuff together. Please, please, uninvite him. Tell him he can't come.'

The blood was thumping in Zadie's temples. She tried to calm herself, to stop herself from saying something she would regret.

Max shook his head. 'I've already asked him. It's fine. Don't interfere between them. Leave it alone.'

Zadie got up. 'I've got work to do, I'm going to the library,' she huffed.

Max snorted. 'Do you need me to draw you a map? It's the big building near the park.'

Zadie slammed the front door, feeling the force shake the glass. She stood on the step, feeling the cool spring breeze move her hair, trying to make herself breathe slowly.

24
NOW

Chloe decided she would give Max twenty-four hours to consider his options. Rav was due home soon and she couldn't imagine hiding all this from him. She hoped against hope, though she had tried not to let it show when they met, that he would do as she asked. Admit to it. Tell Zadie's family. Let them understand that the thing that ended her university career, saw her move home and run out of steam in her attempts to be a real adult, was not her fault. She had no doubt they would have assumed that Zadie had got herself into trouble, that the bruises she would have come home with – if she hadn't covered them up and hidden them – were somehow her own fault. They deserved to know that their daughter was good, and kind, that she was a victim of what Max did to her, just as she was really, truly trying to get her life back together, to get on track and move forward.

But if he didn't confess, she would have to do it. She would have to go through with it. She would have to make good on the threat she had made, to tell one of the worst lies a person could tell. She had watched a parenting programme once – she must have been hung over, or cleaning the house, or on the sofa with a cold. The nanny had told the parents that as soon as you threaten to do something you had to follow through. If you didn't take away the toy or cancel the party or whatever it was you had said you were intent upon doing, you would teach the child not to respect you. It was like that now. She had told Max that she would ruin his life if he didn't do as he was told, and now she was going to have to follow through on that threat, no matter how much the prospect of it scared her. She wished she could find that feeling she had had sitting across the table from him, that she could summon the strength the rage had given her, the power that came with needing to hurt him.

That evening, as she was preparing for her first day back at school, she planned a welcome-home celebration for Rav. He was due back the following evening. She had been a bad wife since he had been away, claiming that she was in the shower or about to eat dinner when he called, avoiding his texts and sending scant replies to his emails. She had claimed that she was feeling inspired, that she was finally working on the play she had been talking about writing for the last ten years and never done anything about. But in fact she was trying to pretend that he wasn't real, or at least that the plan she had been so pleased with didn't involve betraying him.

Only her body had slept with Max, she told herself. Her mind had been completely faithful to her husband. It wasn't as if she had wanted to do it. There had been no choice. Men like Max had got away with whatever they wanted to do for centuries. But now she wanted to make it up to Rav, to make him see that she loved him, and to try a fresh start.

The first day back at school after the summer holidays was always an inset day. Some of the other teachers complained about them. They were all about meetings and organization, piles of paperwork and red tape. But Chloe liked them. She liked going back to school when it had been resting for the summer, waiting and silent, ready to be filled with people and noise. When she was at school herself, she had always loved the moments when she had an excuse to leave a lesson, to go to the loo or take a message to another teacher, where she could wander the quiet corridors, knowing that the building was bursting with people but that she couldn't see any of them. Then a bell would ring and the corridors would explode with teenagers, pushing, laughing, shoving. Her own school was very different to the one she taught at now. It had been a bog-standard comprehensive where she had been summarily ignored by the teachers because she didn't make trouble and didn't need much help. Her school now was quite the opposite. Prestigious. Ordered. Filled with girls who knew they were smart, knew they had potential for brilliance and intended to realize it. They loved Chloe's drama lessons because they were a chance to try different things, experiment, step outside of themselves.

It had been Rav who had talked her into taking the job. She'd been teaching at an underfunded school which was on its knees, a forty-five-minute bike ride away. One day, two years after she had qualified, a child had spat at her and she'd come home in floods of tears. Rav had run her a bath, poured her a glass of wine and made a little speech. 'I'm going to say the thing that I know you don't want to hear,' he had told her. 'Go private. Don't do it for you. Don't do it for the longer holidays or the better pay. Do it for me. I need you to be here in the evenings, not marking until midnight. I need you to have weekends and proper holidays, and a sense of humour.'

Of course, she had felt like a failure. Because, to an extent, she was a failure. Her old boss had made that very clear when she handed in her notice, with a sideways comment about how he was sick of losing his staff to the 'other side'. But she had to admit, every day when she walked the ten minutes to school and taught a small class of girls who adored her and hung on her every word, she felt grateful to Rav for pretending that it was him who needed her to change jobs.

'Right, that's just about everything. Thank you for today. We're looking forward to tomorrow – let's make this a brilliant term.' No one had been listening to the deputy head, who seemed to think that motivational speaking was part of her job description, but by her tone it was clear that they were free to go. Chloe pulled her jumper on, picked up her handbag and took a look at her phone. A message from Rav flashed up.

'When will you be home?'

He was back, then. She had pretended that she wanted to go and pick him up from the airport, that the inset day had prevented her from seeing him and that she was upset about it. But, in reality, she had never really understood the idea of driving all the way to the airport to pick someone up, rather than them just getting a cab.

She looked at the message again. The bluntness of it surprised her – he was a chirpy texter usually, and he always put at least three kisses. She typed her reply with one hand. 'In about half an hour. Everything okay? Xx.'

There were three dots to indicate that Rav was typing, but no message came. She tried to smooth the feeling that was starting to twist in her gut. Something about this didn't feel right.

She picked up various books from her desk, said the goodbyes she needed to say, then walked home more quickly than usual, her new shoes clicking on the pavement. She always bought new shoes at the start of term, as if she were a child who had outgrown her previous pair over the summer holidays.

From the moment she opened the front door to their building Chloe knew something was off. It smelled different. Sounded different. Felt different. The internal door to the flat wasn't locked. It wasn't even closed. There was a millimetre of light coming between the door frame and the door.

'Hello?' she called before she stepped over the threshold. Every single nerve ending in her body was writhing, telling her that something was wrong, that she shouldn't go inside. 'Hello?'

Footsteps on the fake wooden floorboards. Standing in the kitchen, a glass of wine in his hands, shirtsleeves pushed up his perfect forearms, was Max.

25
THEN

Max was tight-lipped about everything to do with the party, and it was driving Zadie completely mad. Every time she came up with an idea – a game they should play, a cocktail she wanted to make – he told her that it was all under control, that he had it covered and that, for once, he wanted her to be a guest, not a host. Chloe could tell that Zadie was trying to be gracious, that she knew it was Max's birthday and that therefore it should be entirely up to him how things were handled. But parties were how Zadie showed her love to people, and every time Max told her he didn't want her to be involved she seemed to move a little further away from him. Chloe wanted to tell him to include Zadie, to let her in on the secret. But he seemed to so enjoy being the only person who had planned this party, and a little part of her was frightened that if she were to tell him off he might take back the invitation she was so proud to have received.

At last, the Saturday morning arrived. Chloe stood outside Archer Crescent with a small suitcase, pulling her coat around her. The spring sunshine looked far warmer than it was. She took out her phone, checking to see whether she was going to be treated to another guilt-inducing voicemail from her mother, asking why she never rang.

'Bang goes my theory.'

Chloe looked up. Of course, it was Rav. 'Theory?'

'I'd been telling myself that you'd almost certainly lost your phone, and that was why you'd gone silent on me.'

'I'm sorry.'

'I'm joking. You don't need to apologize.'

'I am sorry, though. Things have been—'

'Yes, with me, too.'

'Still, this should be fun.'

'Knowing Max, it'll be something quite extraordinary.'

Rav was right. A couple of sleek silver people-carriers arrived on the dot of eleven o'clock. The group – Chloe and Rav, Max and Zadie, the deputy rugby captain and his girlfriend, five of Max's best friends from school and their girlfriends. The drive took a couple of hours, but before Chloe could finish reading *Heart of Darkness*, which she was supposed to be discussing in her tutorial on Tuesday, they had pulled up at a beautiful twisty-turny house.

Like children, they grabbed their bags from the car and ran inside, scattering and looking for bedrooms. Luckily, each door had a name on it, so there were no fights to be had. Chloe ran down the corridor, following

Zadie and looking for her name. Just as she was starting to panic that she had been forgotten, that she didn't have a room and that perhaps her inclusion was one enormous mistake, she spotted another door, which led up a spiral staircase to the eaves of the house. She went up and found her room. It was long and light with huge windows at either end and ceilings which sloped to the floor on each side. It somehow felt like a ship's cabin. On the bed was a typed-up itinerary.

One o'clock: lunch. Three o'clock: hot tub. Six o'clock: cocktails. Eight o'clock: dinner. Midnight: games.

Lunch passed in an easy blur of getting to know the various girlfriends, pale pink rosé and delicious food served by a team of caterers so unobtrusive they were almost invisible. Chloe had been a waitress all the way through school. Every Friday night and Saturday lunch time she had donned her white shirt, black trousers and neat bun, and worked for her mother's friend's catering company. She would pass canapés, dodge questions from elderly guests who mistook her for the host's daughter and leave the kitchen cleaner than it had been when she arrived. But she'd never catered a party like this. She watched one of the teenage girls – far chicer than she had ever been, in tight black jeans and an even tighter black T-shirt, as she topped up the glasses. She looked about sixteen. Would she wonder about them when she was at school on Monday? The group of madly wealthy guests, only a few years older than she was, enjoying a weekend of being waited on hand and foot.

She probably thought they did this all the time, that this was their normal life.

Max's best mate from school regaled the group with stories – the misery of being cold for months on end and their resentment of the teachers, who, seemingly, hated children. Chloe laughed until her stomach hurt at a story of Max parking his first car in the headmaster's office. The only person who didn't seem to be having quite as much fun as everyone else was Zadie. She was laughing in all the right places, and clearly trying her best. But Chloe realized that Zadie only ever really shone in a big crowd. This group was too small, too tight knit. She couldn't thrive here.

'Are you all right?' asked Rav softly, from her left side. Had Max purposely seated them next to each other? She remembered his warning. *Zadie doesn't like to share her toys.*

'I'm having fun,' she answered honestly. 'Just worried about Zadie.'

'Don't worry about her, she's fine. She's got to get used to the idea that it's not all about her this weekend.'

Chloe wanted to defend Zadie, to tell Rav that Zadie wasn't selfish and that her problem wasn't sharing the limelight. But everyone else was telling stories, laughing, interrupting each other, and somehow that seemed more tempting than trying to convince Rav that Zadie was really a good person.

The warm water of the hot tub seemed to unfurl knots in Chloe's back. She'd been nervous about getting in.

Earlier, when someone called up the stairs to tell Chloe that it was hot-tub time, she had thought about pretending to be asleep, or busy, so she wouldn't have to join in. But that would be ridiculous. Like Rav had said, this was Max's birthday. He'd planned this, he'd laid it all on for them. It was their job to have fun – to join in. So she had dutifully put on her bikini, a plain black one she'd bought from New Look in anticipation of today. When she had looked at herself in the mirror she wished that she had thought to put on fake tan – though it might have washed off in the hot tub and that probably would have been worse than being pale. She'd attacked her bikini line the night before, cutting herself twice with a cheap yellow razor panic-purchased from the Boots in town. Not that anyone was going to really be looking. She took a deep breath. It would be fine. She stepped gingerly into the water and noticed that both Max's and Rav's eyes were on her. That didn't mean anything, she told herself. It was just that she was standing up, that was all. They weren't looking at her – not really.

'Where's everyone else?' asked Wilbur, one of Max's schoolfriends. 'They're missing out.'

'Zadie said she'd be down in a bit,' said Max, lying back. 'Not sure about the others, but I'm finding it hard to worry about anything right now.'

There was a murmur of agreement from the others in the hot tub – Wilbur's girlfriend, another friend of Max's and his particular interchangeable blonde girlfriend – and they fell into a comfortable silence, the noise of the bubbles filling the air. Chloe stared up at the clear blue sky, watching a plane trail along. When she was little her mother had told her that there were rips in the sky and that planes were stitching them up, that the vapour trails left behind were actually darns. She couldn't remember where the story had come from. Probably her mother attempting to convince her that having darns in your clothes was a nice thing, not something to be embarrassed about. Her memory was punctured by a great roar from everyone else. She turned her head to see Zadie standing by the back door, completely naked. She was even thinner than she had been the night she had stayed in their shared bedroom. Her breasts were still impressive, further adding to Chloe's questions about whether or not they were real, but her ribs looked like a xylophone and there was an astonishing gap between her legs. She picked a graceful path from the house to the hot tub and slid into the warm water.

'What are you doing?' asked Max, who seemed somewhere between irritated and amused.

'I'm enjoying the hot tub, obviously.'

'You're naked.'

'Aren't the rest of you?'

Everyone shook their heads.

'And there was me thinking this was a party. At least take your top off, Chloe.'

Chloe looked down at her chest and said nothing. Zadie giggled and reached for the string at the back of her bikini top. She caught it and pulled. Chloe grabbed the front and clamped her hands to her chest, gasping. Zadie laughed. The other girls in the hot tub half laughed, but Max's face was stony. 'Zadie, stop it.'

'I'm just playing!' She pulled at the bikini top again. There was a ripping noise as one of the straps came away from the rest of the bikini. Chloe tried to smile. It was only cheap; it wasn't a big deal. Zadie looked horrified.

'I'm so sorry.' She held the strap in her hand. 'I'm so, so sorry.'

'It's okay,' smiled Chloe, frantically making sure she was covered up. 'Just . . . can you grab my towel? Please?'

Zadie kept repeating how sorry she was. Chloe sort of wished she was less sorry, so that she could vent her frustration. But Zadie was so abject in her apologies that saying anything other than 'It doesn't matter, it's not a big deal' felt unreasonable. So she reassured Zadie over and over again. Zadie didn't seem quite herself. She was unfocused, unable to follow the thread of the conversation. It was as if there were music playing that made it too loud for her to hear much, but she was the only one who could hear it.

Later, Zadie decided to stay at home rather than going for a walk. So Chloe stayed with her. She watched the others tramp off, wearing the wellies provided by whoever owned the beautiful house. Their figures grew smaller from her bedroom window as they walked away and she felt a surprising pang of jealousy. If she weren't here with Zadie, she could be with them. Getting to know them. Making them into proper friends, instead of people she had merely spent a weekend with. Zadie was lying on the bed, playing with her phone.

'Who are you texting?'

'No one.'

'You can't text no one.'

'I'm not texting anyone. I'm playing a game.'

It was a lie, unquestionably. But Chloe didn't have the energy to do anything about it. 'Why don't you have a nap before everyone gets back? So you can be on sparkly form later.'

'I'm not tired.'

'You seem a bit . . .' What was the right way to tell Zadie that she seemed weird? 'Not yourself.'

'I don't feel like myself,' she said, her head lolling on the pillow. 'I feel heavy. And strange.'

Chloe's hackles went up. 'Did you take something?'

Zadie shook her head, but seemed to regret it immediately. 'No, no.'

'You know you really can't do that tonight? It's Max's birthday. We have to make him the centre of attention.'

Zadie's eyes narrowed. 'I don't want to be the centre of attention. Why do you always say that?'

'I've never said that.'

'Fine. Not you, everyone else then. They all keep saying that. I don't want to be. I just want to have a nice time like everyone else. But you're having a go at me.'

Chloe got up. 'I'm going to go and read my book.'

'Oh, great, leave me on my own, just like everybody else does.'

'Who else? Max just went for a walk.'

Zadie turned over and faced away from Chloe. Chloe took it as a sign of dismissal and trailed back to her room. She sat on her stairs for a while, meaning to go and get her book but unable to stir herself. It was the first real argument she and Zadie had ever had, and she didn't like it. What if Zadie didn't forgive her? Her first thought was for the loss of her friendship, but quickly afterwards came another: would Zadie take everything away? Would she be left without parties, without friends, without a home from home? Would she still be able to move in with them next year? Her thoughts came thick and fast, swelling in her brain and turning her throat to acid. They were only interrupted when she heard a creak on the floorboards below. Most of the group had gone on the walk. Who was it? She pushed the door open a fragment, looking to see. Had Max come back to see Zadie? She hoped not. She didn't want them to fight. But it wasn't Max. It was Rav. Standing on the landing.

'Hey,' she said, stepping down the stairs. 'You didn't go for a walk?'

He shook his head. 'No, no. I wanted to stay here.'

'Why?'

He smiled. 'I had hopes of catching you alone.'

An hour or so later they were lying in the half-light, somewhere between sleeping and waking. The house was starting to come to life again. 'What time is it?' she asked, her limbs weighted with sleep and pleasure.

'About six, I think.'

The words woke her fully. 'Fuck. I need to go down. I said I'd have a drink with Zadie before we went downstairs.'

'Doesn't it irritate you?'

'What?'

'Doing everything her way, all the time. She's a bit of a brat.'

If she could have foreseen the sentence Rav had said, Chloe would have assumed it would anger her. That she would defend her friend. But to her own shock, a little part of her, a nasty little part, liked hearing Rav speak like that about Zadie.

'You think she's selfish?' she asked quietly, as if she was worried someone might overhear her.

'You don't? Everyone runs around after her – she's completely self-involved. She costs Max – Max's parents – a fortune in cleaning bills for that house, let alone in booze. She's a nightmare.'

Chloe had finished putting her underwear back on and was brushing the evidence of her afternoon out of her hair. 'She's my best friend,' she replied.

Rav raised his eyebrows. 'I know she is. But how much do you do for her? And how much does she do for you?'

Chloe didn't have a response for that. 'I need to get ready,' she said finally.

When Chloe got to Max and Zadie's bedroom she opened the door to see a scene of unbelievable perfection. Zadie facing away, looking into the dressing-table mirror, wearing a white silk robe and white silk underwear, a glass of champagne in one hand. Her hair was freshly washed and dried, shimmering in perfect curls, her lips bee-stung and pale pink. Her skin seemed to glitter and her huge green eyes were rimmed with the kind of lashes people paid for. Chloe hadn't ever seen her like this. She was always beautiful – her amazing genes and seemingly limitless clothing budget made sure of that. But this was a different kind of beautiful. The last few weeks of slowing down, drinking wine with dinner instead of vodka at 4 a.m., had made a world of difference. She looked happy. Right. Max was bending to kiss her neck, wearing the trousers and shirt from his black tie, the bow tie draped around his neck. Sitting above Zadie's collarbones was a diamond necklace so sparkly it could only be real.

'Coco! Look what Max gave me!'

'I thought you were supposed to get presents on your birthday, not give them?'

Max shrugged. 'I saw it and thought of her. Isn't she a knockout?' Zadie giggled, clearly aware that everything Max was saying was true. 'You look lovely, too, Chloe.'

Chloe had felt pretty when she'd left her room. Rav had kissed her neck and told her that she was gorgeous. Her hair had looked straight and sleek, and she'd ventured into the frightening territory of red lipstick, trying to contrast with the pretty green dress she'd spent a week

of her student loan on. But now she felt silly. Frumpy.
Like someone's single older sister, allowed to tag along to
a party out of sympathy.

'What were you up to this afternoon?' Max asked, filling up a glass and passing it to her. 'I noticed Rav wasn't
on the walk either.'

'I was reading,' she lied. If Max noticed that she had
gone dark pink, then he had the civility not to mention it.

Zadie was still looking in the mirror, neatening her
lip liner. 'Don't be ridiculous, Max. Chloe knows Rav is
horrid.'

'Why is he horrid? I like him. That's why I invited
him.'

'He *is* horrid. Everyone says it. You just like him
because he's good at rugby and he laughs at all your
jokes.'

'There are worse attributes for a bloke to have.'

Zadie stood, spritzed herself liberally with a Chanel
perfume then took down the white silk dress which
was hanging from the four-poster. 'Do me up,' she said,
with the silk pooled at her feet and halfway up her body.
Chloe and Max moved at the same time. They laughed
awkwardly.

'Which of us?' asked Max.

'Chloe. She's got smaller fingers. She'll manage the
little buttons better.'

Max flopped on the bed, drinking another glass of
champagne, watching as Chloe slid the zip up, the dress
hugging every perfect inch of Zadie's body. The zip was

covered by dozens of tiny white buttons which went into tiny eyelets. Chloe knelt down to get closer, realizing that if she did one wrong, she would have to start the entire thing again.

'You would make a wonderful lady's maid,' said Zadie.

Max laughed. 'What do you mean, "would"?'

Chloe forced out a laugh. It was a joke. They were joking. But when she glanced sideways to the mirror and saw herself in her plain dress, on her knees, fixing the buttons of the girl in the designer dress holding the champagne, she couldn't help the jolt of rage. She looked away – too quickly. Her lip brushed one of the folds of silk, leaving a tiny red smudge. She looked up to see whether Zadie had noticed, but she was too consumed with her own reflection. She could say something. In fact, because she was her mother's daughter, she even had a little stain-remover pen in her bag upstairs.

'All done,' she said, looking at the red smudge. 'You look perfect.'

'You really do,' said Max, leaning in for another kiss. 'And you look beautiful, too, Chloe.' He placed his hand on Chloe's waist and leaned his head towards her. Her breath caught in her throat, thinking for a moment that he was going to kiss her on the lips. What would she do? What would she do if he suggested that they, all three of them, fell into bed together? A frisson hung in the air, just as it had back at Zadie's parents' place on New Year's Eve. They had more of an excuse than ever, Chloe

241

reasoned. They could claim it was a birthday one-off, that they had tried to be as daring as they always seemed to be. But his lips landed on her cheekbone before she could answer her own question.

'Let's go down,' said Max. 'Let's get the party started.'

ZADIE

While she wasn't exactly pleased with Max's choice to organize the party without her, Zadie had to admit he had done an amazing job. Their bedroom was divine. Earlier that evening they had bounced on the bed like children then pulled each other's clothes off with an enthusiasm they hadn't felt for months. Afterwards, they lay next to each other, staring up at the canopy of the four-poster. The feeling of worry and guilt had started to set in – that somehow she was going to screw the evening up for Max and that he wouldn't love her any more if she did. These past few weeks of living a slower, quieter life had proven to her how much she needed him.

Max had jumped up, keen to start getting ready, and Chloe had arrived, beautiful in a simple green dress, always so tasteful and understated. Zadie felt overdone, like she was compensating for something. She had asked Chloe to do up the buttons on her dress, trying to drink enough champagne to drown the nasty voice in her head telling her that she was trying too hard, that everyone was going to laugh at her for going over the top.

On the way down to the dining room, he had called her back, leaving Chloe to go down by herself. 'Come with me,' he had smiled, taking her back to their bedroom, where he took out a square leather box.

'Don't worry.' He laughed, clearly having caught her expression. 'It's not what you think.'

He opened the box and on the velvet cushion was the ring from his bedroom. Even more rudely beautiful than she remembered.

'It would be mad for me to propose now, I know that,' he said, sliding it on to her finger. 'But I thought maybe you might like to wear it tonight. Eventually, I'm hoping you'll wear it for ever.'

Zadie kissed him full on the lips, then held out her hand to admire the ring against her fingers. Her hand looked so grown-up. 'I can't wait,' she said. And to her own surprise, she meant it. She really couldn't wait. She wanted Max. Just Max. No one else.

'Maybe twenty-one will be a fresh start,' she said, watching Max shrug on his dinner jacket.

'That sounds perfect. No more fighting. Just you and me, against the world. I love how you've been lately, how you've finally started to grow up. I'm proud of you. You've really changed.'

A chill came over her. So that was what this was. A reward for changing. A gift given because she had been a 'good girl'. All those evenings sitting on the sofa, watching TV, waiting for him to come home from practice so she could make him a chicken salad and listen to him talk about sport. He didn't want her. At least, not any real version of her. He wanted the person she had been pretending to be for the last few weeks.

'Shall we go down?'

She followed him to the stairs before her resolve gave in.

'I've forgotten my lipstick,' she lied. 'You go down. Don't keep your audience waiting. I'll be there in a moment.'

She went back to the room, going through her bag, looking for the hip flask she had packed for emergencies. She couldn't find it. Where the fuck had it gone? A noise by the door made her look up. Standing there was Rav, a vial in his hand.

'Hey,' he said. 'Want to share?'

Coke made her more fun. That was certainly true. She glanced down at the ring finger of her left hand. Max's words repeated themselves, making her feel hot and claustrophobic.

'Yes,' she said, taking the vial from him and tipping the white powder on to the back of her hand. 'I really do.'

26
THEN

There may not have been as many people as Zadie would have liked, but the party felt ten times its actual size. Everyone was so swollen with the excitement of it all they counted as two or three of themselves. Drinks were served in a pretty drawing room painted pale blue and filled with flowers. It had huge French windows that spilled out on to a terrace, and the remnants of the late-evening sun seeped through the glass. The chandelier chinked gently in the breeze and cast little rainbow lights all over the room. There was yet more champagne, and cocktails as well. Gentle music came from somewhere unseen, and everyone was laughing, talking, pretending to be a grown-up. After what felt like minutes but was actually an hour Max clinked his glass and a hush fell across the room. 'I'm not going to make a big speech,' he said, to much crowing and shouting from the room, Zadie loudest of all. 'I just wanted to say thank you for coming, I love you all, and I will consider any sobriety a personal affront. To dinner!'

They followed Max into a dining room, again predictably beautiful. A mahogany table was laid with more glasses and cutlery than Chloe could ever have imagined what to do with. She'd heard someone say once that you should start on the outside and work your way in, which she was grateful for. Though, she supposed, she could always copy Max if things got really bad. Each place had a little name card on it. Once again, Chloe found herself seated next to Rav; Wilbur was on her other side. Zadie was at the far end of the table, between two of Max's other friends. The group around Zadie was riotous. They were laughing, shouting, talking over each other. At Chloe's end, everyone was talking politely about rugby and whereabouts in the Home Counties their parents were from. Chloe watched Zadie as she filled wine glasses in between the top-ups from the waiting staff, asking wild questions which somehow seemed to make everyone laugh even harder. The strap of her dress was slipping down her shoulder and her eye make-up was starting to smudge under her eyes, which only served to make her look more dangerously beautiful. Rav was staring at Zadie across the table, a slight frown creasing his forehead.

'I wish she would let it be about Max tonight,' Chloe ventured. 'It is his birthday, after all.' Rav turned, as if Chloe had pulled him back from thousands of miles away. 'What?'

'Zadie. I know she doesn't mean to do it, but she draws focus. Makes things about her.'

Max was watching her from the other end of the table, clearly trying to seem as if he was fine with her behaviour, with hearing her voice cutting over every discussion, with how loud her laugh was. But he wasn't. It was his birthday. It was fair that he didn't want Zadie to be the centre of attention, wasn't it? Every time there was a lull in the conversation Zadie's voice would fill it. Louder than anyone else's. Talking faster than anyone else. How could anyone talk that fast? Chloe watched as Max caught Zadie's eye and discreetly put one finger to his lip, signalling her to be a little quieter. Zadie's eyes flashed dark, a storm brewing. She mouthed 'fuck off' at him, still smiling, but obviously unamused. Chloe scanned the table to see whether anyone else had noticed. It seemed they had not.

Max had seated himself between two of the prettiest plus ones, a girl named Cora on one side, and a girl named Lisbette on the other. He was laughing at something one of them had said, a hand on Cora's arm, a hand on Lisbette's leg. Her gaze flicked between Max and Zadie. Both were laughing, both seemingly happy. She caught sight of herself and Rav, reflected in one of the silver pitchers of water, untouched on the table. Perhaps neither of them was the problem.

Dinner went on for hours, course after course of barely eaten food, all of which was delicious but got in the way of drinking, talking and laughing. Eventually, once an enormous cake had been brought out so Max could blow out the candles, a surprise organized by his parents, he stood up.

'Not another speech, I promise,' he said, laughing. He was especially handsome in the candlelight, 'but a game.'

There were cheers of approval. 'It's Hide and Seek, of sorts. Only a little more grown-up. The lights go off – all the lights – and the girls hide. The boys look for them. And whatever happens when you're found is entirely up to you.'

For a moment there was silence. Then a sort of rush of approval. The girlfriend contingent looked at each other, trying to assess whether they had the message right. Was this really going to turn into boyfriend-swapping? Max added, 'You can of course hunt down your partner. But you're not obliged to. Right. Ladies, you have ten minutes to hide. Let the game begin!'

Someone had clearly been instructed to follow his cue, because the lights went out. The few candles still burning in the dining room stayed, but as soon as Chloe, along with the other girls, fled to find a hiding place, she realized just how dark 'dark' meant. She was used to suburban darkness, diluted by the lights through her window from passing cars or an orange glow on her ceiling from the streetlamps. This was the kind of darkness you could only experience if you were in the middle of nowhere. Chloe paused by a window, looking over the drive at the back of the house. The waitresses from the party were loading their things into a car, laughing and chatting. Finished for the evening, off home for a cup of tea and bed. A strange part of her wished she could join them, to go back to a normal house with normal people, the kind of people who would have found this game shocking.

She heard footsteps behind her and realized that she couldn't stay where she was. Who did she want to catch her? Rav, she supposed. So she should hide near his bedroom, on the far side of the house from hers. That way he would be more likely to stumble across her. She could go to her own bedroom, of course. Lock the door to her staircase, lock the door to her room. Let people assume she wasn't alone in the locked room. Go to bed. Make elusive comments tomorrow about not wanting to kiss and tell. But something inside her, the same something that had kissed Rav in their first term and let him do delicious things to her body that afternoon wanted to know what might happen next. Zadie always said that they were too young not to be having an adventure or making memories. And she was right.

The game had gone on for almost twenty minutes when Chloe was caught. Strong hands on her arms. Thick arms. A thrill ran through her as she recognized a hint of CK One. Max held his hand out to her and stroked her upper arm, clearly trying to work out which of the girls she was. 'You smell delicious,' he whispered in her ear. Did he know? Had he realized that it was her? His lips traced her neck. She allowed herself a moment, his lips sending signals from her neck all around her body like electricity. Then she stepped back. 'It's okay, Coco,' he said in a low, hungry voice, 'I'm allowed.' He slipped his arms around her waist, gripping her tightly, and dipped his head to meet hers. She sank into the kiss, her heart soaring. She knew it was wrong, but it felt amazing.

Then she felt his hands sneaking under her dress, tickling her thighs as he searched for her underwear, and came back down to earth. This was moving too fast. She pushed him away. 'What are you doing?' he said, sounding exasperated. 'I told you, Zadie won't care. It doesn't matter.' But Chloe couldn't do this, even if that were true. Could it be true? Was she so insignificant that sleeping with her would mean nothing? 'I'm sorry,' she whispered, and slipped out from under his arm. He muttered, 'For fuck's sake,' under his breath and turned away. She heard his footsteps go towards the master bedroom. Where should she go now? She gripped her way down the stairs, along the corridor. The dining room still had a couple of candles burning, thankfully. She sat for a moment, listening to the noises of the house, the loud silence. She searched for a water glass then took a candle from the table. She'd take it with her upstairs so that she could manage the spiral stairs without tripping and breaking her neck. And tomorrow she would pretend that she had been just as debauched as the rest of them, keeping silent out of modesty.

Afterwards, she tried very hard to remember what made her stop outside Max and Zadie's room. She tried to find some internal excuse for it, something less perverse than wanting to see Max and Zadie together. Something less desperate than hoping they might ask her to join in. But both of those things were true, however hard she pretended to herself that they weren't. The door was ajar and she paused when she heard soft groaning. Holding up the candle to see who it was, she almost dropped it.

Lying on the floor, looking like a fallen angel, was Zadie. Her dress was torn. Chloe moved lightning quick, raising the candle, trying to assess the damage. Zadie's lip was split and bleeding, dripping on to her ripped silk neckline. Her eye was turning purple, matching similar bruises on her arms. The ring on her finger was bloody from a cut on her knuckle, as if she had tried to fight back. Her eyes were moving under the lids and she was breathing, but she looked half dead. 'Zadie,' she whispered. 'Zadie, what happened?'

'Max,' Zadie whispered.

27
NOW

Chloe's blood was up. Should she turn around and run? Why was he here? And should she be scared? She knew Max could be nasty. Look what he had done to Zadie. Was he still like that? Did a person ever really stop being like that?

'What are you doing here?' she asked after what felt like an hour.

'Very rude. Aren't you going to come in?'

'You've got some serious gall, inviting me into my own flat, Max.' She pushed past him and put her bag down on the hall floor. 'Why are you here? Get out before Rav sees you.'

Max pointed through the hall, through the kitchen and living room into the garden. 'Oh, Rav's already home. We've been waiting for you.'

'What the fuck is going on?'

Max went through to the kitchen. He opened the fridge and seemed to be perusing the contents. 'Do you want a glass of rosé or a glass of white? It's too hot for red, and I know you hate champagne.'

'I don't want a drink.'

'Oh, I think you do.'

Chloe's hands were by her sides and yet, for some reason, her index fingers were twitching. She stretched them, trying to make it stop. 'It's my kitchen, Max. I'll get my own wine.'

'Fine. Come and join us outside when you're ready.'

Chloe watched the wine glass flood with pink liquid and took a steadying breath. Max was only here because he was trying to call her bluff. Rav was only home early because Max had summoned him. This would be a work meeting. In a moment, when she went outside, she would find that Max and Rav were talking about some boring building project and Max had just been trying to scare her. She took another deep breath and willed her feet to move. The longer she stayed in here, the longer she didn't go into the garden, the stranger this seemed.

'Hello, darling,' she said brightly, kissing Rav on the lips. 'Welcome home.'

'How was the inset day?'

'It was great, actually. Everything's in order, I think. Or at least as much as it ever is.'

'Max popped by to chat to us about something. I was thinking we'd give him supper.'

'Oh, I don't know if that's going to work.' Chloe tried to keep her voice even. 'We've hardly got anything in the fridge.'

'That's no problem,' smiled Rav. 'I'll pop to the shops

and grab a few bits. You two will be all right here for a bit, won't you?'

Chloe forced lightness into her tone. 'Yes, of course.'

Rav patted himself for his keys and his wallet, whistling as he closed the front door. The local supermarket was only at the top of their road. It would take him fifteen minutes at most to get back. Could she get rid of Max in that time?

'So what happens on an inset day?' asked Max jovially. 'I've always heard people talking about them but I've never really understood what one was.'

'What the fuck are you doing here?'

'Jesus, you're not very nice after a day at the coalface. I think I'll insist that Verity gives up work when we get married if she's anything like you. Don't want to come home to a row every night.'

'Does this mean you've decided?'

'Decided what?'

'If you think Verity is sticking around, I assume you're going to tell Zadie's parents what you did.'

Max laughed. 'No, no, I don't think I'm going to do that.'

'So what, then? You want me to tell everyone what happened? You want to lose your job and your friends and everything else you have?'

'No, that's not it either. I'd very much like to keep those things.'

Max was talking infuriatingly slowly. Every time she asked him a question, hushed in case one of the neighbours might overhear, he would lean back and stretch. Take a long drink from his glass.

'I gave you twenty-four hours to decide and it's almost up. If you don't tell them by tomorrow, I'm going ahead.'

'I don't think that's a good idea.'

Chloe tried to adopt an expression of amused indifference, but Max was so calm. So confident. She couldn't manage it.

'What are you playing at?' she asked. Her voice came out higher than she wanted it to.

'I'm not going to tell the Listers anything. And you're not going to make any accusations. You're not going to talk to Verity, until you see her at our wedding, at which point you're going to limit yourself to "Congratulations" and "You look beautiful."'

'Why would I do that?'

'Because you no longer have any evidence that we slept together.'

Chloe ran inside for her bag, heart pounding as she scrabbled in it for her phone. Nothing. She took it back to the garden, brandishing it at Max. 'How did you get my phone?'

'I didn't. Rav did. I imagine he's resetting it right now, just as soon as he wipes any back-ups from your laptop.'

Chloe tried to form words but couldn't. She stumbled backwards and let the garden wall take her weight.

Rav was the most honest person she knew, the most trusting. He knew all her passwords and pin codes yet never showed even the slightest hint of wanting to use them. He trusted her entirely. She trusted him. Always had. What could Max have over him? Surely this couldn't be about Rav wanting to be his friend? He couldn't want to be Max's friend more than he wanted to be her husband? 'I can still tell people. Even without the pictures, even without the video.'

'You could,' said Max, recrossing one leg over the other. 'But I have the video you made. Which I think you'll remember showed some rather enthusiastic consent. You probably should have been clearer on the plan before you filmed us.'

'That film doesn't prove I consented. It shows you hitting me.'

'It does. And your brand-new search history on your laptop is full of all sorts of dirty goodies, nasty little video clips of women begging for things like that. And Rav threw in some extra search terms, too, which make it look like you've been obsessed with me.'

She turned at the squeak of the patio door opening. Rav stepped out into the garden, a resigned look on his face.

'It's done,' he said quietly.

She looked at Rav, searching his face for something that would help her understand, but he was staring at the ground.

'Why would you do that?' she asked, because there were so many questions and it was almost impossible to know which one to ask first. 'You want to work for him that badly?'

'No,' said Rav, finally making eye contact. He pulled up a chair, sharing Max's painful slowness. 'It's not about that.'

'Then what? Why the fuck would you do something like this to me? He beat the living shit out of his girl-friend and left her on the floor, bleeding. Why are you protecting him, Rav? Why?'

'It wasn't Max,' he said.

Chloe's gaze flicked between Max and Rav, back and forth. 'What?' she said, breathing heavily.

'It wasn't me,' said Max. There was no pleasure in his voice. 'I told you back then. I told you when you came to dinner, when you came over the other day. It wasn't me.'

'Then who was it?' asked Chloe.

'It was me,' said Rav quietly. 'I did it.'

28

THEN

'Take me to your room,' said Zadie, her voice heavy. 'There's a torch in my drawer.'

'What? Why?'

She started to get up, wobbling slightly. 'Please. Come on.'

It took them a long time to make it up the stairs, Chloe holding the torch in one hand and helping Zadie with the other. When they got there, Zadie sat tentatively down on the bed. All the blinds were open and the sun was starting to come up. She stared at Zadie's ruined face in the blue light. 'Zadie, what happened? Was it Max?'

He had been so angry with Zadie at dinner; Chloe had seen it hidden behind his pseudo-calm expression. But surely Max wasn't like that? Surely Max wasn't the sort of man who would hurt his girlfriend because she was loud and annoying at dinner? Chloe thought back over the previous months, trying to work out whether she had ever had a sense of Max being violent towards Zadie, or towards anyone else. There wasn't a single moment. She had often wondered why Max and Zadie were together, when they seemed to wind each other up and want such different things. But she had never, not for a second, worried that Max might mistreat Zadie. If she had speculated that one of them might be violent, it would have been Zadie, not Max. But there was no question that someone had hurt her.

Zadie moved her head. Was she nodding? Or shaking? 'I just want to go to sleep,' she said.

Chloe helped her to take off the white dress, unhooking each button as if she were doing the rosary. When the dress fell to the floor it revealed that her ribs were stained blue and purple. Chloe couldn't help asking again, 'What happened?'

'He was so angry,' she breathed as she pulled the covers tight around her shoulders, like a little girl who was afraid of the dark.

'Zadie, I'm calling the police. He can't get away with this.' Chloe started searching for her phone and was surprised when she felt Zadie's vice-like grip on her arm.

'No,' she said forcefully, her eyes welling up. 'Please.'

It was the first time Chloe had seen her cry. She nodded, feeling helpless. She waited until Zadie's breathing was perfectly even, knowing after so many nights sharing a bed that Zadie was easily woken initially. Then she slid in next to her, careful not to move or even touch her at all, and fell asleep.

29
NOW

Chloe's head spun, and then she was throwing up into a plant pot by the back door. A pretty blue-and-green one they had bought at a farmers' market and planned to plant with lavender. The two men watched her, and when she had finished vomiting she sank down on to the step which led from the living room to the garden. Rav got up. Keeping a metre or so away from her, he passed her a glass. She drank the wine thirstily, hoping that the alcohol would numb her, even a little.

'She said your name,' she said, looking at Max. 'She said your name, that night.'

Max shrugged. 'Maybe she wanted to talk to me. She was drunk. She'd had a huge shock. Not sure that was really enough to condemn me on, Coco.'

'She was wearing the ring. You have the ring that she was wearing.'

'She left it for me at the house. She knew it was a family ring. Presumably she thought that my parents would be in touch to get it back from her if she didn't.'

'You always seemed so . . . guilty.'

He smiled, a sad sort of half-smile. 'I felt guilty about that night. But not because I hurt Zadie. Because I kissed you. Because I liked kissing you. She told me I could do whatever I wanted that night, as long as I didn't touch you. But I couldn't resist.'

She tensed at the idea of Rav hearing this, knowing that she and Max had kissed when they were together. Then she laughed at the ridiculousness of it all, at her own stupid reaction. Rav had done something a hundred million times worse.

'Why?' she asked him now. 'Why would you do that to her?'

'We had a fight.'

'What could you possibly have had to fight about? You barely even knew her.'

'I was in love with her.'

The world swam for a few moments.

It was too much.

The 'psycho' Zadie was seeing at university, the one Louella had told her about in the conversation that had made her so completely and utterly sure about Max – it hadn't been Max. It had been Rav.

He had hurt Zadie. He had hit her hard enough that she bled. Left bruises all over her perfect skin. Which meant that he had the capacity to do something she could never, ever have imagined him doing.

Rav had been in love with Zadie. Of the people who had known them both, she had thought he had chosen her, liked her best. But he had in fact liked Zadie better. Loved her. And moreover, she had spent the last fifteen years talking to him about Zadie, about where she was, about what had happened to her, while he held this piece of the jigsaw out of her reach.

'Did you and she ever . . .' She trailed off, praying that the answer was going to be no, that he would say they'd never had any contact, that nothing had ever happened between them.

Rav sat down. His skin was grey. 'Yes.'

She closed her eyes. 'When? How many times?'

'We were sleeping together for six months. I wanted her to tell Max. I wanted her to end it with him so that we could be together. I told her that night that unless she came clean with Max and called it quits with him, we were over. She said no. She laughed at me, said she couldn't believe I would ever think she'd choose me over Max. And I saw red. I lost it. I hit her.'

'Six months.'

'Yes.'

'All the time that you and I were getting together.'

'Yes.'

'When did it start?'

'The party where we met. I met her there, too.'

A wave of nausea passed through her. 'She told me that I shouldn't see you. That you didn't seem that inter-ested in me.'

'She was jealous. She didn't like that I liked you. But she was with Max and, I don't know, I guess I wanted you both. Chloe, I'm so sorry. This was a long time ago, I was very young, and very fucking stupid. And then that night, during that awful fucking game, she told me that we were over. She was wearing Max's ring. She said all this stuff, she baited me . . .'

Chloe looked up, trying to focus on Max. 'You knew?'

Max nodded. 'Yes.'

'You knew the whole time?'

'I knew she was sleeping with someone else. I suspected it was Rav. And then the party happened. He came to me that night, told me what had happened.'

'And you covered for him?'

'You always forget, you didn't know her for very long. You had no idea what she was like. She could get into your head. She could make you absolutely fucking crazy. I'm not saying she deserved what she got. He shouldn't have done it. He knows he shouldn't have done it. But would you really have wanted Rav to go down for that? How would it have looked? Angry brown kid beats up a beautiful white girl with millionaire parents? They'd have thrown away the key.'

Chloe drank from her wine glass again. 'Don't.'

'Don't what?'

'Don't try and act like this is normal. Like what he did was okay.'

'It wasn't okay,' said Rav gently. 'I know that. I've regretted it every day since and I'll regret it for the rest of my life.'

'It's your fault she died!' Chloe shouted, for a moment

forgetting to keep her voice down for the neighbours, forgetting to pretend that she was calm, that she was in control of the situation. Zadie would have known that she and Rav had stayed together all those years. That they got married. Had she thought that Chloe knew? That she didn't care?

'That's not true,' said Max, who did at least have the good grace to drop the smirk he'd been wearing earlier. 'Everything I said to you – about her being ill, unstable – it was all still true.'

'She wasn't like that.'

'Don't you care that she was sleeping with him? She knew about you two, and she didn't stop,' Max went on.

'Stop it.' Chloe shook her head. 'Stop it.'

'She listened to you talking about him. She watched you check your phone to see whether he had sent you a message. And then she went back to his room and fucked him. You don't care about that at all? That doesn't matter to you?'

She looked at Max. At Rav. Back to Max. She could smell the vomit from the flowerpot behind her. The light was glinting off Max's glass of wine. A plane whined overhead. What did she do now? Where did she go? How was it possible for a life that she had lived for so long, so easily, to be smashed up, broken, annihilated like this, in a matter of minutes?

Max got to his feet. 'I think I'll be off. Rav, I'll see you next week.'

She watched him go inside, pull an expensive jacket

over his pale blue shirt and close the door behind him. He would presumably get a car back to south-west London. Sit in the garden with a glass of wine. Talk to Verity about work. Keep moving, keep living, keep everything just exactly the same as it had always been. Chloe dropped her head into her hands, looking at the dusty patio between her fingers.

'What now?' Rav asked, eventually.

'I don't know,' she whispered. 'I don't know.'

30
THEN

When she woke the next morning the first thing Chloe thought of was Zadie. Sometimes she needed a moment to remember where she was, what was happening, why she was worrying. But today, it came back before she'd even opened her eyes. She turned to the side of the bed, but Zadie was gone. Trying to breathe calmly, she got up, pulled on a pair of jeans and a jumper and went down to the second floor. She knocked on Max's bedroom door and it swung open. Zadie's make-up was strewn over the bedside table. Her robe was slung over a chair. Max was lying in bed, snoring gently. She closed the door and went down to the breakfast room. A couple of last night's waitresses were back, setting up breakfast. 'Have you seen a girl down here? Tall, blonde hair, pretty?'

One of them shook her head. 'You're the first down. Did you want a cup of tea, or a coffee?' Chloe shook her head, unconcerned about being rude. She went back upstairs and shook Max awake.

'Max, where's Zadie?'

He opened his eyes blearily and gestured towards a glass of water on his bedside table. She didn't pass it to him.

'Zadie. Where is she?'

'I don't know.'

'When did you last see her?'

He ran his hands through his hair then stretched his arms wide open. 'I don't know. Last night. Before the game? During the game? I don't really remember much.' He grinned. 'Did you have fun?'

'I found Zadie lying on the floor last night. Covered in bruises. Her lip was bleeding.'

Max looked confused. 'In here? Had she fallen over?'

'No, she hadn't fallen over, someone had beaten the living shit out of her.'

'I don't think that's possible, Chloe.'

He never called her Chloe. Always Coco.

'I know what I saw. She was in here, she was bleeding, she'd been beaten up. She slept in my room. I wanted to call the police, but she wouldn't let me. When I woke up she was gone.'

Max started to get dressed. 'Okay, let's look for her.'

By the time everyone else had filtered down to breakfast it was clear that Zadie really had gone. They ate pancakes and drank black coffee while Chloe silently fumed. Why didn't they care? Why weren't they worried? Why weren't they doing anything to help? After breakfast her anger boiled over. She grabbed Max by the arm as he walked along a corridor.

'What's wrong?'

'I want to call the police.'

'The police? What the hell for?'

'About Zadie, about what happened last night.'

'We have about £500 worth of coke in this house, plus God knows whatever else. If you call the police, there'll be hell to pay.'

'I don't care—'

Max took her arm, gently. 'If I get in trouble, they'll take my scholarship away. I won't be able to go to Australia. I might not even be able to play rugby here any more. That's my whole career – fucked. Please. Don't do this. I promise you, we'll get back to the house and she'll be there, and she'll understand.'

Chloe studied his face. He was calm, but earnest. 'They'd really take your place away?'

He nodded. 'It's a morality clause. They have them for our places at uni, too, you know. We could all get kicked out. You're on thin ice with the tutors, right?'

That hadn't occurred to her. Was it true? Could she get kicked out? She imagined having to tell her mother that she had lost her place. Her mother having to tell everyone in their town she had boasted to about her clever, clever daughter. The first in the family to go to university.

'And you're really not worried?' she asked, searching for a reason to do as he asked.

'No. Trust me, Zadie does stuff like this all the time. She slices up her arms then calls an ambulance, takes an overdose just when you're due to arrive home. This is who she is. I love her, but she's a chronic attention addict. I promise, she probably just fell over and bashed herself last night, the booze made it seem worse than it was, and now she's gone off in a huff because I took her up on her offer of a free pass.'

Max reached out and stroked Chloe's hair. She flinched at his touch. 'You're a good friend. Better than she deserves.'

'I should go home. She'll be at the house, or in our room. I can take care of her.'

'Or you could stay and take care of yourself. You're not her mother. Eventually, she is going to have to look after herself.'

'Eventually, yes, but I can't just leave her right now.'

'She left. Not you. Listen, I adore Zadie, but she doesn't want anyone to be happy. She doesn't mean to be like this, so selfish, so dramatic. She loves you. She loves me. But she doesn't know how to love us, and if you give her an inch, she'll take a million miles. She sees you getting close to Rav and making your own friends and it scares her. She wants to take you away from everyone else so you're just hers. But if you let her, she won't want you any more.'

Chloe sighed. She knew she should tell Max he was wrong. Call the police. Never mind what that meant for his future. Or hers.

'I've been going out with her for six years. I know how to handle her. The best thing you can do is get back in the hot tub, have a glass of rosé and try to enjoy what's left of the weekend. Give Rav the snog he's clearly been chasing all weekend.'

So she did as she was told. And every time the guilt knife twisted in her stomach, she told it that she was only staying another twenty-four hours, that Zadie hadn't wanted to talk, or to be looked after, and that, when she got home, Zadie would be there, telling herself she was being practical, not just trying to save her own skin.

But of course, Zadie wasn't there. On Monday they were due to be going back to university around midday. Chloe woke earlier and couldn't wait. The guilt had become too much, too loud, too insistent. She got a lift to the station with one of the waiting staff, who seemed to have been instructed to bend over backwards. She paid an eyewatering amount for a train ticket and willed the train to move faster, cursing every single pause on the line. Chloe went to her own room first. Everything Zadie owned was gone – all her clothes, all her books, everything – and the scent of her was a little stronger in the air than it had been when Chloe had left. She walked to Archer Crescent double quick, counting her steps, praying that her every instinct was wrong. She rang the doorbell for minutes at a time, then pounded on the door until her hands ached. She sat on the doorstep, listening for any tiny noise, praying to hear Zadie's feet on the wooden floor. But there was nothing.

Chloe called Zadie's mobile. Then called her again. And again. And again, until her phone was hot and the buttons had made an outline on her cheek. Then she called directory enquiries and found the number for Zadie's parents' house. She rang them until it rang out, again and again and again. She wrote Zadie a text. And then an email. And then, out of complete, sheer desperation, she wrote a letter. By the time she had walked to the postbox and shoved it in she was starting to hyperventilate. She stumbled back to Archer Crescent, eventually found the spare key and sat on the stairs to wait for Max to come home.

Finally, he came through the door, throwing his heavy leather bag into the hall and chucking his suit carrier over a sofa. He didn't seem to have noticed that Chloe was sitting, watching him.

'She's not here,' Chloe called down, after a while.

Max jumped, looking up at where she sat on the stairs. 'Fucking hell, Coco.'

'Zadie isn't here.'

'She's probably gone home to blow off some steam. She does that sometimes.'

'I called her all day. She didn't answer. I even called her parents' house. She's gone.'

Max disappeared into the kitchen and reappeared with a pint glass of water. 'I don't know what you want me to do about this.'

'Did you do it? Did you hurt her?'

Max shrugged. 'I don't know what you're talking about.'

'I don't believe you.'

'I don't need you to believe me.'

'She said you could be awful when you were angry.'

'I'm sure she did.'

'Don't you care whether she's okay or not?'

Max ran his hands through his hair. 'To be completely bloody honest with you, Coco, right now, I couldn't give less of a shit. I'm knackered, I'm hung over and I've got a meeting with the coach about my Australia move. I'm not going to let Zadie's latest stunt derail anything for me.'

Chloe hadn't ever known anger like this. She got to her feet and looked Max square in the eye. 'You disgust me.'

'Get out of my house.'

Chloe didn't know who else to call, so she dialled Rav's number. He arrived half an hour later with a bottle of white wine. Then they crawled into her single bed and he held her to his chest.

'I can't believe I didn't do anything,' she whispered.

'There wasn't anything you could do.'

'I could have called the police. I could still call the police.'

'That's not your choice. That's up to Zadie. She might want to, she might not. But you have to let her have that.'

Chloe nodded, feeling her tears soaking into her hair. She sat up.

'Can I ask something?' Rav asked.

Chloe nodded. 'Yes.'

'Why are you so sure it was Max?'

'She said his name. It was the only thing she said, afterwards. Just his name. And as soon as I saw him the next morning, I knew. I could see it all over his face. He did it. He's got a temper. She told me before he had a temper, but I had no idea he would do something like this. Can you imagine?'

Rav waited a few minutes, stroking her gently. Then he sat up. 'You don't look very well. When I first met you, you had this look about you, this glow. And it's gone. All that time with Zadie. When did you last eat properly?'

'We were doing better. She was doing so much better. She was happy.'

'I'm not talking about Zadie. I'm talking about you.'

Chloe nodded again.

'Come with me,' said Rav.

She followed him down the chilly corridor to the bathroom, an ancient one with peach-coloured tiles and a chipped white bath. He ran the water so that the room filled with steam and stole a generous lug of someone else's bath oil from the shelves next door. Then he undressed Chloe and leaned over the bath, using her flannel to wipe the make-up she hadn't taken off since the party. He washed her hair with what he told her he had judged to be the most expensive-looking shampoo on the shelf and followed it with conditioner. He said nothing while she quietly sobbed, and when he was finished and she was clean, the water a murky beige, he wrapped her in a towel, led her back to her bedroom and found her some pyjamas which hadn't been touched since the first week of term. He made a decent stab at drying her hair with a little portable hairdryer and then he told her to get into bed.

'I should be embarrassed,' she said sleepily. 'You're treating me like a baby.'

'Sometimes we all need to be looked after,' he said quietly. The sun had only just gone down. When was the last time she had gone to bed at a sensible time, in her own bed?

Rav stroked her hair. 'You can stay if you like,' she whispered. There was no way he could have done all this without expecting something.

'I'll stay until you fall asleep, then I'm going back to my room.'

'You don't want to sleep with me?'

'I do. But not like this.'

She drifted into a heavy, irresistible sleep. While Zadie's loss still thumped in her head, she had to admit that she needed this.

For a long time after Zadie disappeared, Chloe kept looking for her. She went to the History of Art department, but they told her they couldn't release details about another student. She left messages on Zadie's voicemail until the mailbox was too full and she couldn't leave any more. Sent text after text after text. She wrote letters to Zadie's parents' house, addressed to Zadie, addressed to her parents. She disguised her handwriting on the envelope. She even found an email for Zadie's father at work and sent him a missive pleading with him to tell her that his daughter was okay. She harboured hopes of going to their house, of turning up on the doorstep and somehow being able to tell Zadie how sorry she was. Rav told her not to, and she knew that he was right. Zadie clearly didn't want to be found. She still dreamed of her most nights. Long, banal dreams of walking around Archer Crescent, washing up glasses in the kitchen, helping Zadie to pick an outfit.

After three weeks of concerted effort she received a very short email from Zadie's parents telling her that Zadie wasn't coming back to university and that she would get in touch with Chloe if and when she was ready. Its tone frightened her. Reminded her that Zadie's family were powerful, that they were real adults. She had burned with shame after reading it, horrified by the idea that they might know what she had done, or rather what she hadn't done. She told herself over and over again as she lay awake at night, her heart pounding with guilt, that she hadn't done anything wrong. But she didn't believe it.

The weeks wore on and, finally, the Easter holidays came. Then the summer term. And before long, Chloe was spending two days packing up her bedroom – the bedroom that she and Zadie had in some sense shared. She got a lift back to Surrey with Lissy, who lived nearby, and when she arrived back at her parents' house it seemed smaller, just like the cliché always said.

Lissy helped her to unload her things, made polite conversation with her mother, who seemed charmed and relieved in equal amounts, then threw her arms around Chloe.

'I'll call you next week and we can find a date to go

house shopping. We can do a proper Ikea trip! I'm so excited!'

While living with Lissy wasn't quite what she had dreamed of, Chloe found she was almost looking forward to it. There would be Marilyn Monroe and Audrey Hepburn prints on the walls. Heart-shaped candles on the table. Herbal Essences shampoos in the shower. It would be normal. Not what she had planned, but nice. Obviously, moving into Archer Crescent was no longer an option. The house was to be rented out to a family, which would presumably be an enormous relief to everyone who lived nearby.

Lissy had moved heaven and earth to find a place for Chloe in her house, convincing the three other girls that they should give up the four-bed that they'd found close to campus and the big supermarket in favour of a five-bed so that Chloe could join. She'd seen a steeliness in Lissy, as she strong-armed the girls into picking a slightly smaller, slightly shabbier house, which surprised her.

'Why are you doing this?' Chloe had asked her.

'Because we're friends,' she had answered.

Her reply had surprised Chloe. What sort of a friend had she been to Lissy? Occasional chats and texts, a few nights out. Nothing spectacular or dramatic. Nothing like what she had had with Zadie. But then, Lissy was here, and Zadie was gone.

Rav liked Lissy. He hadn't said it outright, hadn't admitted that he liked Chloe more when she surrounded herself with gentler, more normal people. But it was implied. Chloe wondered if maybe she liked herself more now, too. She often felt like the smartest, funniest person in the room. She didn't replay everything she said back in her head to try to work out whether she sounded stupid or not. She'd managed to scrape a 2.1 in her end-of-year exams. But despite all of that, she knew, without a shadow of a doubt, that if her phone rang tomorrow and it was Zadie summoning her to anything, whether it was a party or to help her bury a body, she would smack aside any obstacle that prevented her from being there.

31

NOW

Her mother's self-help books hadn't, as far as Chloe could remember, had much to say about what to do when it transpired that your husband had been having an affair with your best friend, who was now dead, and that he was, at least in part, the reason she had died. So she had spent the following weeks sleepwalking. Going to work. Avoiding her friends. Ignoring the hundreds of calls from Rav. He had apologized a thousand times, and then, when he had finished apologizing, he had been defensive. 'I know I cheated, but this was years ago. We were kids. We've built a whole life since then. I've forgiven you for what happened with Max. Why can't you forgive me?' Eventually, she supposed, she would tell him that she didn't care that he had cheated on her all those years ago. It wasn't the infidelity that bothered her. It was the fact that he had watched her constantly wondering what had happened to Zadie for almost the entirety of her adult life. He knew how confused and guilty and angry she felt. And all along it had been entirely within his power to wave a magic wand and make all that not knowing disappear. But he had chosen not to. That was the betrayal. But she didn't feel ready to say any of that to him. And it made the constant ache in her chest worse when she allowed herself to think about the fact that her husband knew her so little that he wasn't able to work any of it out. So instead she spent late nights and early mornings walking the pavements around her house, as if, if she could keep moving fast enough, she could escape everything that had happened. She slept alternately for hours and hours, and then not at all, falling asleep at her desk then staying awake all night. Trying to work out whether it was even possible to rebuild her life from here. Trying to forget Rav's ashen face and Max's expression of righteous anger. And then, before she had even begun to untangle the whole thing, she found herself with another, more pressing issue to deal with.

Chloe had never really felt that she knew her own body. She didn't admire herself in the mirror while she got dressed. She didn't have a specific feature that she liked to highlight with her clothes. She had barely ever even masturbated, and when she had attempted it it had been more through a desire to understand the fuss than out of anything resembling lust. She'd been given a vibrator years ago, and she used it intermittently, but only really in an attempt to understand why other people liked them. And yet now, she could feel that something was different. It wasn't just that she felt sick from the moment she woke up to the moment she fell asleep. Nor was it the fact that her breasts were so swollen that putting on a bra made her wince. Her jeans were tight, she slept longer and deeper than she ever had before, and she woke with a ravenous hunger she had never previously experienced. But that wasn't why she knew she was pregnant. She would have known without any of the symptoms. She just – and she couldn't really explain how or why – knew. There was something different. Something inside her which was undeniably, unquestionably, alive.

She bought a pregnancy test at a chemist's a mile or so from the house, making sure that no one from her school was lurking behind her. Then she went to a pub, bought a pint of sparkling water and went to the bathroom to confirm what she already knew. She sat, her jeans and knickers around her ankles, feeling completely and utterly calm. Even the bleachy odour of the pub bathroom smelled sweet to her. In films, people always peed on the stick then placed it face down while they waited. But Chloe watched the urine seep down the little window. The two pink lines appeared, vivid and rude, without waiting a second, let alone the three minutes the test suggested.

It was the first pregnancy test she had ever taken. Thanks to good contraceptive fortune, and having clockwork periods, she had never had so much as a scare before. She had sat with Zadie, once, while she took one. Zadie had been ashen-faced when they bought it, and they had walked back to the house in silence. She had sworn Chloe to silence. 'Max would have a fit,' she had said. 'It would ruin his whole future.' Chloe wondered now if it might have been more about the fact that a pregnancy would have aroused Max's suspicion that Zadie was sleeping with someone else than a concern for his future. It was weird. Every time she had a memory of Zadie, now, she found something mean to say about her. Little digs. She had never said a single bad word to, or about, Zadie, until recently. And now she couldn't stop.

Zadie's test had been negative, and they had laughed about it afterwards, throwing it into the bin, covering it up with tissues because Zadie claimed it 'wasn't worth the stress' of telling Max that they had had a near-miss. They had celebrated by getting drunk, because that was all they ever did. And Zadie had half joked that she was going to name Max's first baby after herself, just as his father had named him after himself. 'Zadie Two.' She had smiled. 'Men do it all the time. Why can't I?'

So, there it was. She had been right. How far along was she? She tried to count on her fingers, but the previous weeks and months were so nebulous, running together into a mass of confusion, excitement, misery and pain. There were ways to find out, of course. She could go to the doctor. Go to the hospital. She could sit down with a calendar. Or she could wait. And hope that, when it came to it, she just knew.

ZADIE

The sky was a purple-yellow colour when Zadie woke. She sat up without thinking. Her ribs screamed in objection. Looking down, she saw that she was naked. Her arms were a mess of livid bruises, as if someone had dipped a brush of purple paint in a jar of water. She stood up, almost admiring the spectrum of damage across her arms, her thighs, her neck. Her lip was crusted with blood, her eye socket swollen. She looked horrific. Chloe lay asleep in bed, her hair spread out over the pillow, her snub nose perfect in profile and her eyelashes long on her cheeks. What must it be like to be so uncomplicated? So fundamentally good?

Chloe had been such a good friend to her, and Zadie had paid her back with betrayal. She deserved everything that had happened to her. She knew Chloe would be better off without her around.

Zadie picked a pair of jeans off the floor, next to the ruined white dress, which lay in a puddle next to Chloe's green one. What else? She needed a top. On a chair, she found a jumper which she didn't recognize but looked like it was a boy's. A pair of socks, probably Chloe's.

'I'm sorry,' she whispered as she zipped up the jeans, a little too big, but wearable. Making the word cracked the scab on her lip. She winced.

Her handbag was in the hall, and her trainers. Everything else could stay here. Then she started walking. One foot in front of the other. What time was it? Light, but not very. After a while, she reached the village, a sleepy little place just coming to life. The station clock said it was eight a.m. The next train was mercifully soon. Only when the train started moving did she open her phone and dial.

'You were right,' she said. 'I can't do this. Please come.'

By the time the train had ground to a halt her father had arrived at the station. He didn't ask any questions. If he wondered where Max was, what had happened, how his daughter could have crashed out of university so spectacularly, he didn't ask. And if he noticed the bruises that she had covered with make-up, he said nothing.

Her phone vibrated incessantly. Chloe called. Texted. Called again. Messages begging her to answer, asking where she was, threatening to call the police. Zadie watched the display light up but couldn't convince her fingers to move to open the phone. And even if she did, what would she say? Guilt hung heavy in her stomach. The first real, proper friend she had ever had, and look where it had ended. But this was what she did. She ruined things. She curdled the things she touched. It was stupid to think that she could belong here, that she could manage it. She would be safe at home, far away from people who she could hurt. Or people who could hurt her.

Her father didn't want to take her back to the house. He said *he would send someone for her things later. But she had to go. She unlocked the door with shaking hands. Put the ring, in its box, on the kitchen table. Max's parents wouldn't leave her alone until they had it back. Then her keys next to it. She put her phone in the kitchen bin, where she had put so many bottles before, then poured a bottle of water over it for good measure. It stopped buzzing. Chloe's name disappeared from the display. 'Bye,' Zadie whispered. 'I'm sorry.'*

On the way home, Zadie lay down in the back of her father's estate car. She watched the dappled sky move past the car window while her father played Classic FM on the radio, occasionally humming. Neither of them spoke.

At last, they grew close to their family home. He indicated and turned into the drive, the drive she had run up and down as a little girl, walked up to get phone signal as a moody teenager. 'Thank you,' she said. Her father caught her eye in the wing mirror and smiled.

'That's all right,' he said. 'You're going to be okay.'

But she knew that wasn't true. She couldn't make it work, because that was the sort of person she was. She wasn't ever going to be able to have what other people had – friends, relationships, jobs. Lives. She watched the back of her father's head for a while, pressing her finger into one of the bruises on her leg and wishing for his sake that she had been the kind of person who knew how to build a life and resist the temptation to raze the whole thing to the ground.

ONE YEAR LATER

Chloe's hands were freckled on the bar handle of the pram. She hadn't thought she'd been in the sun much lately. But she must have been. She peeked over into the basket of the pram, smiling at baby Rose, who lay on her back, holding her foot in her hand, seemingly transfixed by the leaves on the trees overhead.

'Thank you for coming with me.'

'You're welcome,' said Lissy. 'It's nice to get out of London.'

'You don't think it's a bit morbid?'

Lissy shrugged. 'I don't think so. It's all part of life. The sooner this lot get used to it, the better.' She pointed at Claudia, who was toddling ahead, fat legs in little white bloomers, a pale pink hat jammed on her head. 'Anyway, as far as she's concerned, it's not a graveyard, it's just another park to play in. Do you know where we're going?'

Chloe shook her head. 'No. Her mum didn't say where it – where she – was. Just that it was here.'

The graveyard was a pretty one, known for playing host to the graves of various Victorian poets who'd met their end from opium or consumption. It sat behind a beautiful, ancient church where upper-middle-class couples fought to get married every summer, attending Mass for six months beforehand just so they'd have it in their wedding photographs. It was as chic as being buried could be. Not that Chloe would have expected anything else from Zadie. Tasteful to the last.

If Lissy had found the request to come to the graveyard strange, she hadn't said so. In fact, she had been brilliant in almost every way over the last year. From the moment Chloe had stood on the doorstep, sobbing, Lissy had been there, just as she always had been, calmly unbothered. Chloe had stayed with them for several weeks after the Revelation, as she had taken to thinking of it. She and Lissy had sat up night after night, Lissy breastfeeding an apparently endlessly starving baby, Chloe weeping, obsessing, questioning what she should do. Lissy had offered very little advice, realizing, as friends so rarely do, that Chloe didn't need direction but time. She offered no judgement when Chloe said she wanted to stay with Rav, no judgement when she said she wanted to leave. She helped make lists, do sums. Asked all of the questions that have to be asked.

It had been too late for the kind of abortion that Chloe felt comfortable with. And anyway, she was nearly thirty-six. It was probably now or never. And as she looked down at Rose, she struggled to stir up any guilt from inside herself at having brought her into the world. She was too perfect to regret.

Rav's mother had been, to Chloe's immense surprise, generous and kind. 'I told you I would buy you a house if you had a child,' she had written in her now weekly email. 'And I meant it. It will be up to you whether or not Ravinder lives with you both. But my grandchild must have a home.'

So she had purchased a little two-bedroom with a tiny garden, a mile away. Close enough that she could walk to Lissy and Guy's house, come rain or shine, but far enough that she never had to walk past her old flat again.

There were strict rules about what could be left on graves. Zadie's mother had instructed her not to bring all sorts of extraordinary things, like teddy bears, for example. Chloe had tried not to be offended that it seemed plausible she might bring such a thing.

She had also answered Chloe's questions. It had felt selfish to ask her about Zadie, about the fifteen years that had passed between the party and the day that Zadie had died. She had heard herself ask Astrid to talk about her and, to her great relief, it seemed Astrid wanted to. The words had come spilling out, story after story about Zadie and her attempts to wrestle with life, to be a person in the same way that everyone around her had found so easy to be.

Astrid said that after Zadie moved back home she had gone travelling. Tried a term at art school but dropped out when a teacher said something crushing about her work. Then it had been yoga, more travelling, a whirl-wind marriage with someone she met in Bali who turned out, to no one's surprise, to be a complete shit. She'd painted intermittently. Moved back home, moved out, moved back home again. And as she'd got older and all her good-time friends found the straight and narrow, she had become sadder. Every failure seemed to leave her more bruised and more delicate.

Chloe had found herself pouring with silent tears as Astrid described how Zadie had moved back home for the last time three years ago. Only then, she rarely left. She had a dog she adored, a puppy she'd adopted from the streets on one of her travels. She liked the gardens, and being outside. But according to Astrid, Zadie had found less and less that she could bear, and towards the end she spent most of her time walking alone in the countryside or in her childhood bedroom, painting. Astrid had told Chloe she was welcome to visit, to come and see the family. She had apologized for allowing Zadie to disappear so comprehensively. 'I thought it was what she needed,' she had said on the phone. 'I wanted to make things easier for her. But I'm not sure anyone could have done.'

Astrid believed, rightly or wrongly, that Zadie wasn't a person who could live in the world, at least not like her siblings and her friends could. 'Life was such a battle for her,' she had said. It sounded as if her death had come as absolutely no surprise. Zadie had taken an overdose in the woods, left an uncharacteristically short letter for her family, apologized for hurting them, but explained she had nothing left in her any more.

Finally, Chloe had told Astrid she was sorry. Sorry for pretending that Zadie was living in their shared room, sorry for everything she did or didn't do. She told her she was horrified by what had happened to her at Max's party. She had wanted to confess about Rav and Max and everything that had happened in the previous months. But that wasn't for Astrid to contend with. She already had plenty of weights strung around her neck.

'Darling girl,' Astrid had said before they finished the conversation, 'Zadie was like this for as long as I can remember. What happened to her was awful, but it's not why she ended up the way she did. That was written in the stars for her from day one, I am afraid. I could tell from when she was a little girl that something about her was different. That life was going to be harder for her than it was for other people.'

She and Lissy continued walking, scanning the names on headstones.

'How are things with Rav?' Lissy asked.

Chloe shrugged. 'I'm not sure yet.'

'He's good with Rose.'

'He is.'

'And he still loves you.'

'He does.'

'But maybe you need a fresh start.'

'Maybe we do.' Chloe kicked a lump of grass. 'I know it should have a conclusion. An ending with a bow on it.

Either back together, in love, having more babies. Or broken up. Over.'

But the truth was, they weren't either of those things. He had been in her life for so long that she didn't know how to be without him. And even if she had, she didn't want to be without him. But she could never unlearn what she knew about him. It would always be true that Rav had something inside him which had allowed him to do a terrible, unforgivable thing. Could you forgive the unforgivable? Or could you learn to live with it well enough that you could be happy?

'He's having therapy,' she ventured. 'Has been for a while. Then I think we might try living together. I don't know. Some days I want to get it all back, to be together soon enough that Rose won't remember us apart. Other days I want to start all over again.' She stopped. 'That's it,' she said.

Lissy took the pram. 'Take as long as you need,' she said, turning away and pushing the pram back towards the church, little Claudia sitting on her hip.

The headstone was white, with neat black writing. 'Zadie Elizabeth Henrietta Barber Lister, 1985–2020. Beloved daughter and sister. What we keep in our memory is ours, unchanged for ever.'

Chloe wondered who had chosen the quote. One of her parents, she supposed. Or perhaps a sibling. All those children who had tumbled around the house would be adults now. They would never have known Zadie as Chloe had, as a raging, laughing, burningly brilliant party girl. They would remember her as Astrid had described. Erratic. Unreliable. Unhappy. She tried to push away the memory. In order to say what she needed to say, she couldn't feel sad for Zadie. She needed to allow herself her anger. She took out the flowers she had placed in her handbag. A little bunch of hyacinths she had grown herself. They smelled sweet and sharp. She placed them in front of the headstone, and then, having looked around to make sure that no one was there to see, she sat down on the grass.

'Long time no see.' She paused. 'I don't know where to start, Zaid. You'd talk for me, if you could. If you were really here. I wish I knew what you would say. I imagine it, sometimes. I guess what you'd tell me to do, what you'd think. When I'm picking an outfit or trying to decide something, there's this voice in my head, and I always tell myself that it's you, that you're still with me. But how could that possibly be true, when I didn't even really know you when you were alive?'

The late-afternoon sun was on her shoulders, seeping through the cotton of her dress. She looked up at the sky, bright and brilliantly blue.

'I wish I'd known you as well as I always told myself that I did. I wish I hadn't spent the last sixteen years comparing every single friend I made to you and always finding that they came out wanting. Lissy's my friend. I never wanted you to meet because I knew you'd think she was boring. I thought that, too. But she's not. She's kind. She drove us all the way here so that I could talk to you, and she's looking after my baby so that I can sit here and tell you – tell you what? I don't know what to tell you. That I'm angry with you, I suppose. I'm angry that you didn't tell me that you wanted Rav, or that he wanted you. Angry that you slept with him all those times when you knew I was falling in love with him. Even angrier that you didn't tell me what he did. I know it wasn't your fault. I know it was him. I don't know if I'll ever forgive him.

'You weren't kind to me. You know that? You weren't kind. And you weren't a good friend. I've spent all these years trying to convince myself that you did like me and that I was important and that you did respect me, because I thought that if you didn't it said something about me, that I was too suburban, too boring, too provincial, too unspecial to be worthy of your friendship. But it wasn't that, was it? It wasn't about me. It was about you. You couldn't be my friend, not properly, because you didn't know how to treat people. You didn't know how to treat Max, or me, or anyone in your life.

'I wish you were still here. But I don't know if I would like you if you were. Because you weren't a good friend. You weren't kind. You didn't love me like I loved you. You weren't any of the things that I've spent the last sixteen years telling everyone that you were. And I'm angry with you for that. I forgive you for sleeping with Rav and lying to me about it, and making me lie to your parents, and telling me not to make friends with people who you thought were dull. But I can't forgive you for that. I don't forgive you for that. I do miss you, though.

'I think about what kind of a godmother you would have been to Rose. Whether you'd have been the one who noticed that she looks so much more like Max than Rav.' She paused, somehow expecting the admission to have changed the world around her, not quite believing she could have said the words out loud without them changing things. But there was no one here. At least, no one who could hear her. Her chest felt a little lighter. It felt good to confide in her friend. And they were, she supposed, by some warped logic, sort of even now.

She got to her feet. 'Bye, Zaid.'

ACKNOWLEDGEMENTS

Two Wrongs was predominately written during a very strange time, when the whole world sort of ground to a halt because of Covid-19. I can honestly say that it has never been harder to be creative than it was during those weeks where the only contact with the outside world was an hour-long walk in the evening or an occasional trip to the supermarket. I spent a lot of time not writing but comparing myself to other writers on Instagram and feeling sorry for myself.

But, while finding the motivation to write was almost impossible, eventually I came to see *Two Wrongs* as the structure that held my life in place. It gave me a reason to sit at my desk every morning, and something to focus on when being so far away from friends and family felt especially hard. So, in rather a meta way, I think the first entity I have to thank is the book itself.

By extension, I must thank Tash Barsby, who edited *Two Wrongs* with such thoughtfulness and skill, taking it from a collection of chapters to a real book. I am for ever grateful both to Tash, and to Transworld at large, for the purpose, joy and escapism that writing these books allows me. I would also like to thank Darcy Nicholson, who is no longer my editor but whose editorial voice will for ever live in my head when I am writing.

I also owe Eve White, my agent, to whom this book is dedicated, a huge thank-you for the ongoing work that she has done, along with Ludo Cinelli, to help me build this career I love so much. Without Eve, I'm not sure what I would be doing right now, but I'm pretty sure it wouldn't be this.

There are also a whole host of people who I have to thank, for too many various reasons to go into: Angelica Malin, Madeleine Spencer, Chloe, Pete, Catherine, Ivy and Oak, Emma, Jon and Erin, the Oakfield girls, the Mayfield girls, Steph and all my wonderful cousins.

Lastly, as ever, I have to thank Tim, Charlotte, Lucy and George, and my divine husband, Marcus. There are no people on this earth who I would rather have lunch with. Apart from possibly Taylor Swift.

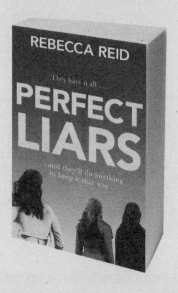

Sixteen years ago, best friends Nancy, Georgia and
Lila did something unspeakable. Their crime forged
an unbreakable bond between them, a bond of
silence. But now, one of them wants to talk.

One wrong word and everything could be ruined: their lives,
their careers, their relationships. It's up to Georgia to call a
crisis dinner. But things do not go as planned.

Three women walk in to the dinner, but only two will leave.

Murder isn't so difficult the second time around . . .

*****

Available in paperback and ebook

What is more dangerous, a secret or a lie?

When Poppy meets Drew, she's at rock bottom: broke, jobless and with nowhere to live. So when he proposes after a whirlwind romance, she says yes – even though he has suggested they don't tell each other anything about their lives before they met.

It's unconventional, but it suits Poppy's needs perfectly. Because Poppy has a secret – and she isn't so sure Drew would still want to marry her if he knew the truth.

But, of course, this is a two-way deal – and Drew has secrets of his own. But surely they can't be worse than what Poppy's hiding . . .

*****

Available in paperback and ebook